P9-CQY-386

--- ★ ---

LIEUTENANT LUIS MENDOZA WENT TO WORK WITH A VENGEANCE ON CASES LIKE ROSALIE YBARRA'S

Rosalie Ybarra had been eight years old, and by her picture, a pretty, solemnly dark-eyed girl. She attended St. Ignacio's parish school on Mozart Street in Lincoln Heights; she had six blocks to walk from her home on Gates Street. Last Friday afternoon she hadn't come home, and eventually was reported missing. Neighbors went out looking, the squad car along that beat hunted, questions were asked. Rosalie and her best friend Alicia Romero had walked together up to the corner of Griffin and Darwin Streets, and Rosalie had turned down Griffin and left Alicia. They hadn't found anyone who had seen Rosalie after that, and there hadn't been any sign of Rosalie anywhere until five o'clock yesterday afternoon.

They would work this one hard.

--- ★ ---

Dell Shannon is the "reigning doyenne of the U.S. police procedural."
—*Kirkus Reviews*

"Readers should be warned, Luis Mendoza is habit-forming." —UPI

Also available from Worldwide Mysteries by
DELL SHANNON

BLOOD COUNT
CHAOS OF CRIME
COLD TRAIL
MURDER MOST STRANGE

Forthcoming Worldwide Mysteries by
DELL SHANNON

DESTINY OF DEATH
EXPLOIT OF DEATH

SHANNON DELL

The Motive on Record

WORLDWIDE.®

TORONTO · NEW YORK · LONDON · PARIS
AMSTERDAM · STOCKHOLM · HAMBURG
ATHENS · MILAN · TOKYO · SYDNEY

This one is, belatedly,
for my longtime agent and friend
Barthold Fles
with gratitude and affection

THE MOTIVE ON RECORD

A Worldwide Mystery/June 1990

First published by William Morrow & Company, Inc.

ISBN 0-373-26049-0

Copyright © 1982 by Elizabeth Linington. All rights reserved.
No part of this book may be reproduced or transmitted in any
form or by any means, electronic or mechanical, including
photocopying, recording or by any information storage and
retrieval system, without permission in writing from the
Publisher. For information, contact: William Morrow &
Company, Inc., 105 Madison Avenue, New York, NY 10016
U.S.A.

All the characters in this book are fictitious, and any
resemblance to actual persons, living or dead, is purely
coincidental.

® are Trademarks registered in the United States Patent
Trademark Office and other countries.
TM is the property of Harlequin Enterprises Ltd.

Printed in U.S.A.

Up from Earth's Centre through the Seventh Gate
I rose, and on the Throne of Saturn sate,
And many Knots unravel'd by the Road;
But not the Knot of Human Death and Fate.
                    —*Rubaiyat of Omar Khayyam*

This is the porcelain clay of humankind.
                    —*Don Sebastian*
                    JOHN DRYDEN

ONE

NOBODY, SAID ALISON—with a very few exceptions—was writing solid decent mystery novels these days. She had taken to reading true-crime collections instead. She had been yawning over *Murderers' England* for the last couple of hours, and upending it on her lap said to Mendoza, "All I can say is, it's so much more plausible in fiction. Some of the things that happen in real life—no self-respecting author would dare put them in a novel. There doesn't seem to be anything in between the merely mindless violence—knock the elderly storekeeper on the head for four dollars out of the cash register—and the most unlikely goings-on imaginable. That Bartlett case, with that idiotic minister running around buying chloroform—and Mrs. Bravo and Dr. Gully—it's more ridiculous than dramatic. And people doing murder for no motive at all or the silliest flimsiest motives—it's all terribly implausible."

Mendoza grunted sleepily. "I see enough crime reports on the job. Human nature tends to be implausible. Monotonously."

Alison yawned. "Well, I'm going up to bed—it's after eleven." She laid *Murderers' England* on the ottoman. "I wonder if some enterprising travel agency has ever thought of a murderers' tour—a lot of people are interested in crime—Whitechapel and the East End for Jack the Ripper, and Bognor Regis for George Joseph Smith, and so on—" She stood up and stretched.

"Not one of your brighter ideas," said Mendoza somnolently. He put down *The Day's Work* and stood up. The old Spanish hacienda with its high ceilings and large rooms was silent and sleeping around them; the twins would have been asleep for hours, and ten-month-old Luisa; the four cats were in a tangled mass on the long couch, and Cedric the Old English sheepdog raised a reluctant head at Alison's feet.

She prodded him out the front door for a last run before bed, and started up the wide spiral staircase. Mendoza stood yawning before the open door to let him in again. And as she reached the landing, Alison was thinking sleepily, a tour— it's ridiculous, we never go anywhere, and Luis has weeks of vacation coming to him—Mairí and the Kearneys here to look after the children, we really ought to take a holiday and go somewhere. A cruise or something. Say in August or September, to get away from the heat. The South Pacific, or Europe, or somewhere— It would do Luis good to get away from the job, though he'd never admit it. Tomorrow, go and see a travel agency. She thought vaguely, the West Indies?

Unaware that he was about to be uprooted from his daily routine, Mendoza let Cedric in, locked the front door, and proceeded upstairs after her. After twenty-six years at the job, he could put the current cases out of his mind overnight, but tonight he was thinking about Rosalie Ybarra, and feeling some faint curiosity about the body found in the Southern Pacific yards. But tomorrow was also a day.

IT WAS the second Tuesday in June, a gray cool morning. June was usually a respite before the long fierce summer struck southern California, lasting sometimes into mid-October. But the heat would be lurking, ready, and within a month would turn Los Angeles into a little humid hell. Why anybody lived in this climate, and why a great city should have grown up here, was an unfathomable mystery.

The Ferrari, which had had its nose smashed in when the electric eye on the gate had gone out of kilter, was repaired and running smoothly as Mendoza slid down the hill toward the gates of the House of Happy People, *La Casa de la Gente Feliz*. On the way he passed the Five Graces, the woolly white sheep imported to keep the underbrush down;

they usually moved *en masse*, and were a peaceful pastoral sight grazing on the slope of the hill beyond the house. The concrete-block wall was now up around the house, to keep the sheep from eating all the expensive landscaping. On the other side of the curving drive Ken Kearney was energetically maneuvering a Rototiller; he waved casually as the Ferrari passed.

What the hell, thought Mendoza resignedly, it was only money... Kearney the ex-rancher, recommending the sheep as cheap lawnmowers, had lived for years far north in the state, and had been disconcerted at the long dry season this far south; unless they wanted to buy supplemental feed, he said— As it was, the two ponies for the twins got through a surprising amount of hay. For the last couple of weeks, Kearney had been busy installing an underground sprinkling system over a couple of acres, and would sow permanent pasture as year-round grazing for the sheep, and what that was going to do to the water bill— Only money, reflected Mendoza. Not any of his doing that the money was there; it had been a surprise to everybody, his grandfather unexpectedly leaving a fortune behind, probably founded on the proceeds of crooked gambling. At least the permanent pasture would look nice and parklike, said Kearney—and hopefully next spring he could shear the sheep himself, having studied a textbook. He hadn't been able to find a shearer nearer than Santa Barbara, and the bill for his mileage—

Only money. At least the electric eye on the gate was behaving itself now; Mendoza shoved the gadget on the dashboard and obediently the gates swung open, let him through, and closed smartly after him. He started down through Burbank for the Golden State freeway, and now he was thinking again, grimly, about Rosalie Ybarra.

The usual run of heisters they were hunting would get dropped on or not; hopefully some time the newest body would get identified; that bank job might get cleared up some time; but the ones like Rosalie Ybarra they went out to work with a vengeance.

Rosalie Ybarra had been eight years old, and by her picture a pretty, solemnly dark-eyed little girl. She attended St. Ignacio's parish school on Mozart Street in Lincoln Heights; she had six blocks to walk from her home on Gates Street. Last Friday afternoon she hadn't come home, and eventually was reported missing. Neighbors went out looking, the squad car along that beat hunted, questions were asked. Rosalie and her best friend Alicia Romero had walked together up to the corner of Griffin and Darwin Streets, and Rosalie had turned down Griffin and left Alicia. They hadn't found anyone who had seen Rosalie after that, and there hadn't been any sign of Rosalie anywhere until five o'clock yesterday afternoon.

A couple of scared ten-year-old boys had come home with a tale of a dead kid under some bushes in the playground, and the parents had called in. The squad had called Robbery-Homicide just before the end of shift, and Mendoza and Hackett had gone to look. By the description, the clothes, it was Rosalie; and no experienced detective needed a formal autopsy report to know what had happened to her. She had been raped and probably strangled, probably on the day she had disappeared. She had been thrust under a big sprawling juniper bush, naked, and her clothes put in on top of her—all but her underpants—the cotton slip and blue school uniform jumper, white blouse, white socks and strapped black shoes. The jumper and blouse were torn and bloody; the lab would be going over those, and some time tomorrow or the next day there'd be an autopsy report.

They would work this one hard, for whoever had killed Rosalie was one of the wild ones who might go looking for another little girl tomorrow or next day or next week.

Mendoza was a little late getting into the office; the morning traffic on the freeway was heavier than usual. He came in past Sergeant Lake at the switchboard, said, "Morning, Jimmy," and went down the hall to the big communal detective office, sweeping off the black Homburg. It was Jason Grace's day off. Palliser and Hackett were missing; Higgins was typing a report, hunched over his desk scowling. Tom Landers was half sitting on a corner of Henry Glasser's desk and they were both laughing. Mendoza went on into his office and found the night report centered on his desk.

It was an expectable one for a weeknight. More of the same, but not as much as it might have been. Another heist, by the description the same boy who had pulled two others in the last ten days, at a liquor store and a pharmacy: a big blond hulk waving a big gun around, and on this one—at another liquor store just before closing time last night—as on the pharmacy job, the victim said he thought the heister was high on something, wild-eyed and acting irrational. A body had been found on Skid Row, probably a wino dead of natural causes. There had been a mugging in the old plaza, the victim sent to Emergency in Cedars-Sinai.

The phone on his desk buzzed and he picked it up. "Yes, Jimmy?"

"I just got a call from Narco. Goldberg wants to see you about something—he'll be up about ten, he said."

"Bueno," said Mendoza inattentively.

"And Art and John are just back with the parents. It's a positive identification."

Mendoza got up, abandoning the report, and went out to the other office. Hackett had talked briefly with the parents on Friday; they hadn't been questioned since. It wasn't very likely that the parents could contribute anything helpful, but you never knew.

They were sitting beside Hackett's desk, with Wanda Larsen and Palliser hovering behind. Hackett said, "This is Lieutenant Mendoza, Mr. Ybarra."

He was a big, dark, stocky man, clean-shaven, looking uncomfortable in a formal dark suit and white shirt. He nodded heavily at Mendoza. He worked on the janitorial crew at a public elementary school. The Ybarras were both in the mid-thirties; they had three other children, one older and two younger than Rosalie. Mrs. Celia Ybarra had been crying; she mopped her face with a crumpled handkerchief. "I told the sergeant," said Ybarra, "it's Rosalie. In the morgue down there. Our Rosalie. We were so afraid—ever since she didn't come home. The awful things that happen—"

"But we'd told her—about not taking presents or listening to strangers—" Mrs. Ybarra sobbed once, dryly. "Not getting into cars with people she didn't know. But I said to Joe, she's so little—if some man just grabbed her off the street—oh, mother of God!—but somebody would have seen it, all the streets right around with people—" she rocked back and forth. They were both a type once commoner in California than now, their families probably resident here longer than most Anglos, since before California was a state. They both spoke unaccented English.

"I don't know," he said heavily. "Not so many people around, middle of the afternoon." He accepted a cigarette from Hackett with a nod. "Naturally we told her all that—like Celia says—things that happen nowadays, in the city or anywhere— You wouldn't believe what goes on at that school. Where I work, I mean. It's why we skimp ourselves other ways, send the kids to the parish school. It costs, but it's worth it—the sisters make them behave, they get taught manners and a better education all around. You got to do the best you can for your kids, you owe it to 'em. But I don't understand how Rosalie—how anybody could've got hold of her—just on her way home from school, and daylight—she always came straight home—"

"You were pretty upset on Friday when we talked to you before," said Hackett. "You said your son attends St. Ignacio's too—wouldn't he and Rosalie have walked home together usually?"

"Bob went home with Jimmy Lopez—his best friend. He does that a lot—they do homework together. He got home just before—before we usually have dinner. We'd called the police by then—" Ybarra was shaking his head blindly. "I don't understand how anybody could've got hold of her—she was a good girl, she knew to be careful of strangers, she wouldn't have gone up to any stranger—"

Hackett met Mendoza's eyes and gave a small shrug of his massive shoulders. The parents didn't have anything to tell them. Later on it might be different, when they were thinking straighter; they'd be questioned about family friends, relatives, any adult Rosalie had known. It wasn't always the wild one coaxing the child into a car, snatching her off the street; sometimes it was the known, trusted acquaintance. Right now they had what they needed from the parents, the formal identification.

Hackett explained about the necessary autopsy, the release of the body. "We'll be in touch with you, Mr. Ybarra. You know we'll be at work on this, try to find out about it."

"Yes, sir. You all been good," said Ybarra. His wife sobbed into her handkerchief as she stood up. Palliser said gently he'd take them home, and shepherded them out.

"There are still a lot of people to talk to," said Hackett, taking off his glasses to polish them. "All along the way she'd have been walking. It's a bastard, Luis. Working-class neighborhood, a lot of people not home. And they're such nice respectable people, the Ybarras."

"What's that got to do— Oh," said Wanda. "Oh, yes, I see."

"Words of one syllable." Mendoza flicked his lighter and ejected a long stream of smoke. "Rosalie was brought up to be a polite little girl. If a car pulled up and somebody asked which way was Darwin Street, she'd have gone over to answer."

"It could be as simple as that," agreed Hackett. "Well, go on working it as we can. Nick's down in records looking for the local sex freaks."

"And it could be as simple as that too," said Mendoza sardonically. "Some nut with the right record let out on parole by the softheaded judge. Or it could be the first time out for some character nobody's ever suspected."

"You needn't say it," said Hackett. He stood up, looming over Mendoza, and put his glasses away. "At least it's nice cool weather for the legwork. I want to see the sisters at that school—they were going to talk to the kids. It could be one of them noticed something." Landers and Glasser had vanished, and now Higgins was on the phone. "I suppose we'd better get with it. You like to help out?"

"I've got a date with Goldberg on something, I don't know what."

"Well, wish us luck." Hackett went out with Wanda trailing him.

Higgins put the phone down and sat back looking annoyed. He passed a hand over his craggy face. "We can use everybody we've got on one like that, all those damn streets to cover, and I sit here waiting for this damned witness— that Conover, on the pharmacy heist. He's very sorry, he overslept, he'll be in as soon as he can make it. And I waste time taking him down to look at the books of mug shots and he won't make a damned one."

"It can be a frustrating job, *compadre*. Tom and Henry seemed to be enjoying a joke when I got in. Anything interesting?"

Higgins chuckled. "You hadn't heard? Matt left a note with the night report. It's very funny in a way, Luis—all happening at the same time, I mean. You know Tom's wife is expecting a baby in December, and now it seems so is Matt's wife, they just got it confirmed. And the first thing John said this morning was that they think Roberta's pregnant too, she's got a date with the doctor on Thursday."

Mendoza laughed. "The young people will do it," he said amusedly, and Sergeant Lake came in with a manila envelope.

It was the autopsy report on Saturday's unidentified corpse. He took it back to his office to read; but it didn't tell them much.

The corpse had been found as soon as it was light, last Saturday morning, huddled up against the fence around the Amtrak freight yards along Alhambra Avenue. It was completely naked, with nothing on or around it to provide a clue to identity: just the body of a man, and all that could be deduced when Higgins saw it was that it had been dead for a day or so, rigor just passing off. None of the railroad employees had recognized it.

The autopsy said a little more. The corpse, which bore no scars or tattoos or any useful identifying marks, was that of a man between thirty and forty years old. He had been five feet six and half inches tall, weighed a hundred and forty pounds. He was a white man with thinning brown hair and blue eyes, and he had all his own teeth except for a bridge with three teeth in it in the upper jaw; he had probably worn that for ten years or so. He had sustained, in lay language, a severe bang on the head, to the left temple, but that wouldn't have killed him; he had actually died of manual strangulation, probably sometime between nine A.M. and nine P.M. on Friday. He had eaten a meal about three hours before he died. There was no evidence of alcohol or any controlled drug present in the body. It was just an anonymous body. Fingerprints had been taken, and a dental chart could be made up if requested, but the doctor didn't sound optimistic about the idea: there hadn't been much dental work evident.

"Así," said Mendoza to himself, and picked up the phone and asked for SID. He got Marx, and asked about the anonymous corpse's prints.

"They weren't on record with us," said Marx. "I sent them on to the feds, lessee, on Sunday, it may be awhile before you get a kickback. Of course they may not know him either."

"Thanks so much."

"He was a harmless-looking little guy," said Marx. "He reminded me a little bit of Crippen."

"Who?"

"You know, Dr. Crippen—I like the true-crime stuff sometimes, classic cases, you know. Crippen's the one who killed his wife and cut her up. Not that she didn't deserve it. He was a mild-looking fellow with gold-rimmed glasses and a sort of apologetic expression, by the pictures."

"True crime!" said Mendoza. "I haven't seen the corpse."

"Well, it just put me in mind of Crippen. I'll bet he was a henpecked husband."

"And the lady lost patience because he wouldn't stand up for himself and strangled him?"

"Oh, was he strangled? I wouldn't know. You ought to hear from the feds sometime," said Marx.

As soon as Mendoza put the phone down it buzzed at him.

"Goldberg and Callaghan are here," said Lake. "And there was a new call—a body. Palliser just got back, he went out on it."

"*Bueno.* Both the Narco experts at once? Well, shove them along."

PALLISER MET LANDERS just coming back after having left one of the heist witnesses poring over mug shots down in R. and I., and they went out on the new call together.

"Is that right, you're expecting too?" asked Landers.

"We're pretty sure. Robin's feeling what you might call ambivalent about it," said Palliser with a grin. "On the one hand, Davy's nearly two and it'll be nice spacing between them, but she's been talking about getting farther out of Hollywood into a better area, and you know what interest rates are."

"Indeedy," said Landers with a groan. "We ought to have made a down payment on a house when we got married, but there it is, we didn't. Phil can go back to work after six months without losing any seniority, but— Hell, I don't know, we can look and maybe find some little place we can afford." Phillippa Rosemary was one of the policewomen in the Records office. "And then, as she says, there'll be the baby, and it'd be nice just to stay home and be a housewife for a change. But on just my salary—"

"At least we got in on the lower interest rate," said Palliser sympathetically.

"Where are we heading for, by the way?"

"Dead body somewhere on Bonnie Brae Street." They took Palliser's car.

When they got there, it was an old and shabby apartment house, and the squad car was waiting in front with the uniformed man—Waring—and a civilian in it. The civilian was a paunchy middle-aged man with an unshaven jowl, wearing a soiled plaid shirt and jeans. "This is Mr. Boman," said Waring. "He found the body and called in."

"Don't know why you kept me hangin' around," said Boman. "I don't know one goddamned thing about it—don't even know the guy's name. He lives in the next apartment, that's all. I'm on vacation, I work for Firestone, only who can afford to go away anywheres now, just means I sleep later in the morning, 's all. And I forgot I was out of coffee, so I'm on my way out to the market to get some, and come past the door and it's open and he's lying there in plain sight—I thought he was just passed out at first, and then I saw the blood. Looked like there'd been a fight or something."

He followed them up the stairs, puffing slightly. No manager on the premises, he said, so he just called the police himself. "And I haven't had a cup of coffee or no breakfast yet, damn it. It's nothing to do with me."

At the back of the second floor, he pointed out the door. "You can see I couldn't help but see him when I come past."

"Yes, sir," said Palliser. The apartment door was nearly wide open, and five feet beyond it the body of a man sprawled face up on the worn ancient rug. "Did you go in?"

"Just inside the door, to look good—and I see he's dead, so— No, I never touched a thing."

"You live in the next apartment? Did you hear anything like a fight in here last night?"

Boman shrugged. "Things got a little noisy in there sometimes. Not too bad—music and partying, like—you know. He was just a young fellow, like you see, no wife or nothing, sometimes he'd have people in and they'd be a little noisy. I never said nothing because it wasn't that often and it didn't go on long. Nor it wasn't that rock music crap either, it was a funny kind of foreign music. And just some loud talking and laughing, young people enjoying themselves."

"Did you hear that last night?"

"No music. There was some loud talking just for awhile, that's all. It was, oh, I guess maybe about nine o'clock or around there."

"Nothing that sounded like a fight?"

"Nope."

Palliser said, "Well, these older buildings are pretty solid. It's possible you wouldn't have."

"Said I didn't."

"Yes, sir. Thanks very much for calling in. We'll want a statement from you, but later on will do." Boman went out gladly, and they looked around.

The body was that of a very good-looking dark young man; the classic-featured face was virile and handsome, and the rest of him matched: he was tall and well-built, with a wide chest and narrow hips. He was wearing gaudy bright green pajamas and a scarlet nylon bathrobe. There was blood on one temple and down the side of his face and throat, and on the floor beside him was a metal statue about a foot long, also bloodstained: the figure of a naked girl striking a ballet pose, arms uplifted.

Landers squatted over it. "One of the arms is bent. Looks as if somebody used it to hit him with. It's good heavy metal by the look of it."

"Um. See what the lab says. Who was he?" said Palliser. They prowled around, not touching anything. It was a cheap, shabby apartment, obviously rented furnished; only a portable color TV in one corner of the living room wouldn't have come with the place. In the bedroom, a double bed was made up with an old-fashioned chenille spread, and the half-open closet door showed a little wardrobe of slacks and shirts neatly on hangers.

"Those pajamas—" said Landers. "A couple of fags having a ruction?"

"Time should tell," said Palliser. "Here's his billfold." It was on top of the dresser, with a wristwatch on a stretch band, some loose change: a worn plain billfold with no snap fastening. Palliser maneuvered it open with his pen, and the first little plastic slot held a driver's license. The darkly handsome face of the dead man stared up from the left-hand corner. Nicholas Zemenides, twenty-five, six-two, a hundred and ninety, black and brown. This address was listed; the license was good for another three years, which said he'd had an excellent driving record. Palliser went on leafing over the slots, and the third one contained a standard I.D. form: under "whom to notify in emergency" was scrawled two names and addresses—Mr. William Waller, *Herald-Examiner* office, and Mrs. Peter Zemenides, 14 Horton Street, Concord, Massachusetts.

"Some place to start asking questions at least," said Palliser. They went downstairs and told Waring to call the lab. Fifteen minutes later the mobile lab truck pulled up, and they let the squad go and left Horder and Scarne taking photographs.

At the *Herald-Examiner* office up toward Hollywood, they encountered a vague-eyed female who denied any knowledge of a William Waller. She had never heard of Zemenides either. Palliser asked for the personnel manager and showed her the badge; she fled and didn't come back, but in her place they got a fussy gray-haired man by the name of Hancock, who said really it was the first time they'd had police here and what was it about?

"William Waller," said Palliser. "Does he work here?"

"Mr. Waller? Well, not precisely here—in the other building—what on earth do you want with Mr. Waller? He's head of Circulation, but really—police—" He sputtered, finally gave them directions—the old building directly across the parking lot.

Waller, run to earth in an untidy office on the second floor, stared at the badge in surprise. "Zemenides?" he said. He was a tall, spare man in the forties, with a good-humored mouth and friendly eyes. "Sure I know Nick. What about him?"

"Does he work here?"

"Yes, that's right. He's one of our delivery drivers. There's one crew bales up papers for the carriers, and another crew supplies all the drops—you know, the automatic containers all over town. Nick's one of those drivers. What do the police want with him?"

Palliser told him, and he was astonished. "Murdered!" he exclaimed blankly. "Well, I will be damned! I will be goddamned! What? No, I never knew Nick to have any trouble with anybody—he always seemed to be a very nice guy, I don't think I ever saw him lose his temper or— Of course, you understand I don't see much of the drivers, my job's assigning routes and so on."

"How long had he worked here?"

"Oh, a little over two years, I can look it up. He was a reliable man, he had a good record with us. I couldn't say if he had any particular pals among the other drivers, but I can give you the names—"

"Would you know," asked Landers, "if he was a fag?"

Waller looked even more astonished and then burst out laughing. "Now you have got to be kidding!" he said. "Nick? My God, about the only other thing I do know about him—from some of the other boys and a couple of the typists out in front—he was hell on wheels with the girls."

"Oh, is that so?"

"By what I gather, no female could resist him, and he played the field."

"But you wouldn't know any names? Any of the girl friends or his men friends?"

"Sorry, no. My God, this does shake me. Happy-go-lucky handsome young fellow like that, getting himself murdered—my God. I don't know if any of the other drivers could tell you anything, but you can talk to them. They're on more or less regular hours, seven to three. The other crew supplying the carriers, that's part-time work, just afternoons. As a matter of fact, I ought to have had it reported before now when he didn't turn up for work—I suppose the other men took it for granted he'd called in sick." He glanced at the wall clock. "It's all pretty organized. That crew's been out with the first edition, they'll be showing up by eleven to pick up more papers."

"Here?"

"That's right—out there in the parking lot by the garage. Another thing," said Waller, "not that I suppose it'd be much help to you, but he was Greek, you know—he went to the Greek Orthodox church. I remember hearing him make a joke about it, how he'd promised his mama always to go to church, but it was only one day a week. Maybe somebody at the church would know more about him."

"Maybe," said Palliser. "Thanks very much."

In the parking lot, waiting for some of those other drivers to show up, Landers said again meditatively, "Those pajamas. Damn it. John, nobody but a fag would wear kelly-green pajamas and a red nylon robe."

"You're forgetting one thing."

"What?"

"He was Greek," said Palliser. "Very gay, happy people—same like Latins, they go for the bright colors."

"Well, maybe," said Landers. A boxlike truck tagged with the *Herald-Examiner* logo swung into the lot and pulled into one of the slots in front of the big garage under the building. They started over there as the driver got out, and showed the badges. The driver, a stocky, blond young fellow, stared.

"Detectives?" he said. He looked at tall handsome Palliser, at tall slender Landers. "Hell, you don't look old enough to be a detective," he said to the latter, and Landers suppressed wrath.

Maybe by the time Phil's expected baby was grown up and married, people would stop saying that to Landers.

HACKETT AND WANDA had started out at St. Ignacio's parish school, and talked to Sister Mary Grace, who was young and nice-looking and friendly, and Sister Mary Frances, who was elderly and grim. Neither of them was any help.

They had both questioned all the classes, jointly, and got nothing from any of the children. "And if any of them had seen anything, Sergeant," said Sister Mary Grace, "I'm sure they'd have told us. Over a terrible thing like this—it wouldn't be anything like keeping a friend's innocent secret, something like that. Oh, yes, we heard about the body being found—it was on the radio last night—dear Lord, what a terrible, terrible thing—she was such a sweet child, so well brought up, and a bright little girl too—" She looked very troubled. "Poor Alicia—her mother called to excuse her from school, she's so upset—they'd been best friends since kindergarten."

"Tchah!" said Sister Mary Frances. "Giving in to emotions. The sooner we all learn to cope with the power of the devil in this world—"

"She's only eight," said Sister Mary Grace. She looked at slim, blond Wanda. "You see, most of the children live within walking distance but some of them take the bus—up along Main Street. We're a fairly small school—just eighty pupils this year—and only a few of them would be walking the direction Rosalie and Alicia would, down Griffin Avenue."

That was only reasonable: with the tale of what had happened to Rosalie running like wildfire through the school, if any of the kids had seen anything—Rosalie talking to a stranger, getting into a car—they'd have spoken up.

Hackett had talked to Alicia Romero on Sunday: a rather homely, pug-faced little girl who had cried and said, "If only I'd walked home with her! If only I had—I nearly did, but the Ybarras don't have a color TV and I wanted to see Cartoon Parade—if I'd just walked home with her nothing bad could've happened! If I'd only—"

Robbery-Homicide had not been officially involved, of course, until the body had been found, but it had been nearly a foregone conclusion what had happened to Rosalie, and they had already started asking questions around the general neighborhood, on Sunday. They knew that Rosalie had been all right when she parted from Alicia at Griffin and Darwin, and she'd only been four and a half blocks from home there. But they were four and a half blocks of old, shabby single houses, duplexes, a few apartments, along the narrow old streets of one of the older areas of Los Angeles—a mixed neighborhood, about half Hispanic with an interspersing of a very few blacks, and in the last couple of years anonymous Orientals with a poor grasp of English. A great many of these people would be at work all day; and those four and a half blocks were all residential, quiet and largely empty at three-twenty on a weekday afternoon.

They split up and started ringing doorbells and, where they found anyone home, asking questions. Were you at home last Friday afternoon? Did you happen to notice a little girl in the St. Ignacio school uniform walk past? Was she alone?

There weren't many people at home. At one apartment and one side of a duplex, Wanda was frustrated by Vietnamese females who shrugged and chattered and waved hands uncomprehendingly. "If we get many more of these people coming in," she said, comparing notes with Hackett briefly, "we'll have to hire interpreters to do the leg-work. Damn. It could just be that one of those women saw something."

"And I don't suppose we'll ever know," said Hackett. He looked tired and troubled, and she thought he was probably thinking about his own small daughter. A man would.

They were joined midway along Eastlake Avenue by Nick Galeano. He met Hackett just coming away from an empty house and said, "I figured you could use some help. I've got a list of possible sex nuts out of records, but how much it says—"

"Yes, we'd better go looking and lean on them," said Hackett. Stocky, dark, amiable Galeano was looking strangely slim and spruce these days; he had been married to his charming, efficient German Marta for two and a half months, and it was apparently an improvement on a bachelorhood of thirty-five years. "We're not getting anywhere here. When are you joining the sweepstakes, Nick?"

"What sweepstakes?"

"Babies. I'm thinking of getting up a kitty—guess which arrives first, Landers' or Palliser's or Piggott's, we could make it a straight gamble or a combination for higher stakes—"

Galeano laughed. "Palliser too? I hadn't heard about that. It's a thought, Art. Give me a little time. You haven't turned up anything yet? Well, it's early—we've only just started looking."

"So let's see the list of nuts, and we go looking some more."

WITH RED-HAIRED ALISON, to think was to act, and she said energetically to Mairí MacTaggart that morning, "A cruise or a tour—Europe or the South Pacific or somewhere. He never gets away from the job, and it's ridiculous. Here you all are to look after the children, and it'll be good for him."

"Mmhph," said Mairí, smiling. She regarded Alison benevolently, patting her silver-gray curls. "I can see well enough he's to be haled off on holiday whether or no. Verra guid. Doubtless you'll both enjoy it. You could take a nice tour of the British Isles, now—your father having been a Weir, you'd like seeing the Highlands, and all that part and the Hebrides will be showing their best at this time of year."

"Marvelous," agreed Alison. "But the South Pacific—"

The twins, with school out, were down at the corral caressing the ponies Star and Diamond and waiting for Ken Kearney to supervise rides. Luisa Mary, who had suddenly decided to walk at ten months and was developing a jargon of her own instead of Spanish or English, was contentedly sitting in the back yard picking dandelions.

Alison was looking up travel agencies in the Yellow Pages when Angel Hackett called her. "It is really the funniest thing—everybody pregnant at once—I was just talking to Roberta Palliser. Tom Landers' wife, and Piggott's, and now Roberta. Well, the reason I called her—you know we want a dog for the children. Now we've got a nice fenced yard on a nice, quiet dead-end street. Roberta's been really working at training that big shepherd for obedience, and she's got her entered at the Pasadena dog show next Sunday. I'm going with her—I thought it'd be a good way to take a look at all the dogs, and talk to breeders—"

"Yes, that's a good idea— What I've been thinking about, you know Luis never will take a vacation, and it'd be good for him, we never go anywhere, and I thought—"

"—Just a small dog, I got that AKC dog book from the library, with all the pictures, and I thought something like a West Highland white terrier or a Scottie—not to need much exercise—"

"Yes, that'd be fine. And what I thought, I couldn't care less about Hawaii, the climate impossible, and the prices— but possibly Jamaica or Haiti—"

"Yes, marvelous," said Angel. "Or possibly an Irish terrier—"

"WELL, AND SO what do you want with me?" asked Mendoza, leaning back in his desk chair.

Captain Goldberg blew his nose and Pat Callaghan, bigger than Hackett and redder-haired than Alison, gave a disgusted snort.

"I'm tired of telling the story," he said. "You and every other precinct and the sheriff's boys and the Highway Patrol. It's a bummer and we'll probably never get anywhere on it."

"So tell me the tale."

"We want to ask you," said Goldberg, "to be on the lookout for a body."

Mendoza laughed. "We don't generally have to go looking. Whose body?"

TWO

CALLAGHAN LEANED back in the chair beside Mendoza's desk and shut his eyes. "His name is Tony Quinlan and he's a dealer. The Hollywood boys have had an eye on him for a while—they got tipped by an ex-con who disapproves of the foolish powder, he had a job for awhile as a chauffeur gardener for one of our brighter young starlets. My God in heaven, these show-biz people. Do I need to spell out the details? You know the story—the dope floating around by the pound, all varieties. The uppers and downers, all the prescription stuff, there are a dozen and one doctors who'll write the prescriptions for the asking, but the hard stuff is a little bit harder to come by. Just a little. Quinlan was one of the sources. You understand that this is all pure speculation, no usable evidence. He was one of the boys obliging the boys and girls of studioland, at the fancy prices. Ostensibly the young playboy about town, money of his own, only no background of money shows. It's all kind of vague, but for about ninety percent sure his wholesale supplier was Al Crossland. One of the six or seven wholesale suppliers in the general area, and—"

"Tied to the Syndicate?" asked Mendoza, making a steeple of his long hands.

"What else?" Goldberg folded Kleenex away, taking up the tale. "We got Crossland's name on the q.t. from the Chicago boys, after they'd pulled a raid and come across this and that. But it's all up in the air, no usable evidence at all, God damn it. He's not the only Albert Crossland in existence. He's got a very nice front, all open and honest and a beautiful record with the IRS. A garment manufacturing business, ladies' dresses and accessories, a big plant out on

San Pedro. It's doubtful that he stashes the supply there, and we've got no idea how and where he takes delivery.''

"In other words, it's all up in the air,'' said Mendoza. "I'm waiting for the corpse.''

"God damn it, we deduce the corpse,'' said Callaghan querulously. "There's no real evidence on either of them—the Hollywood boys have had an intermittent tail on Quinlan, and we've been keeping an eye on Crossland. We deduce this and that. To each his own vice, and Crossland's a gambler. Poker, the ponies, you name it. About four months back, we got from a snitch who claims to know, he dropped a big bundle at Vegas. It could have caught him short enough that he couldn't hand over the percentage to the bosses. Anyway, the word is that he borrowed a bundle from Quinlan, and still owes him.''

"Up in the air!'' said Goldberg with a snarl. "We've got a girl friend of Quinlan's—ex-girl friend—who heard a couple of phone conversations, Quinlan calling Al a damn welsher and threatening action. We've got the cleaning lady last Thursday afternoon—''

"Ahead of yourself,'' said Callaghan. "Quinlan's got no link to the Syndicate, of course. But he could make Crossland a little trouble. You know how smooth and legit the Syndicate is set up these days—the nice legal fronts, the channels. It's possible that Crossland is in a little hot water with the bosses already, when he's showing as a big-time gambler at Vegas.''

"What about Quinlan?'' asked Mendoza.

"Well, he's disappeared.'' Goldberg sneezed and reached for more Kleenex. "The last we can place him is about five o'clock last Thursday afternoon—with one exception—when the cleaning lady heard him talking on the phone. He'd thrown a party the night before, and she spent the afternoon cleaning up after it. Fancy apartment out in West Hollywood. He was talking to somebody named Al, and he didn't sound friendly—said something about a showdown, or he'd hire a collection agency. He was due at a party that night at Sally Ann Blanchard's place—you know, one of our newest TV starlets—''

''It rings a faint bell.'' Mendoza was not a TV fan.

''—And he called her about eight, said he'd be late, he had to see a man about a dog. He never showed. So far as Hollywood can find out, he hasn't been seen since.''

''Interesting, but what's it got to do with me?'' asked Mendoza.

''Well, damn it,'' said Callaghan, ''we can add two and two, Luis. Quinlan had had dates with Crossland in his office—Crossland's office in the manufacturing building—before. Hollywood had tailed him. It looks as if he set up a date that night, for a showdown over the money. And abracadabra, he's gone. Very convenient for Crossland, you can see.''

''If you're asking me to delve into Syndicate contracts—''

''Be your age, God damn it,'' said Callaghan. ''When the Syndicate puts out a contract the evidence is a mile deep—they're way behind all the legit fronts. This was just between Crossland and Quinlan, and the hell with the Syndicate, Crossland wouldn't have any henchmen helping out. His bosses would take a damn poor view of an unauthorized homicide.''

''Mmh,'' said Mendoza to his steepled hands. ''Which is what you think happened?''

''Well, it's a little suggestive. We've got Quinlan on the phone making threats, and missing the party, and incidentally not turning up for a date with the current girl friend the next night—''

''Hollywood's been busy.''

''Yeah. And then Saul sometimes has useful ideas.'' Callaghan glanced at Goldberg benevolently. ''Quinlan got a traffic ticket that night—last Thursday night. Along Venice Boulevard just this side of the Stack. For running a red light.''

"*¿Es cierto?*" Mendoza laughed. "That's very pretty. Very astute of you to look for it, Saul."

"Just being thorough. He seems to have had a reputation as a careless driver. But that places him on the way to Crossland's building, in a way. The ticket was handed out at eight thirty-five."

"*¿Cómo no?* And he hasn't turned up anywhere since?"

"Well, for God's sake," said Callaghan, "he could be over in Vegas watching the girly shows, only we don't think so, Luis. Just deducing, it could very well be that he had a private meeting with Crossland, there was a fight, and Quinlan ended up dead. Unintentionally on Crossland's part, because that would make the bosses very cross with him, you know."

"Understandable. And?"

"Well, he'd try to cover up. He already knew we were sniffing around Quinlan. Hollywood, that is. He'd have been running scared. But he's a cool customer, he hasn't been in the business for years without occasional trouble, and he'd come up with a plan."

"So what would he do with the corpse? If any?"

"You can use your imagination on it," said Callaghan. "He didn't take it home to bury in the back yard. He and his wife, who is just as talented at spending money as he is, live in a two-hundred-thousand-buck condo in Bel Air. The sensible thing would have been to take it four miles out in the Pacific, but he doesn't own a boat and he wouldn't want any accomplices in on it. What we both think he'd have done was try to disguise it. Stash it somewhere inaccessible—under the bushes up in Griffin Park—but in case it was found, the fake I.D. on it. Not much, maybe, but enough to look legit—standard I.D. form, John Joseph Brown, who to notify."

"If the corpse was an obvious homicide—"

"Well, how far would you look?" said Callaghan reasonably. "How far would Hollywood? Anybody? Nobody's got Quinlan's prints as far as we know. A body maybe six months dead, labeled with a name? The press of business we get, you'd take a look around and end up shoving it in Pending. But you can see what we're after. There's not one goddamn piece of evidence on Crossland on the Narco charge. It'd be very nice to put him out of business. God damn it, in a month the bosses would have somebody new in his place, but— And it'd be even more gratifying to nail him on a homicide charge. We're just alerting everybody to take a second look at any stray bodies that show up."

"Mmh," said Mendoza. "Where's Quinlan's car?"

"Talk about astute," said Goldberg dryly. "Peacefully at home in its carport at the West Hollywood apartment. A year-old Caddy Coupe de Ville."

"And Hollywood hasn't any legal reason to look at the apartment."

"Nobody's reported him missing. It's all our nasty imaginations."

"Oh, yes. Well, we'll take a second look at any stray bodies on our beat. Have you got a photograph?"

"Only a description." Goldberg handed over a photocopy. "He seems to have been leery about being photographed, even if he hadn't a pedigree anywhere."

Mendoza glanced over the description, couched in official language, and grinned. "At least there's the tattoo. Very pretty." Anthony Quinlan was five-ten, a hundred and seventy, brown hair, blue eyes, about thirty. On his left forearm he bore the tattoo of a six-pointed star with beneath it the legend *born under a lucky*.

"Yes, if you come across a body with a piece cut out of its left arm you can look three times," said Goldberg.

"At least," said Mendoza absently, "Quinlan's not the gent from the Amtrak yards. No tattoo, and quite intact. Well, we'll keep you in mind and let you know if any possible corpse shows up on our beat."

HACKETT HAD LEFT Wanda and Galeano to finish the leg-
work on Rosalie's way home, and armed with the list of sex
offenders out of records went back to the office and picked
up Higgins. They started out after lunch looking for those
men to question, at their last known addresses. They found
just one—Lester Freeman, with a record back to age fourteen, the expectable record starting out with underwear
thefts from clotheslines, Peeping Tom, attempted assault,
attempted rape, finally abduction and rape of a twelve-year-
old girl. He had spent six years in Susanville, been out six
months and was still on parole. He was twenty-seven. He
lived in a two-room apartment on Michigan Avenue in Boyle
Heights and had a job at a gas station on Adams Boulevard, which was where they found him.

Freeman was a big hulk of a black man, not very bright,
and he said sullenly that he never did that, they couldn't put
nothing on him, he hadn't done nothing. Friday, well, Friday he was here at the station all day, Mr. Coates could say.
Coates, who owned the station, said that was right, Les had
been there all day Friday. So was he, so he knew. There'd
been two radiator jobs in, and one had given him the hell of
a lot of trouble, and it was promised for five o'clock, so he'd
never got away for lunch—just sent Les across the street for
sandwiches.

"You can say definitely," asked Hackett, "that Freeman
was here after three o'clock?"

"Yeah. To about five-thirty. He wasn't gone twenty
minutes after the sandwiches—besides, his car was here all
day, parked right against the garage," and Coates nodded
at an old heap of a Ford.

They went looking next for Harold Custer and John
Schultz, who both had records similar to Freeman's, and
didn't find either. They were both off parole. Custer had
just quit his job as parking-lot attendant and moved from
his single room at an old hotel. At the address they had for
Schultz they found his mother. She was a defeated-looking
middle-aged woman who told them that Johnny thought he

might do better up north, he'd gone up to San Francisco a couple of months ago. "Have you heard from him?" asked Higgins.

"Oh, yeah, I had a postcard last week. He got a job in some big hotel up there, it pays pretty good."

There were six more names on the list, all the addresses farther afield than the downtown beat. Those wouldn't be the only likely sex offenders in records; Galeano had just culled the hard-core cases of violent assaults on children; and there'd be a lot more of those around in other peoples' records. One like this was always a bastard to work.

It was four o'clock; they went back to the office, and ten minutes later Wanda and Galeano came in with Mrs. Inez Cabrillo.

"I think we've got a little something," said Galeano. "See what you think."

Mrs. Cabrillo was a large deep-bosomed dark woman with soulful brown eyes and a warm voice. "Mother of God!" she said dramatically. "I never heard a thing about this until you come asking—this poor child killed, this monster, such fiends there are around—but it's like I told you, it was on Friday—last Friday—my husband's birthday, and I'd just taken the cake out of the oven and put it to cool, I went to see if the mail had come—usually it comes two-thirty, three o'clock—and it hadn't, I just went out on the porch to look in the box, and I looked up the street to see if the mailman's coming—I don't see him, but I saw the little girl in the street, and it must be it was that one. I never heard about the murder—such things happen these days— I've been busy the last week making clothes for my daughters—I have three, thanks to God all grown and married— but it must be it was that little girl. It was after three o'clock—yes—and she had on that blue uniform those kids at the parish school wear—she was right down by the curb, she was talking to somebody in a car there—nearly in front of our house, yes. The motor was running—I couldn't see who was in the car, I don't know if it was a man, but it must have been this fiend, I couldn't see into the car, but if it was that poor child, it must have been—''

"What about the car?" asked Hackett.

She gestured violently. "Do I know about cars? What could I say? I didn't notice! If I think about it at all, I think the little girl's talking to a friend, brother, father, maybe just got out of the car—how should I know? I was thinking about the mail, I expected a letter from my daughter Maria— About cars what do I know? I couldn't tell you much about it—it wasn't new, it wasn't old, it was a tan color all over, it was a car with a back seat but I don't know if it had two doors or whatever—'' Another massive shrug. Wanda was scribbling shorthand efficiently.

It wasn't much, but it was the first break they had had. Wanda typed a statement and Mrs. Cabrillo signed it. The chance had always been that a car was involved, an abduction in the middle of the afternoon, and Rosalie would have been the only little girl from St. Ignacio's walking up that block at that hour. Mrs. Cabrillo lived in the middle of that block of Eastlake Avenue. Rosalie had been within a block of home.

All it gave them was a rudimentary description of the car.

MENDOZA HAD HEARD about that, everybody else had left and he was on his way out when a messenger from Communications dropped off a manila envelope. He stayed to open it, and it was the kickback from the FBI on the corpse by the freight-yard fence. His prints had been on record because he was a federal employee. His name was Edward John Foster and he had worked for the Post Office.

Rather a surprising end for a civil servant, reflected Mendoza vaguely. He dropped the report on his desk and went on out to the elevator.

Traffic on the freeway was moving briskly for once, and he was driving up the highest street in Burbank half an hour later. The wrought-iron gates swung politely open as he shoved the dashboard, and closed silently after the Ferrari.

Kearney had one set of the new sprinklers going, up on the hillside, and the westering sun struck rainbows in the silvery flashes of arching water. He slid the Ferrari into the garage beside Alison's Facel-Vega and Mairí's old Chevy, and walked around to the front door, glancing down the hill to admire the flashing fountain-play of sprinklers again. The Five Graces were grazing pastorally down the other side of the hill, and Alison's gracious old estate was looking handsome altogether. Cedric was lying regally in the middle of the courtyard, and wuffed at him genially, came up to trail him in.

The wide entry hall was empty except for El Señor ensconced on the credenza, paws well folded in; he gave Mendoza a dark inscrutable glance. The other three cats—Bast, Sheba and Nefertite—were in a tangle on the long couch in the living room. Mendoza went down to the large square kitchen at the back, and found Alison and Mairí talking animatedly.

"¿Qué tal tu día, mi vida?"

"Oh, Luis—" Alison pounced at him. "I went to the travel agency, and there are lots of possibilities but I really think this South Pacific cruise sounds just the thing. There's a stopover in Honolulu but only one night—twelve days, Tahiti and Papeete and Bora-Bora—"

"¡Dios me libre!" said Mendoza. "What's this all about?"

"Now don't rush the man," said Mairí amusedly. "Give him a chance to have a drink before dinner. Everything's hot in the oven when you're ready—I'll just fetch Johnny and Terry for their baths."

"A nice ocean cruise—you'll enjoy it, it'll do you good," said Alison robustly. "The end of August, and not really as expensive as you might think, Luis."

Mendoza opened the cupboard over the sink and took down the bottle of rye. El Señor could sense when that cupboard was opened, and arrived speedily on the counter, begging in his raucous half-Siamese voice for his share.

Mendoza laughed at him, poured him half an ounce in a saucer. "I don't want a vacation. Anywhere."

"But I do," said Alison firmly. "It'll do you good, *cariño*. All right, I'll have a glass of sherry."

He poured his rye, the sherry for her, and started back to the living room.

"We fly to Honolulu and pick up the cruise ship there. And there's an optional cruise out of Papeete to Rangiroa, I thought that sounded—"

"No," said Mendoza. "It's too far off. Why this sudden craze to visit such outlandish places? You remember what happened the last time you dragged me off on a vacation."

"Oh, don't be silly," said Alison. "Art couldn't get himself half murdered twice. A nice restful ocean voyage will be good for both of us."

"It's too far. And I wouldn't like to lose you to the headhunters." Mendoza swallowed rye.

"Really, Luis—"

But at that point the twins erupted into the room, yelling at the tops of their voices. "Daddy, Daddy, Uncle Ken put Luisa on Star and she like it! She laughed and laughed—"

"Daddy, we have to get another pony for Luisa—"

"My God!" said Mendoza. "Maybe in another five years, *niños*—" The hay those ponies got through—

"Now! Now! Luisa liked it, she laughed—"

"And she can't have Diamond," announced Terry firmly.

"Can't have Star neither! We got to get her own pony—Daddy—"

"*¡Qué camada!*" said Mendoza.

"I want you to look at the brochure," said Alison loudly.

"For God's sake let me finish my drink in peace."

THE GALEANOS had started to buy a house in Studio City. It was nice to have a real house to come home to, Galeano thought as he pulled into the garage beside the secondhand Ford they had found for Marta. He went in the back door; she was busy in the kitchen, and there were appetizing smells; a bonus to get a good cook as well as a beautiful wife.

"Darling!" she said. There was a suitable interval for the newlyweds. Presently he told her about the sweepstakes.

"Have to hurry to get in on that maybe."

Marta chuckled richly. Her tawny-blond hair was a little untidy, her dark eyes warm on him. "Yes, indeed, we will have two, perhaps three—but not until I have the garden in better order, much cheaper to grow some of our own food. You will see! And what do you think, Nick? You know I have wanted a nice cat, and today I hear of people up the block who have kittens, and I go to ask—we will have a pretty gray tabby puss when they leave mama."

"Wouldn't you rather have—"

"In a little while," she told him, laughing. "Now go and wash, and we will have dinner."

WEDNESDAY WAS HACKETT'S day off. He got up a little later than usual, and mowed the back lawn while Angel went out to market. The children played quietly enough in the sand-box near the house. For all that Mark was just out of first grade, he was good about playing with Sheila, who was only four.

With half the lawn mowed, Hackett sat down to have a cigarette. The children were prattling about the nice doggie mama was going to get them. "It'll be loverly," said Mark, and Sheila echoed dutifully, "Lovally." When Mark found a word he liked it got constant use; for the last month anything and everything had been tagged as "loverly."

Hackett yawned and reflected that Angel was right, a dog would be nice for the kids. This was a bigger yard to take care of, but a better place for the kids, on a quiet dead-end street high up in Altadena. A little dog would be company for the kids. Just as well to have a watchdog, too, the crime rate was up everywhere now.

He wondered if anything more was turning up on Rosalie, on the other jobs on hand.

HIGGINS HAD INTENDED to go out with Wanda and Galeano to finish up the legwork along Eastlake and Gates: not
that there was much in it, for without much doubt that had
been Rosalie Mrs. Cabrillo had seen, but you had to be
thorough. It was unlikely that anyone else had noticed anything, but you never knew. But Mendoza intercepted him on
his way out, agreeing with that. "Damn it, Luis," said
Higgins, hunching his wide shoulders, "I can't help thinking, if that woman had stayed on her front porch another
minute she might have seen that driver make a grab for the
kid—and she'd have yelled, interfered some way right then,
and nothing would have happened—damn it, it makes you
wonder—"

"Never any point in thinking what might have happened, George. I think we've got what we'll get from the
neighborhood. Follow up on the nuts out of records. But
meanwhile, we'd better ask some questions about this civil
servant. Edward Foster. The body over on Alhambra."

"Oh, did he get identified?"

"The feds knew him. He worked for the Post Office."
Mendoza brushed at his narrow moustache absently; as
usual, he was dapper in silver-gray suit and snowy shirt,
discreet dark tie. "I've been on the phone to find out where,
and he was working out of the Terminal Annex right down
here. Evidently he was living alone, nobody reporting him
missing."

It was only about eight blocks up to the enormous bulk
of the main Los Angeles Post Office, but across freeways,
and they took the Ferrari. It was a big and busy place, but
the assistant postmaster Mendoza had talked to was waiting for them, a small spare man who must be near retire-
ment: the name block on his littered desk identified him as
Brian Early. He had a round bald head and a querulous
voice.

"I didn't recall the name when you called, Lieutenant, but
I've looked out Foster's record for you. It's a common
name, we have eleven Fosters working out of this station.

Really, I was quite staggered when you said he was dead—but I see by his time sheet he's supposed to be on vacation. Otherwise, of course, he'd have been missed when he didn't report for work.'' Early had a little sheaf of papers in front of him. "He'd only been with us about three and a half months, he'd been transferred from a Hollywood station. You understand, it would be impossible for any of us to know everyone here personally, there are literally hundreds of people working at this station—it's the main sorting center for greater Los Angeles. But in any case the man had only been here a short time—''

"Yes, I see," said Mendoza. He offered Early a cigarette and Early declined with something like horror, got up hastily to open the window as Mendoza flicked his lighter. "When did he start his vacation?"

"By what I have here, last Saturday."

"Oh. Then he would have been at work on Friday?" The autopsy had said that Foster had probably been killed on Friday, but gave it leeway through Friday evening.

"Presumably. Yes. Yes, his time sheet's up to date, he reported for work on Friday morning as usual."

"What was his job?"

"Oh, he was a carrier. He was assigned to a route around the Echo Park area."

"And you're sure he was at work all day on Friday?"

"Unless someone else checked in for him," said Early stiffly, "that's so."

"I suppose some of the other mail carriers would have known him? Would any of them be here now?"

Early shrugged and glanced at the clock. "Most of them will be going out about now, but we can go and see. The carriers have to sort the mail for their routes, you see, before going out to deliver—of course some days the mail is lighter or heavier. I'll take you down to their sorting room."

They followed him down a long corridor in the bowels of the building; glimpses into boxlike cubicles revealed that they were passing behind the great public area of this vast place, where the actual mail slots were, windows for purchasing stamps, the long rows of post-office boxes. Early ushered them into a large square room filled with long tables, a door at the rear leading into the parking lot. Only a handful of men were working at a couple of the tables, over bundles of mail; as they came in, several more men were leaving by the rear door, trundling their wheeled carts in front of them. Early went up to the nearest table where three men, all black, were working, and asked if any of them had known Foster. Mendoza produced the facial shot taken at the morgue; it wasn't flattering, but recognizable. Foster had been nondescript, with scanty eyebrows and rabbity teeth.

Two of the men shook their heads at it; the third said, "Oh, him. Yeah, I seen him around—couple of times we was at the same table, sorting. Last Friday? I couldn't say, I don't remember. Never heard his name. See, you're busy, sorting, you don't have time to talk." He looked at Mendoza and Higgins curiously.

"It's very funny," said Early, back in the corridor, "but ever since you called, Lieutenant, I've had the vague impression that someone else had mentioned Foster's name to me recently, but I can't recall—unless it was Al—Al Lowry, he's the next senior assistant postmaster—but I can't imagine why he should—and of course he's on vacation too, took the family up to Oregon on a fishing trip. Well, if you'd like to look at Foster's record—"

Foster had worked for the Post Office for nine years. He had a clean record with the government, a good work record. He had worked at two different branch post offices in Hollywood, been transferred to the Terminal Annex at the beginning of last February. His home address was on Romaine in Hollywood.

"Typical colorless civil servant," said Mendoza back in the car, remembering what Marx had said. "Now how in hell did he end up strangled?"

"Even civil servants have acquaintances—and girl friends," said Higgins.

"True." Mendoza switched on the ignition.

The address on Romaine was one of the fairly new and garish small apartments going up in central Hollywood. It was built on three sides of a small courtyard, and the doors on the second floor led off communal balconies. One of the ground floor doors bore a sign, *Manager*; Mendoza shoved the bell.

The woman who opened the door was fat and elderly, gray-haired. She stared at the badges, listened to what Mendoza had to say. "Well, for the Lord's sake!" she said. "If that doesn't beat all! You'd better come in. Fred, you'll never in this world believe this—"

"I heard what he said." The tall thin old man looked up interestedly from his newspaper. "Beats all, all right. Why, Foster couldn't have been forty. But you said, killed? By somebody? I will be goddamned. That's one for the books. Always seemed an awful quiet sort—never much to say for himself."

"Had he lived here long?"

"He was here when we came, and that's four years, I guess he'd lived here since the building was new. Sit down, won't you? I'm Mrs. Farley, by the way—this is my husband." They were probably retired, eking out a pension, Social Security, with this small job; they would get the apartment rent free.

"You didn't know him well, who his friends would be?"

Farley shook his head. "He was quiet as be damned. Hardly knew he was there. All we knew about him was that he worked for the Post Office. I don't think he ever had anybody come to see him, if they did we never noticed. Paid the rent on the dot, and except for seeing him come and go that's the only times we ever laid eyes on him."

"Well, we'd like to look at his apartment. Try to locate any relatives, for one thing."

"Surely," said Mrs. Farley. "This is really something—first time we ever had police coming, even when the blond hussy was living in Fourteen. I'll get the key. It's Eighteen, at the rear upstairs—"

"Did he have a car?" asked Higgins.

"Sure. It's a four-door Chevy, about six-seven years old. His carport's the last one, other side of the building." They went to look, and it was empty. Farley had gone with them, and said, "Friday, you said. I couldn't say what time he might have come in. It was usually around five, the few times I saw him. Last Friday—well, we had an early supper, there was an old movie on TV we wanted to see. You can see the driveway's the other side from our place, he could have come in and gone out again or never come in at all, far's I could tell you."

She bustled up the open staircase and let them into the apartment. "There'll be some more of us coming," said Mendoza. She looked pleased and excited.

It was a curiously anonymous apartment; the rather sparse furniture was starkly modern. There was a tape recorder and a collection of tapes, mostly classical music; no TV, no stereo. The kitchen was very neat and clean. In the single bedroom, the bed was precisely made up; there was a wardrobe with a sliding door, and Higgins shoved it open with one finger. A modest row of clothes, including a blue Post Office uniform, several regulation Post Office shirts, was neatly put away on hangers. "There you are," said Higgins, nodding at the uniform. "He came home, changed out of his uniform, and went out again."

"Yes," said Mendoza. "Apparently."

The phone was in the kitchen, but there was no sign of an address book. It didn't look as if anything had happened to Foster here, no indication of a struggle. They opened drawers and looked, but failed to find an address book. "He carried one on him," said Higgins.

"He seems to have been the typical old-maid bachelor, by the looks of the place." Mendoza wandered back to the living room and contemplated the contents of the one modest bookcase. It was a peculiar little collection: the only fiction was a hardbound trilogy, *The Lord of the Rings*; the rest was a conglomeration of popular occult lore, a couple of solid tomes on English history, and the entire works of William Shakespeare.

"Funny sort of civil servant," said Higgins.

"You have said it. I don't suppose the lab would turn up anything, but we have to look."

They went back to Parker Center, stopped off in Communications and queried the DMV in Sacramento about Foster's car. The plate number was relayed in five minutes, and Mendoza put out an APB on it.

BY LATE WEDNESDAY morning Palliser and Landers had been round and round on Nicholas Zemenides, and hadn't found out much. None of the other *Herald* drivers they had talked to yesterday had known him except casually; nobody at the apartment had known him. The nearest Greek Orthodox Church was on Olympic Boulevard, a renovated store building; the sign in front gave them the priest's name, Stephen Maniklese, and he was in the phone book, a modest address in Hollywood.

He was friendly, behind a magnificent black beard, but unhelpful. He remembered Zemenides—"such a very handsome young man"—but hadn't known him personally. Zemenides hadn't been a regular church member or attendant. All he did remember was that several times Zemenides had sat with the Bakas family. Mr. Gregory Bakas and his family.

Bakas was in the phone book too. It was a middle-class house in Hollywood, and nobody was at home. A next-door neighbor told them that Mrs. Bakas was probably out at the market, might be home in the afternoon.

They stopped at a coffee shop for lunch and headed back to the office. Sergeant Lake, who as usual was trying to stay by a diet and consequently feeling disgruntled, said, "I

swear the jungle's getting wilder by the day. Would you believe a heist at eleven-thirty A.M. at a drugstore on Hill?
Jase and Henry went out on it."

"And the hell with it." Jason Grace came in with Henry
Glasser behind him; they were both looking annoyed.
Grace, usually as dapper as Mendoza, had pulled his tie
loose; his chocolate-brown face registered disgust, and he
was brushing his narrow moustache with a thumbnail in
unconscious mimicry of the boss. "Not one solitary goddamned witness! He walks through a busy drugstore—
there's a sale on—and waves a gun at the pharmacist and
gets away with a sackful of pills and all the take from the
register, and even the damn pharmacist can't describe him!
He was kind of, you know, medium—color, size, voice.
Augh!"

"And we haven't had lunch yet," said Glasser plaintively. He produced a quarter and tossed it, and Grace said,
"Tails." "You called it. So I get to do the report."

Palliser said, "We've been having some of the same.
Don't invite the high blood pressure, Jase."

Grace looked at him bitterly. "I guess what's really annoying me is all you damned prolific husbands. Everybody
expecting babies. We spent yesterday afternoon at that
adoption agency again and now they're saying maybe a
three-year wait—all these goddamned abortions—" He sat
back and lit a cigarette moodily.

Palliser and Landers tried the Bakas house again at two
o'clock, and this time found Mrs. Bakas home. She was a
tall handsome woman in her fifties, and she was shocked to
hear about Zemenides. He seemed a nice ambitious young
man. But she didn't know much about him, about his
friends. Nick was her son Philip's friend. "You know young
people," she said. "They're off places together, dates,
movies—he'd come to pick up Philip, or they'd meet somewhere. All I could tell you, what Phil says," and she smiled,
"it was never the same girl twice, that Nick dated." But apparently Zemenides had had a serious side too; he'd been

interested in music— "The music of the old country, you know? He and Phil would exchange records."

And of course Philip Bakas wasn't available. He'd been working at a restaurant in West Hollywood, but just last week got a better job at a bigger restaurant in Beverly Hills. He wasn't due to start that job until next week, so he'd gone off on a trip with his sister and her husband, in their RV camper, over to the desert. They wouldn't be back until Sunday.

"Phil will be—" she gestured, at a loss for the word. "They were good friends. Sentimental young men—our families have been here for many generations, I think Nick's people too, but they had to be the romantic patriots always talking about the old country— Boys. Just boys. Poor Nick. Oh, if it would be any help, there was a place they went often—a bar, a restaurant, it's a Greek place, Ari's, on La Cienega."

They found that address, and went out there; it was a hole-in-the-wall restaurant and there was a hand-lettered sign on the front door: *Closed for funeral.*

Landers uttered a rude word.

They got back to the office at four-forty. There wouldn't be a lab report on Zemenides' apartment for a while; those boys always took their time; but the lab had kindly sent up a cheap fake-leather address book from the apartment. They had a look at it. Nearly every page was covered with barely legible scrawls: girls' names, phone numbers, Anne, Jean, Gloria, Norma, no surnames at all, and about half of them scratched out.

This time it was Palliser who uttered a ruder word. "Sweet Christ!" he said. "Hell on wheels with the girls all right. It looks simple—he was making time with somebody's best lay, and the somebody got mad and had a fight with him—"

"Adding up to Murder Two," said Landers.

"And how in hell we could ever drop on the somebody— call all these numbers and ask does anybody there know

Nick? And the somebody's best lay, who knows all about it and is probably preening herself because the somebody loves her enough to murder for her, says sorry, wrong number.''

"And to think," said Landers, "that I could have been enjoying a middling good veterinary practice in partnership with my father. I think I'll go home early."

FOR NO VERY GOOD reason, Higgins was feeling tired when he got home. Tomorrow was his day off, thank God. And it was just a job, and after all the years he'd spent riding a squad, and out of uniform as a detective, he'd got used to shelving the job and forgetting it until next day; but there were jobs you couldn't so easily put out of your mind.

Rosalie. Well-brought-up Rosalie, eight years old. Had the driver of that middle-aged tan car asked for directions?—"Excuse me, little girl, which way is Darwin Street?"—What pretext had he used?

You brought up kids to be polite and helpful.

Margaret Emily. He hadn't had a family in so long he'd nearly forgotten what it was like. Bert Dwyer dead on the marble floor of the bank— And he'd gone with Mendoza to tell her. Mary. It seemed a long while ago.

They'd been married for three and a half years, nearly four, and their own baby Margaret Emily was nearly two. Steve Dwyer more like Bert every day, and Laura would be fourteen next month—

You tried to bring the kids up right. But in the jungle, the wild ones coming out of the bushes—

He was glad they'd bought the old place in Eagle Rock; a better area than where they'd been living.

The little Scottie Brucie welcomed him exuberantly as he came up to the back door. "Good day, dear?" asked Mary, turning from the stove.

"Reasonably," said Higgins. Laura was pounding the piano, but her teacher said she was some kind of genius so they had to put up with it. Steve was probably out in his darkroom. Margaret Emily was crooning over a stuffed toy on the living room floor.

Higgins sat down and lit a cigarette and thought about Rosalie. Unprofitably.

THE NIGHT WATCH came on—Piggott, Schenke and Conway—and settled down to catch any calls. Rich Conway was feeling slightly more reconciled to a spell on night watch; he was a man for the girls, and it had ruined his social life, but he'd recently met a girl who worked nights too, swing shift at an electronics assembly plant, so he could arrange dates. He and Schenke, the confirmed bachelor, weren't particularly interested in Matt Piggott's incipient fatherhood.

They didn't get a call until eleven-fifteen: a heist. Piggott and Schenke went out on it.

The heister had not only got the take from the register at the little bar in Olive, but had stripped the bar patrons of cash and a little jewelry.

"Listen," said the bartender, who was a scrawny little fellow, "this mountain of a guy comes in with a great big gun, do I act like a hero? I do not. I was scared—I admit it." He had a nervous Adam's apple.

There had been five people in the place, all men. They took a confused count; probably the heister had got about a hundred bucks from the customers, another hundred from the register. Nobody could give a good description—as usual, the bar was dark and a big TV blaring in one corner. He'd been a white man, big, waving a big gun around.

Schenke said resignedly, "Well, the devil still pretty active, isn't he, Matt?"

"He is indeed," said Piggott seriously: but then Piggott the fundamentalist really believed in the devil.

THREE

On Thursday morning, with Higgins off, there wasn't much to be done about the overnight heist job. They were still ostensibly working six heists from a month back, that they'd never get anywhere on: vague descriptions, no solid evidence.

Palliser had sent a wire to the address in Concord, Massachusetts, from Zemenides' billfold, and just after he came in a long-distance call was relayed from downstairs. A neutral male voice identified itself as Stephen Zemenides, Nicholas's uncle. "His mother asked me to call—we were most distressed to hear—" the voice faded. "If you could tell me—"

"Oh, yes, sir," said Palliser. It wasn't a good connection, and the uncle didn't have much to say. Nicholas had been away from home, out in California, for four years, they didn't know any of his friends here. His mother wanted the body sent back for burial there; could that be arranged? Palliser explained about the necessary autopsy, release of the body; he gave the uncle the name of a local mortuary which would make the arrangements.

That restaurant on La Cienega wouldn't be open until eleven or so. At the moment he didn't see anywhere else to go on Zemenides, pending the autopsy and lab reports. He sat back in his desk chair and looked at that address book again—hopeless, of course.

Everybody else—Hackett, Galeano, Landers, Grace, Glasser—had started out after the list of sex freaks. Wanda, ever eager for street experience, had tagged after Glasser. That was the kind of heartbreaking, slogging routine they so often ended up doing, the only indicated way to go at a job like hunting Rosalie's killer. Yesterday Higgins had used the computer in records and collected another list of names, men with the records of sexual violence, of child molestation. It was a hell of a long list. They had to work by logic; they would look first for men on that list who lived or worked more or less in the area where Rosalie had been abducted, bring them in to question, ask for alibis. And as usual, some of those men, perhaps most of them, would stay up in the air—no alibis: any of them could be X. They'd look at their cars, and if they were lucky they might come across a middle-aged tan sedan, and the lab might find something significant in it. They might not, too. They wouldn't find all of the men on that list, some of them moved and absorbed into the anonymous maw of the city, not to be traced. And the X on Rosalie might have come downtown from Pasadena or Santa Monica, but as experienced detectives they knew that in a majority of cases the child molesters didn't move far out of their own orbits—except for the exceptions. They went looking as they could. It was tedious, tiresome work and it took a lot of time, and they might spend weeks at it and get nowhere, but it was part of the job they had to do.

And Palliser wondered if anything new would go down today. Robbery-Homicide was usually kept busy.

He went down the hall to the coffee machine, thinking about the heisters, about Zemenides, about Rosalie. He passed a uniformed man approaching Sergeant Lake's desk; when he came back to the communal office with his coffee, Mendoza was leaning on Hackett's desk reading a report.

"Here we are, the autopsy on Rosalie. It doesn't tell us much." He sat down in Hackett's desk chair and snapped his lighter, thrusting the report at Palliser.

It didn't make pretty reading, but it was short and simple. She'd been raped vaginally and anally, beaten and strangled; the cause of death was manual strangulation. The time elapsed before the body was found made the time of death uncertain, but she had probably been dead by early Saturday morning.

"And you know," said Mendoza, taking the report back to look at again, "there's something else, John. It's the last week of school, most public schools. The kids starting to wander around. I don't think she was under those bushes in the playground long before she was found on Monday afternoon. It's not a very big playground, and if she was stashed there on Saturday she'd been spotted long before."

"He left the body in the car a couple of days, maybe?" Palliser massaged his jaw thoughtfully. "He wouldn't have dropped the body there by daylight—it's a fairly crowded neighborhood—"

Mendoza shrugged. "Early that morning from midnight on Sunday. But if she was in his car any length of time, the lab might get something significant from her clothes—more likely, if we're very damn lucky and ever drop on him, something significant from his car to link it up, the nice scientific evidence."

"Yes," said Palliser. And the unexpected did happen; it could be that the first possible suspect on that list of sex nuts might come apart and confess. It didn't usually come that easy, but—

He supposed he ought to try to follow up Zemenides. He called the lab to ask what they'd got in the apartment, and Scarne said, "I was just on my way up. Hang on ten minutes."

When he came in he had a manila envelope of glossy eight-by-ten prints and a one-page report. "A lot of prints in that place, good, bad and indifferent, but all we could identify were his—the corpse's. That metal statue thing, the naked lady, there were only smudges on it. It was a dandy weapon, the damn thing weighs nearly five pounds. His blood on it—his type anyway, O."

"Yes," said Palliser, "it looked as if there'd been a fight and somebody grabbed that up and hit him—"

"No fight," said Scarne. "You saw the scene. Haven't you got the autopsy yet? Well, take a look at the photos—" he spread a sheaf of them on Palliser's desk, shots of the shabby apartment living room from all angles, the corpse. "Now that was a big strong young fellow, he'd have been able to put most men down in a fight, wouldn't you say? At least he'd have put up the hell of a fight if he'd been attacked. And look, the place is neat as hell, furniture all in place, no sign of any kind of struggle. You know what it looks like to me? Whoever went for him did it without any warning—or it was somebody he never expected trouble from. And it was just by chance the first or second blow got him in a vulnerable area." Scarne laid a blunt forefinger on one close-up shot of the body. "The temple where the skull is thinner. I'd have a guess there were half a dozen blows, he'd bled, but I'd have another guess the autopsy'll say simple skull fracture."

"Yes," said Palliser. "I see what you mean." That big strong young fellow Nick Zemenides wouldn't have been afraid of many men. Somebody he didn't expect trouble from—somebody he wasn't remotely afraid of— Hell on wheels with the girls, Zemenides. Some girl he'd finished with, trying to get him back—some girl jealous? Boman had said, loud voices, just a little while. These old apartments solidly built, he might not have been able to tell, male or female voices. And how in hell to locate such a girl— Or just as probably the boyfriend of some new girl Zemenides had annexed—

"Hell," he said mildly. "All up in the air."

"Well, you're the detective," said Scarne. "We just man the microscopes, thank God."

Palliser took one of the photographs, a good close-up of the dead man's face, and drove up to that hole-in-the-wall restaurant on La Cienega. It was just open, and there were no customers in. The proprietor, Ari Dimitrios, was there, and the one waiter, Stavros Papoulas. Dimitrios was fat and wholly American and anxiously helpful. Papoulas had a thick accent; he was a gangling young man in the early twenties. They recognized the photograph; yes, that one had been a regular customer, in maybe once a week. Sometimes alone, or with a girl, with other young men. They hadn't known his name, or the names of the people he'd been with.

"Except that one girl, now I think," said Dimitrios. "Yeah, he picked her up in here once, maybe four, five months back, they were here together a couple times after that. She used to come in for early supper, she liked our stuffed-grape-leaf casserole. She was hostess at that Knight's Rest Inn up the street, I think her name was Jeanie or Ginger or something. Knockout of a girl, black hair and big black eyes—this guy, he usually had a good-looking dame."

Papoulas couldn't add anything to that, just nodded violently in agreement. Palliser found the Knight's Rest Inn in the next block; it was just open, and a rather bleary-eyed manager looked at the badge and asked what the hell the police wanted. Palliser asked about Jeanie or Ginger, passed on the description. "Oh," said the manager, after thought. "That could be, I guess, Ginger Kinsella. She was a hostess here up to around last March, quit to take another job, I don't know where."

"Would you have an address for her?"

"Oh, hell, I don't think so—but I know she was a pretty good friend of Fay's. Fay Bush, she still works here, I got an address for her."

It was on Dover Place up in the Atwater section, an apartment over a garage in the rear of a single house in front. He climbed rickety stairs and shoved the bell. He shoved it three times before, five minutes later, the door opened and a sleepy-eyed young woman peered at him. She had tousled brown hair, and she was clutching a pink bathrobe over a nightgown. "Who the hell are you?"

He showed her the badge. "I'm trying to find a Ginger Kinsella. Would you know where she lives?"

"Ginger? My God, come along just after dawn to ask stupid questions—what do the cops want with Ginger? She's perfectly straight, a nice girl, strictly square."

"Do you know where she is?"

"Sure I know where she is. She used to share this place up to six weeks back. She got married to Doug last month—Doug Lamont—and they went back east to Detroit, he just got transferred to the main Ford plant there."

"Thanks so much," said Palliser. She shut the door smartly in his face.

"Your husband didn't like the South Pacific cruise?" The narrow-faced clerk at the travel agency gave Alison a sympathetic smile. "I'm sure you'd have enjoyed—well, of course we have a great many to offer. If I might suggest something, ah, perhaps more educational?"

"Educational?"

"Since it's been possible to arrange travel there, a good many of our clients have found it most interesting to visit China—we have an all-inclusive fourteen-day tour, really quite inexpensive, with a two-day stopover in Hong Kong—"

"Communist China?" said Alison. "Why on earth would anyone want to go there?"

"Oh, many people find it interesting, I assure you, to see the way such a formerly backward country is being modernized, assimilated into the modern—"

"By Communists? With slave labor?" said Alison. "Thank you, no."

"Well—" he leafed over brochures. His toothy smile was only a trifle discouraged. "Er—Scandinavia? We have a very nice sixteen-day tour among the fjords, with four days in Copenhagen—"

Alison looked at pictures of the fjords uninterestedly. But a vacation somewhere they were going to have, whatever Luis said. It would do him good to get away from the job.

She couldn't work up any passionate interest in the fjords, but somewhere—

"Perhaps you'd be interested in one of our newest cruises—Buenos Aires, on a very new cruise liner, the latest word in design—"

Marimbas, and everybody speaking Spanish; not very different from Los Angeles. "Well—" said Alison.

He looked at her disappointedly, but he was game. "Switzerland. Now we have a five-country fifteen-day tour—Bern, Munich, Vienna—" He pressed the brochure on her hopefully.

HACKETT AND GALEANO had just brought in a possible suspect from the sex list, at three-thirty, and shepherded him down to an interrogation room; Mendoza trailed them to sit in on the questioning, but Lake waylaid him in the hall.

"You've got Carey on the phone."

"Oh?" Mendoza took one look at him and made back for his office to pick up the phone. "Carey?" Lieutenant Carey was attached to Missing Persons a couple of flights downstairs.

"I thought you'd want to know," said Carey tersely. "I see that missing juvenile turned into a homicide. We've got another one, just now. Missing, I mean. Another eight-year-old—Brenda Dodson—just reported missing from roughly the same general area."

"Dios," said Mendoza. "So what's the story?"

"Well, it's the last week of school, there aren't such regular classes, at elementary schools anyway, and she was supposed to be home by noon, she had an appointment with the dentist at one o'clock. Her class was out at eleven-thirty, but she didn't come home—her mother drove up to the school, it's a public one on Third, but there's no sign of her and nobody claims to have noticed her after the class was out. She was in class all right, but nobody remembers seeing her later. I've just had the mother in, she finally called a squad—she's saying all the usual things, a good obedient girl, something must have happened to her, she'd been warned about strangers, and so on. She had the sense to contact Brenda's best friend, a kid named Ann Dahlgren, but she'd stayed at the school to play volleyball and all she knows is that Brenda intended to go right home. I've got a few squads out looking. She'd have been going down Third and then Virgil, the Dodsons live on Geneva.''

"¡*Vaya!*" said Mendoza. "All right. Keep us informed." He stabbed out his cigarette viciously. Another little girl missing—and maybe she'd gone home with another girl friend, forgotten the time, but it didn't sound likely. And those were busy crowded streets— But! Next to the last day of school, the kids wandering around, and the distracted mother couldn't have talked to everybody at the school, on the playground. He swore. That would be a big public elementary school, and once it was closed for the summer, try to chase down all the kids, the teachers— If Brenda Dodson had been somehow picked up by the same pervert who had picked up Rosalie—

"¡*Condenación!*" he said violently. He went out to the big office. Landers and Grace were just coming in, towing a sullen-looking young black fellow. Mendoza passed on the news, and they both swore.

"It's early," said Grace. "Or is it? Three-twenty, and she was supposed to be home by noon. Kids—maybe Rosalie's made us all nervous. Carey's got men out—do we go looking too? Would it do any good?"

"*No sé,*" said Mendoza, brushing his moustache. "I don't really know, Jase. Wait and see. And hope she just went home with a new pal and is peacefully watching TV. Inviting the sound spanking."

"Three hours," said Landers speculatively. "It's no time really, but—yes. Wait and see, and hope she turns up."

PALLISER HAD FINISHED the afternoon on a wild-goose chase after one of the sex freaks named Aaron Lopez. Lopez had a large family, and an aversion to steady work; the relatives apparently took him in turn, and he had moved seven times since he got off parole from a charge of child molestation. All the relatives lived right around the Central beat, and Lopez had the right record to have been the X on Rosalie; Palliser would like to talk to him. He never caught up to him until five o'clock, and when he found him, five assorted Lopezes were voluble on an alibi. Aaron had had a little accident last Friday, a little bit drunk and fell off the porch and broke his arm, and all afternoon he'd been at the hospital getting it fixed. The splint and sling looked authentic.

So Palliser went directly home and never heard about Brenda Dodson until next morning.

He left the car in the port at the side of the house and as he opened the gate Trina gave one polite welcoming bark. He reached to pat her; no longer did she jump up or pounce from behind: Roberta had really done a fine job of training her. She was full-grown now, a very handsome black German shepherd. She followed him in the back door sedately.

"You're a little late," said Roberta, smiling at him; she was busy over a big bowl of salad on the counter.

"So what did the doctor say?" He came to kiss her, his lovely tall dark Robin with the grave dark eyes.

She kissed him back soundly. "Oh, it's positive all right. It's due about the middle of February."

"You really mind?"

"Of course not, idiot, I'm very happy about it, we always said we'd have two. I just hope this one is a girl." Davy came running up, discovering that daddy was home, and Palliser picked him up.

"Thought about any names?"

"Not definitely. It's just," said Roberta ruefully, "that it'd be nice to move to a quieter area—out farther—but we've got a little equity in this place. We can't afford another baby and a new house, with interest rates what they are." Davy slid down Palliser's pants leg and grabbed Trina's tail, and she began to wash his face lovingly.

"Mmh. At least we've got the dog to bark at burglars."

"I wish you could come to the dog show on Sunday, John. See her in action. She's really good at all the exercises, I'll bet she'll make a good score, if the other dogs don't make her nervous. I never saw much sense in ordinary dog shows, but the obedience thing is interesting."

"Well," said Palliser, "just watch yourself, don't trip over any leashes and lose the baby."

"Don't be silly, I'm healthy as a horse according to the doctor. Angel Hackett's going with me, she wants to see all the different breeds."

ALISON WAS sitting up in bed at ten-thirty, desultorily reading *An Encyclopedia of Murder* while she filed her nails, and Mendoza was wandering around undressing. "Honestly," she said, "I can see the fascination in a way—but it's all so formless, it's frightening. People committing senseless murders for no reason and not always the lunatics—and then once in a while the really offbeat thing and no answer to it. This Wallace case is just a big blank, and now nobody'll ever know what happened or why—"

"I am familiar with crime reports." Mendoza buttoned his pajama top and took off his watch to wind it.

"All so untidy. But it's quite nostalgic in another way," said Alison.

"*¿Cómo dice?*"

"The way most of the accounts end. Hanged at Pentonville such and such a date. Most of this stuff was published twenty or thirty years ago, of course."

Mendoza laughed sharply. "*¡Hermoso!* It's the hell of a lot cheaper way to deal with them. Nostalgic indeed—"

The phone rang shrilly. There were phones all over Alison's big hacienda, and one here in the outsize master bedroom, on one bedside table. He sat down on his side of the bed and picked it up. "Mendoza."

"I thought you'd better hear right off," said Rich Conway's voice. "The Dodson girl just turned up."

"Where and how?" asked Mendoza tersely.

"Couple coming home from shopping found her in their driveway about an hour ago—Eleventh, just down from Vermont, you know it, dark little old residential block. They called a squad, and the beat man called the paramedics. We just heard fifteen minutes ago."

"She's alive?"

"Yes, but in critical condition, what I got from emergency just now. They say she's been raped and beaten—she's still unconscious. I hope to God she makes it okay, poor kid, but they say she's lost some blood, and there's concussion—"

"Let's pray she makes it, Rich," said Mendoza grimly. "Because that has to be the same one picked up Rosalie, and maybe Brenda can tell us something about him." He put the phone down.

"The other little girl?" Alison asked soberly.

He nodded and told her. She looked at her book thoughtfully. "It's really not so entertaining—in real life. Not while it's happening, to real people."

MENDOZA GOT INTO THE OFFICE early on Friday morning. Everybody else came drifting in—the only men off on Friday were Galeano and Matt Piggott on night watch. They heard about Brenda as they came in; by eight-fifteen Mendoza was calling the hospital, the emergency wing at Cedars-Sinai.

He got, finally, an efficient-sounding cool-voiced nurse, who told him that Brenda was still unconscious, but responding well and in stable condition. She might be conscious later today.

"You understand, we'll want to talk to her as soon as possible."

"She's had some pretty rough treatment, Lieutenant," said the cool voice. "It might not be such a good idea to remind her of it."

"Damn it," said Mendoza, "we have to get whatever she can tell us, we'd like to pick up the bastard who did it. He's probably the one who killed the other little girl, you know."

"Yes, of course I understand that, but the mind's a funny thing, Lieutenant. She was in deep shock, she may not remember much about it. Merciful in a way if she doesn't."

"Well, keep us informed, please."

"We'll do that, Lieutenant."

"Wait and see if she can give us a lead?" asked Hackett.

"I think so, Arturo. It's a gamble, but I think so," said Mendoza. He lit a cigarette. "And damn it, there's no place to go on Foster—" He looked at Palliser. "What about that Greek?"

"What about him?" said Palliser sourly. "Nothing. Nowhere to go. I think he probably got killed over a girl, it may even have been a woman who clobbered him—" he got out the photographs and elaborated his thinking on that, and Mendoza agreed absently. "When we can talk to this Phil Bakas, he'll probably be able to give us some names. He's supposed to be home on Sunday."

"Yes," said Mendoza, studying the photographs. "Once you get some names it may be simple, John. I think only about a tenth of the population is left-handed."

"Come again?"

"He was struck on the right temple. If X was standing in front of him—"

"Oh," said Palliser. "Oh, I hadn't got that far— But if he wasn't expecting it, he could have been hit from behind."

"De veras." And ten minutes later the autopsy report on Zemenides came in, and it said just what Scarne and Palliser had deduced. He had died of a skull fracture, one of four wounds on the right temple responsible for that. There was no evidence that he'd put up any resistance; his hands were unmarked. He had been a very healthy specimen. He had had a meal about two hours before he died, and the es-

timated time of death was between six P.M. and midnight last Monday night. Interesting, but singularly unhelpful.

"And Foster—" said Mendoza meditatively.

Higgins, sitting smoking moodily, said, "Him. A handful of nothing."

Mendoza grunted. He and Higgins had gone to both branch post offices in Hollywood where Edward Foster had worked, and talked to a few people. They'd heard this and that about Foster, but nothing to suggest who might have killed him. Foster had been better known up there, had worked there longer, but everybody they'd seen said Foster was a loner, not very friendly, didn't talk much. He had a good enough record at the job, didn't go out of his way to be an eager beaver. The postmaster at the first branch could tell them that he hadn't had any family, had been brought up in an orphanage somewhere in the Midwest, around Chicago he thought. He didn't smoke or drink.

Another of the carriers at that post office had said, "Just sort of, there wasn't anything to him, know what I mean. Not much personality."

In fact, Foster seemed to have been so totally colorless that it didn't seem likely anybody would have felt strongly enough about him one way or the other to waste the energy killing him. Let alone take the trouble of stripping the body and lugging him at least some way to the fence around the freight yards.

At nine-thirty a new call came in from a squad, a homicide. The address was Francis Avenue. Hackett looked at Higgins and they stood up.

"If it's male," said Mendoza, "look at it twice in case it's Narco's Tony Quinlan in disguise." They had all been briefed about the vanished Quinlan. It was Mendoza's private opinion that Goldberg and Callaghan were being optimistic to expect a body to turn up. An old pro like Crossland would have contacts outside the Syndicate, probably people who owed him favors. And a lot of the hard stuff was being flown in southwards now. If a body fell out of a private plane over the middle of the Gulf of Mexico, nobody would be the wiser; and by now the fancy tattoo on Tony Quinlan's arm would have been happily digested by some species of ocean-going fish.

AND THEY ALL CUSSED at the jobs that made for the tiresome slogging routine; but sometimes the ones they'd never forget, the really grim ones, were the cases that gave them hardly any work at all.

The block on Francis Street was an old one, its asphalt street narrow. The houses along here had never been impressive: for the most part modest two-bedroom frame houses on forty-foot-frontage lots, and it had been more than sixty years since any of them had been new.

There was a Fire Department truck in front of one of the houses halfway down the block, and the black-and-white squad car. A handful of men in the regulation yellow slickers and billed caps were standing in the street talking to the uniformed man. Hackett and Higgins had come over in Higgins' Pontiac; they left it behind the squad and got out.

There was a woman sitting in the back of the squad.

"What's up?" asked Hackett.

The biggest man, his cap labeled Battalion Chief, said dispassionately, "Christ. You the front office dicks? You can get in there in about ten minutes, we got everything open. The lady kept her head and turned off the valve, but it's a damn miracle it didn't go up with a bang. My God, those old unvented gas wall heaters, they've been outlawed for thirty years, but in old places like this, these old areas of town—" he spat into the gutter. "A goddamn miracle. Except that there'd have been leaks through those old windows, like that."

While they waited, Corbett out of the squad took them over there. "It's a Mrs. O'Donnell," he said. "Mrs. Hazel O'Donnell. She lives next door," and he nodded at the yellow-painted frame house next to this one. He looked shaken.

She was about sixty, not so much fat as shapeless, neat in a printed cotton housedress; she had gray hair and a round face and rimless glasses. She had been crying, but she was coherent, and it all came out in a spate.

"They were so old—Mr. Hall was eighty-six and she was eighty-five, she had the arthritis so bad she could hardly get around—they'd lived here over fifty years, they'd been married more than sixty years—and never any children, they hadn't any relatives left at all. He'd worked as a clerk in a big department store all his life—about all they had was the house, and the Social Security. I've been afraid something was wrong, I didn't know what it could be, and they were proud, liked to be independent as they could be— But I always go out to market on Friday morning and I'd stop by, ask if I could get anything for them. Mr. Hall was getting awfully shaky, it was about all he could manage to get up to the little market on Hoover, and their prices are higher. Up to a couple, three months ago, they'd ask me to pick up this and that, and always paid me right away—but lately they hadn't—and I'd wondered— And when I came up to the door this morning and Mr. Hall didn't come, I was afraid—and the door was unlocked, and then I smelled the gas and went in—"

"It was pretty thick," said Corbett. "She called the fire boys first. Kept your head all right, Mrs. O'Donnell."

"I never was one to go to pieces easy. I've been alone ten years since Frank died, had to manage. If I'd known they had money trouble I'd have offered—not that I've got much—but they'd have been too proud to take anything—"

By the time Hackett and Higgins approached the open front door, the taint of gas had largely dissipated. It was the shabbiest little house on the street, long in need of paint, and one of the front windows was cracked; the wooden porch was narrow. Past the door was a very small living room with a threadbare rug, a sagging old couch, two upholstered chairs, and little else. In silence they went into a tiny hall, with two bedrooms front and back and a bathroom between. The bodies were in the front bedroom: two old, old people lying side by side on the bed, her right hand clasped in his left. They looked peaceful and quite happy. She was wearing an old-fashioned flannel nightdress, he was in ancient faded pajamas. The bedroom was about twelve feet square and held the double bed, a small dresser painted white, and a cane-seated rocking chair. Hackett glanced automatically for the heater: that kind he hadn't seen in years, the gas-jets set right into the wall with a flimsy protective grate.

"There's a note," said Higgins.

It was on top of the dresser, held down with a covered dish meant to hold false teeth. It was a single sheet of standard typewriter paper covered with lines of fine copperplate writing, nearly as easy to read as print. They read it without touching it.

Dear Mrs. O'Donnell,

We have talked it over and decided that this is the only way out for us. I am sorry that you should have to come in and find us, but knowing that you always come on Friday morning, the only one ever comes to see us, it seems the only way. The money from the Social Security was not much but we managed on it, but when it stopped coming it was very hard. The lady at the S. S. office, Miss Marsh, kept saying be patient but it is just too long and there is nothing left. For a while there were things we could sell at the pawnshop, the radio and Martha's garnet jewelry and my watch, but they did not bring much and now there is nothing. It is very hard for me to walk so far to the market and prices keep going up every day. Even being careful we had spent nearly all of Martha's S. S. check and could not buy the pain pills she needs for the arthritis. All we own is the house and if we took a mortgage things would be even worse as there would be payments. There is not

enough food now to last another week and it does not
look as if the S. S. people will ever get the mistake
straightened out. It was supposed to be our own money
kept for us we thought but the government will not admit the mistake. So it is best we go together and as you
have been very kind to us we would like to leave the
house to you. I hope this will be legal if we both sign
this.

His neat signature and her shaky one were appended.
"Now what the hell?" said Higgins.
"We won't need any pictures, anything from the lab."
"No."
They looked through the rest of the house. In sixty odd
years the old people would have accumulated the posses-
sions, but few of them would be pawnable, saleable. Anything like that, that the old man could have carried on foot
to the pawnshop, was gone. In the neat old kitchen the refrigerator was unplugged from the wall socket. "Electricity
rates," said Hackett. There was an old gas range. Dishes,
pots and pans in cupboards; and in the one long cupboard
intended for canned goods, six cans of condensed soup and
a half empty box of crackers.
"Good God almighty," said Higgins.
"I don't think that note's a legal document. Just in case
it is, we'll hand it back to Mrs. O'Donnell after the report's
in to the coroner."
"What do you want to bet the state'll get it instead?"
"No bets." They went out to Corbett waiting in the
squad, and called the morgue wagon. Mrs. O'Donnell had
gone home. There was a key in the inside knob of the front
door, and they took that. When the morgue wagon had
come and the long baskets been loaded in and driven away,
Hackett said, "They had the phone taken out, of course. No
phone book."
"There'll be a public phone booth up on the main drag."

They found one. The nearest Social Security office was over on Wilshire. Higgins found a slot in a public lot a block away, and Hackett fished up a couple of dimes for the meter. Inside the office was a long counter, behind it a lot of people sitting at desks. Nobody looked very busy. Hackett asked if a Miss Marsh worked there.

The spectacled pimply-faced girl at the counter said, "Oh, yeah. You want to see her? Just go on through, it's the desk at the back by the side window."

In fact, there was a name block on the desk: *Patricia Marsh*. She didn't look as if anyone had ever called her Pat. She was about forty, an angular sandy-haired woman with protuberant pale-blue eyes and a prim mouth. She goggled at the badge in Hackett's hand, at big craggy Higgins who might as well have *Cop* tattooed on his forehead.

"About Mr. Hall. Mr. John J. Hall," said Hackett.

"Well, for heaven's sake, has he called the police on it? I've been doing my best! Really, this is—"

"No," said Hackett mildly. "They're dead. Both Mr. and Mrs. Hall."

"Oh!" She looked taken aback. "Well, they were awfully old, of course. Was it an accident?"

"No," said Higgins. "Have we got it straight, there'd been some mix-up about his Social Security?"

"Well!" said Miss Marsh. They felt reasonably sure it was Miss; and the absence of a wedding ring said nothing, but they also felt reasonably sure that she was as virginal as she had arrived in the world. "Of course, that's that— I can let it drop and forget it. All the red tape—it's been nearly eight months, you wouldn't believe what a nuisance, all the endless forms to send in—of course these things always take time, as I kept explaining to him. He *would* keep coming in and calling, at least up to a couple of months ago—"

It would have been a twenty-five-cent bus ride up here, and a public phone cost a dime.

"About what?" asked Hackett.

She laughed a little brittle laugh. "Well, of course it was rather funny really. If maddening to straighten out. John Joseph Hall, it's not that uncommon a name, and the computers got fouled up back in Washington. There was another John Joseph Hall died, and the computers said it was the John Joseph Hall here, and the checks stopped coming. Do you know, it was four months before I could find out anything about the other Hall? He lived in Baltimore, Maryland. And there were all the forms—everything has to go back to the main office in Washington, of course, and—"

"How long had it been?" asked Hackett gently. "Since the checks stopped coming?"

"I'd have to look up the exact date. It was October something. It's been perfectly maddening— I've been doing all I can, but everything's done by computer now and whatever I sent in about this Hall, it kept coming back stamped *Deceased*, and then in March we got all the new printed forms and I had to do everything over again, and—"

"How much had he been getting?" asked Higgins.

"Well, that was another thing. Nothing, really." Miss Marsh sniffed. "A hundred and seventy-five a month, and his wife got half of that."

"My good Christ," said Higgins softly.

"You hadn't got it straightened out in eight and a half months?" said Hackett.

"It's all the red tape. All the forms. And he kept pestering me about it, I told him to be patient, it always takes time when these things happen, and a measly amount like—"

"Miss Marsh," said Hackett, "it was all they had to live on. To buy food and pay the utility bills and the— Would you like to try living on eighty-seven fifty a month?"

Her narrow mouth gaped foolishly at him. She closed it and licked her pale lips. "All?" she said blankly. "Well, for heaven's sake. He never said that to me." The old people had wanted to be independent, living on their own money so kindly saved for them by the government. In what had been a pyramid scam from the first. "Well, really," she said crossly, "if people aren't sensible enough to save for their old age, what can they expect? It's only intended as supplemental income—"

"That wasn't how it was sold to people the Halls' age, Miss Marsh," said Higgins. Both of them in the eighties, when Hall was working it was probably all they could manage to get the house paid for, wages what they were then. "We haven't always had inflationary wages with us, you know."

"I don't know what you mean," she said, and she really didn't. "Anyway, if they're both dead I can forget about the computer goof. Thank God. You didn't say if it was an accident."

"No. They committed suicide. They didn't have enough money to buy food. On account of the computer goof." Higgins stood up.

She stared at them. "Now that's impossible, I don't believe you—there are all sorts of places they could have got aid, all the other government agencies, federal and state—if he'd asked I could have told him—"

"That's right," said Hackett. "That's absolutely right, Miss Marsh. These days. Only there are some people like the Halls who are a little old-fashioned, you see—they're too proud and independent to take charity. All they wanted, all they expected, was what they thought they were entitled to."

"It's not my fault!" she said sharply.

They went out to the street, and Higgins said, "Sweet Christ," in sole comment.

It was the middle of a working day, and they couldn't even have a drink before lunch.

AT FIVE-THIRTY, just getting on to the end of the shift, the hospital called Robbery-Homicide to report that Brenda Dodson was conscious. She was still in serious condition;

they were saying now that she would live; but she couldn't possibly be talked to by the police until tomorrow, if then.

Mendoza relayed that to Hackett, Higgins and Grace—everybody else was still out on something.

"Well, hope we can question her tomorrow," said Grace. "And maybe we'd better take somebody from Juvenile, used to talking to the kids."

"That I'd already thought about," said Mendoza.

BOB SCHENKE and Conway were sitting on night watch alone. They didn't get a call up to midnight—tomorrow night might be busier—and they were playing a hand of gin on Conway's desk at ten minutes of one, wondering if the day men were getting anywhere on the little girls, when without warning two uniformed men came in. One of them was Bill Moss. He had been riding a squad for quite a while, but he looked oddly shook now. He walked over to Conway's desk and put a gun down on it, a Police Positive Colt .38, the regulation sidearm they all carried.

"What's with this?" asked Schenke.

"I was a minute away," said Moss. "Cruising down Second—God damn it, I heard the shots—nobody called in. One of those new fancy restaurants around Little Tokyo—" he shook his head. "I walked in on it. I suppose you'll want the lab out for pictures. They're both dead."

"Who?" asked Conway.

The other uniformed man had sat quietly down in the chair beside Palliser's desk. He looked up and said dully, "I don't know who the man was. She was my wife. Phyllis."

All of a sudden Conway noticed that the breast patch on his uniform jacket didn't say *LAPD*, but *Beverly Hills*.

FOUR

THAT WAS waiting for them on Saturday morning. Sergeant Farrell was sitting on the switchboard on Lake's day off, and Landers was off too. Higgins came in a few minutes before anybody else, and was reading the report Conway had left when Mendoza arrived.

"Let me guess, something new to work overnight." Mendoza swept off the usual Homburg, gray in deference to the season. "What's up?"

"Just more human nature," and Higgins passed the report over as Hackett, Grace and Galeano came in together.

"*¡Por Dios!*" said Mendoza, scanning the report. "Oh, yes. And whatever the hell the facts are, won't the papers blow it up—at least he's Beverly Hills, not LAPD, but one of the boys in blue, the stalwart guardians. Hell."

"Conway just booked him in and called the lab."

"And they got called out on a heist afterward." Mendoza brushed his moustache irritably. "We'll have to get chapter and verse, George."

They got out to the jail on North Broadway by nine o'clock. His name was Bernard Fillmore, and he was twenty-three years old. He was just an ordinary-looking young man, not very handsome or homely; he was fairly tall and well-built, he had short-cut reddish-brown hair and hazel eyes and a stubborn chin. He was just anonymous young America.

They had taken away his blue uniform and given him another, the rough tan jail uniform.

He was quiet and polite and quite willing to talk to them. "They let me make a call this morning," he said. "I called Dad. I didn't know how to tell him, I just said it. I suppose

he and Mother'll be coming." Higgins offered him a cigarette and he said he didn't smoke. "You see, everybody said
I shouldn't have married her," he went on dully. "Mother
and Dad didn't like her, and Betty—my sister—told me I
was a fool, I was mad at her a long time over that. I was
crazy about Phyllis from the first time I met her, we were in
high school together, you know—Santa Monica High
School. I thought—people—were jealous of her, telling
stories about her—because she was so beautiful. You know?
She was just—so—lovely. And I was sorry for her too—she
hadn't had it easy, her father deserted them when she was
just a kid, and her mother was kind of a lush—if her aunt
hadn't taken them in—"

He was staring past them out the high barred window of
the little interrogation room. "She always said she loved me
too. We were married nearly three years. I wanted her to stay
home and have a family, but the apartment she liked was
pretty damn steep rent, and she got that job—at an insurance office. I guess I was a little stupid. It was a while—before I got to wondering—her going over to some girl friend's
two, three evenings a week—Gloria, Marge, Vicky. I was on
day watch then. And then one night she came home pretty
drunk, and she was talking, and I found out she'd been
dating her boss—he'd been giving her things—"

"That was just the first one. I guess. I don't know. She
didn't like to stay home, she liked nice things and going out
a lot, more than I—we—could afford. And then I went on
night watch—and I was awful damn worried about it—I was
goddamn worried." He was looking down at his square
ringless hands clasped together on his lap now. His voice
was nearly expressionless. "I wouldn't get home till past
midnight, and a few times—she wasn't there, came in just
after me, and said—she'd been at Marge's—at Vicky's. I
didn't know. I was worried about it. Worried." He looked
up at them briefly, down to his hands again. "I got—a
friend of mine—he's on day watch—to kind of keep an eye
on her. You don't need to know his name. It doesn't mat-

ter.'' He was silent for quite a long while, and then went on. ''He said—he found out—she was meeting different fellows—nearly every night—going out places, sometimes just to the guy's pad and staying in. He said to me, you get shut of that stray bitch, Bernie—''

He looked up at them then, and he said painfully, ''But it was Phyllis! I loved Phyllis ever since I first met her—she said she loved me, we were married—and I thought—if I talked to her, begged her to stay home quiet and—and—And she promised. She said—she was sorry. But I guess—I always knew—I always knew—I just wouldn't think about it.

''And I kept finding the matchbooks around from the fancy restaurants—that place down in Little Tokyo, the place with the floor show, she was crazy about it—I took her there for her birthday in April, it cost a fortune—but Phyllis— All the time I knew how she was, but I—but I—wouldn't let myself know— And she got a little careless, there was that dress from Magnin's—and a diamond wristwatch, she said it was just fake but it wasn't—

''And—when—I—got—home—last night—and she wasn't there—I thought, just go look in that place, see if she was there—and if she wasn't, just go back and wait for her—and do it when she came home. Home. But she was there—with some man—and I'm glad I got him too. So you can see it's all over and done with, and I just don't seem to give one good goddamn about it any more. Ever any more.''

He had just walked into that restaurant, spotted the girl and her escort, and emptied his gun into them. The lab had been out to take pictures, and had his gun. The man had been Carl Copeland, partner in a theatrical agency on the Strip, with a bachelor apartment in West Hollywood. There'd be the hell of a lot of paperwork on this, all the statements to get from the witnesses at the restaurant, ballistics reports when the slugs out of the bodies had been sent up. And the newspapers would blow it up.

Higgins, Grace and Galeano went out to find the witnesses and get the statements. Mendoza went over to Beverly Hills and saw the Traffic watch commander, who said all the expectable things. Fillmore had a good record on this force, he'd had the highest score of his class at the Academy, and been riding a squad for two and a half years.

"My God, what a thing—I'd better call the captain, it's his day off—and I know Gilroy's a damn good pal of Fillmore's, he's on day watch now—"

They all said the expectable things. Gilroy, who was about Fillmore's age, said in agony, "I told him! I told him to get shut of that bitch—pick up anything in pants offered her a free meal and a roll in the hay—I told him—oh, Christ, but it's a waste! Such the hell of a waste—Bernie's such a good man—a good cop—and she wasn't worth—she wasn't worth a button on his uniform, for God's sake—"

Which summed it up in a way. Mendoza proceeded to Copeland's office found an emergency number on the door, and with some trouble located the partner, Reuben Goldfarb. All he wanted was the name of a relative to notify, and Goldfarb gave him the address of Copeland's father; he was a retired Navy captain.

He got back to the office at two o'clock, without lunch, and called the hospital. Another nurse told him that someone could talk to Brenda about five o'clock, but not for long.

BOTH THE LANDERSES were off on Saturday. Over a late breakfast they had a serious discussion, and Phil had made another pot of coffee; they'd been poring over the financial records.

"What it comes down to, Tom," she said, "is that we've gone at it backwards." She poured more coffee. Pregnancy was becoming to her; her tight blond curls were shining and her eyes very blue; she wrinkled her tip-tilted nose at him. "We always intended to have a family, but we should have got the house first. We should have gone looking last year, only who expected the prices to go so sky-high so fast—''

''And the farther out you go from the city, the cheaper,'' said Landers gloomily, ''only that means higher gas bills to drive back and forth, damn it. Maybe when I get my next pay jump—''

''Yes. Maybe. One thing, we're very lucky the landlord will let us stay on with the baby—but if it yells too loud at two A.M. maybe they'll reconsider.'' Phil sighed, running a hand through her blond curls. ''I can go on working through the sixth month—that's September—and go back after another six without losing any seniority. Only there'd be the baby-sitter— I'd rather be just a housewife, that's just a glorified clerk's job in R. and I., for heaven's sake—but—''

''But, just my pay,'' said Landers. ''Could we swing it?''

''The rent's probably going up in September,'' said Phil. ''And I'll tell you something else, Tom. I really wouldn't like an only child—if you're going to do a thing, better do it properly—and they might let us keep one in an apartment, but not two.''

Landers sipped lukewarm coffee. ''Well, I tell you what,'' he said thoughtfully. ''We can send the second one up to my sister in Bakersfield to raise, and visit it summers.''

She grinned at him. ''We'll manage, darling. No point in anticipating worries—we'll just be careful, and try to save most of my salary, and keep an eye on the real-estate ads. Sometimes the older places that need a lot of fixing up are fairly cheap. I keep thinking of Mehitabel.''

''Who?''

''Of Archy and. You know. Don Marquis. 'It's cheerio my dearie-O that pulls a lady through.' '' Phil laughed. ''We'll manage, Tom. Somehow. It'll all come out all right.''

''Pollyanna,'' said Landers, but he grinned back at her.

THE LAB REPORT on Rosalie's clothes came in about four o'clock. There was nothing in it at all. From semen stains, saliva, they could at least have got his blood type, but apparently her clothes had been stripped off before the rape. And the lab could do some miraculous things, but not without straw to make bricks. If the clothes had stayed in X's car awhile, they hadn't been in any proximity to any analyzable material.

Well, there was Brenda.

Mendoza had talked to Juvenile awhile ago. At a quarter of five he drove Wanda and a policewoman from Juvenile over to the hospital. They had decided it would be better to let a couple of women talk to Brenda. The other policewoman was Ruth Kaplan, a good-looking dark girl about thirty.

"Now you know what we're after—I know you've got to keep it low key, but get everything you can, for God's sake—"

"Yes, yes," said Wanda. "We know."

"And I suppose you can question her again, if you don't get much the first time."

"Don't fuss, Lieutenant," said Ruth Kaplan kindly.

"MEN," SAID WANDA as they followed the nurse down the hall. "At least they showed some sense, not trying to talk to her themselves. George Higgins would likely send her into a fit—and he's such a nice man—"

"Any man might," said Ruth, "right now. The poor kid. And she's only eight, she might have been so scared and hurt she won't remember much." They had wondered about having the mother there, but the nurse had said better not, she was something of a hysterical type and they hadn't let her see the child for long at a time.

Now she pushed the door of the room open and said, "Ten minutes," and followed them in.

Brenda was alone in the two-bed room. There was an I.V. tube attached to one arm, and she lay flat in the high hospital bed. She was a round-faced little girl with light-brown hair and blue eyes and freckles. She looked up at them without much interest.

"How are you feeling, Brenda—better?" asked Ruth.

"Okay, I guess." She had a thin, reedy little voice.

"Well, we're policewomen, and if you don't mind we'd like to talk to you."

"Oh." Faint interest crept into her expression. "I never saw any police ladies—before."

"We want to find the man who hurt you, honey. Do you feel like answering some questions about that?"

"I—guess—so," said Brenda draggingly. "He—that man—hurt me awful bad—I still hurt. It was just awful."

"We know, honey," said Ruth gently. "He's a very bad man, and we'd like to find him and put him in jail so he can't hurt any other little girls. And maybe you can help us. Will you try?"

"I—guess—so. What do you want me to do?"

"Just tell us a few things," said Wanda. "Did you ever see the man before?" Brenda shook her head slowly. "Well, when did you first see him? Was he in a car?"

"It was right—right outside the school ground. I was just starting home—and there was this car—right across from the gate. By the curb."

Now that the judges had listened to the citizens, there weren't the fleets of buses cluttering up the streets around public schools any more, the hordes of kids waiting to board, the drivers. "On Third Street?" asked Wanda.

"The gate's on—the other street. Harvard." And that would be a side street, not so busy, not crowded.

"Did he say something to you—the man?"

"He—said, did I know a girl named Janet Lee or something. He said he was her daddy. Mama always says—not talk to strangers—but he was awful polite. I wasn't scared of him then. There's a girl in my class named Jeanette, I thought—that's who—he meant—and I said I knew her—"

Brenda gave a little gasp. "And then—and then—he grabbed my arm—he grabbed right ahold of me—"

"Take it easy, honey," said Ruth. "You're all right now. Had you gone over to the car?"

"The front door—was open. He yanked me—right in—and hit me on the head. And—when I—when I woke up I was all—tied up with a rope and there was bandage stuff pasted over my mouth—"

"Adhesive tape?" asked Wanda.

"Yeah. And I was still in the car, on the floor in back I guess—and the man—the man—he was singing."

"Singing?" said Ruth.

"Yeah. He was driving the car—and singing—it was all real crazy, he was singing a song about me and my gal—that was the way he sang it, gal."

"Could you see anything? In the car or which way you were going?"

Brenda said miserably, "I was just—so scared—I just kept my eyes shut—and then the car stopped—"

"Go on, honey. I know it's hard, but just tell us— Could you see anything at that place, where you were then?"

She shook her head. Slow tears started down her cheeks. "He—carried me—up some stairs, I guess. I was so scared—and he—and he hurt me just awful bad—" Her mouth quivered and the tears came faster. "And—that's all—I remember. Till I woke up here."

They gave her a minute. "Can you tell us what he looked like?" asked Wanda. "You saw him pretty close just before he grabbed you?"

"Yeah. I guess. Just for a minute. He had on—awful nice clothes. He was sort of all dressed up. I think his pants were brown. And a real bright yellow shirt."

"Could you guess how old he was?" An eight-year-old wouldn't be good at judging an adult's age.

"I—don't know. Maybe—about as old as—my Uncle Dick."

"What about his hair?"

"I don't know."

"Do you remember what color the car was?"

"I was so scared—" She was shaking now, and the silent nurse tapped Wanda's arm and jerked her head.

"Was he a black man, Brenda?"

She shook her head blindly. "That's it," said the nurse.

"All right, honey, that's fine, you helped a lot," said Ruth. They followed the nurse out.

And that was probably about what they'd get from Brenda. An eight-year-old— They passed it on to Mendoza in the corridor. "Singing?" he said. "*¿Qué es esto?* For God's sake—"

"Me and my gal," said Wanda. "But at least we've got something definite, Lieutenant. He wasn't black. He's a sharp dresser. He puts up a good front, not to scare the kid."

"*De veras.* And of course there's scarcely any chance that she'd recognize a mug shot, a child that age—the parents raising a fuss, and understandably, if we asked."

"She's lucky to be alive," said Ruth soberly.

"Yes. Well, thanks very much for the helping hand."

"Any time, Lieutenant. I just hope to God you catch up to this one."

SATURDAY NIGHT was sometimes busy on the Central beat; it was on weekends they got a higher incidence of heists and brawls sometimes leaving the bodies behind. But the first call the night watch got was a first in another way. It was nine-forty when the squad relayed it: the Ahmanson Theatre over on Grand.

That was one of a little cluster of theaters and restaurants, with a big parking lot underground. In the last ten years this oldest part of Los Angeles had had a lot of facelifting, and these places attracted the elite crowds. As Piggott and Conway pulled up in front, behind the squad, they saw by the marquee that the present show here was a play featuring a very famous actress. "My God," said Conway, "she must be in the seventies, I remember seeing her old movies when I was a kid, but she's still supposed to be good."

The uniformed man was Turner, black and just out of the rookie stage. He was waiting for them by the box-office window. "It's a heist, but sort of a funny one." He took them through the one open door into a plush carpeted lobby. The double doors leading into the auditorium were closed, but they could faintly hear the voices from the stage, a vague rustle from the audience in there. At the end of the lobby was a door labeled *Manager*; it was open, and a chair lay on its side on the floor just outside it. It led into an expensively furnished office where four people were sitting: a portly red-faced middle-aged man in natty sports clothes, a thin blond woman, two younger men.

"Mr. Elliott," said Turner.

"That's me," said the portly man. He was past his first shock and now he was just mad. He said, "Oh, a very cute operation. I've been in this business twenty-five years and I never heard of a caper like this. Talk about timing!"

"What happened, sir?" asked Piggott.

One of the younger men spoke up. He and the other one were wearing maroon uniforms with the theater name embroidered on the jackets. "They came in at eight-fifty exactly. I happened to notice the clock in the lobby. I was just going over to shut the doors—we give 'em till nine—the curtain's at eight-fifteen and usually right on the dot."

Elliott snorted. "That's right—there are generally a few people in late, though it hasn't been usual with this engagement, a very popular show—the box office closes at eight-thirty, and that's why I say cute timing—Joy here, this is Joy Fancher, she's in the box office, she'll gather up the money and come along to my office, we check it together and I stash it away in the safe. They came in just as we were starting to count it, they were shoving Eddy and Don ahead of 'em—"

"We're the only ushers downstairs at the lobby doors, after the curtain's up," said the other one of the two. "The other two downstairs ushers are inside the auditorium. Two more in the balcony. These jokers just sort of collected us and herded us down to Mr. Elliott's office."

"And all the receipts in plain sight on my desk!" said Elliott. "They had a paper bag, they just stuffed it all in and out they went, inside three minutes—my God— How many? Two—stocking masks over their whole heads, you couldn't see—they both had guns—"

The blond woman spoke up. "I think they were young, something about the way they moved. They both had on dark clothes."

"And I don't pretend to be a hero, but I was damn mad— I started after them, but they'd shut the door and shoved a straight chair from the lobby under the knob, we had the hell of a time forcing the door open—of course by then there was no sign of them—"

"How much did they get, you have any idea?" asked Conway.

"Oh, my God," said Elliott. "So very cute." He sounded savage. "Saturday night! We get more people on weekends, naturally—and more cash. You see, some people will get tickets ahead, but not too many. The majority of the customers phone in reservations, and stop to pick up the tickets and pay for them on the way in—and mostly it's cash. We've been sold out every night but two for this engagement. You can call it somewhere in the neighborhood of forty-five hundred bucks."

"My God," said Conway. "Did they touch anything in here?" All four of them said definitely no, so it would be no use to call the lab out. None of them could say anything about the guns—just big handguns.

"Quite a cute little caper indeed," said Conway. They went back to the office and Piggott typed up a report. An hour later they were called out to a heist at a bar, and by the description it could have been the same hulking customer who had held up the bartender and patrons at that other place; he'd done that here. Only this time he'd been drunk.

"As a skunk," said the bartender, "only not falling down drunk. And I wasn't about to argue with a gun anyway, but a gun in the hands of a drunk—"

They thought he'd got away with another hundred or so, seven watches and a couple of rings. That was a nuisance; those people would have to come in and give descriptions to be added to the hot list sent to all the pawnbrokers—another job for the day watch.

When Piggott got home he found Prudence curled up in the big living-room chair reading real-estate ads in the *Times*. "What are you doing up? You need your sleep."

"I couldn't get there," said Prudence, yawning. "It was that nap this afternoon. There's not a possible house listed, Matt. The prices— Anything exciting on the job?"

He told her about the heist at the theater. "Oh, I'd just love to see that play—I always liked her so much—I noticed the ads when it was coming. But the cheapest tickets are twenty dollars."

That had been quite a little caper indeed.

MENDOZA WAS ALWAYS LATE on Sunday if he came in at all; it was supposed to be his day off. But Sunday was just another day to Robbery-Homicide; the routine was always there to be done.

Higgins got in a few minutes early, the freeway had been nearly empty. Sergeant Lake wasn't in yet and the switchboard was flashing busily. Higgins frowned at it; they really did not need a new call down the first thing on Sunday morning. He passed it by and went on into the office; five minutes later Landers came in.

"You heard what the girls got from the Dodson kid?"

"No—nobody else is in yet. If she gave us some lead, at least we can stop beating the bushes for the sex nuts."

"Which would make a little change." They heard Lake come in.

"It being Sunday," said Higgins suddenly, "maybe Luis left a note, on anything definite—" He looked, and Mendoza had left a note propped in the carriage of Hackett's typewriter, listing the gist of what the girls had heard from Brenda. "Well, so we can screen out some of the nuts," said Higgins, reading it.

"At least a couple of you in," said Lake from the door. "You've got something new, and a very funny one. The Traffic man said to hurry, he can't keep the people out of the church and they'll ruin any evidence."

"What church?"

"Place called the Calvary Bible Church over on Hoover. When the minister came to open up he found some bodies there."

"Bodies plural? My God. What's the address?"

As they started out they passed Hackett and Palliser coming in, and Higgins said, "Luis left a note, it's on my desk."

They didn't talk much on the way; they'd find out what they had when they got there. Most of the day-to-day business was mundane, but now and then the surprises came along.

The Calvary Bible Church was not very large. It was an old building on a corner, and unlike some churches these days it really looked like a church, with a little steeple with a bell in it, and a flight of shallow steps up to double front doors. It was a frame building painted white, and there were about twenty people milling around in front of it, talking excitedly, and two uniformed men guarding the double front doors. Higgins and Landers made through the little crowd; the two beat men were McConnell and Barrett.

"This has got to be the damndest thing I ever saw," said Barrett. "We finally convinced the minister he couldn't go back in. All I can say is, these people must be hell on religion, whatever brand it is—a first service scheduled at eight-thirty."

"There he is back again," said McConnell. "I hope to God he didn't get through a back door. Oh, sir! Mr. Macklin! Here are the detectives, sir, they'll want to talk to you—he's the minister here, he—"

The man who came loping up reminded Higgins vaguely of Ray Bolger as the Scarecrow. He was a tall loose-limbed man with an untidy shock of black hair and a sheeplike face with a wide mobile mouth. He was wearing a formal dark suit and an ordinary white shirt and tie. "This is a terrible thing!" he told them agitatedly. "I simply can't believe it—and how did they get in? It's simply not a thing that could happen! And why? And why?" He flung both arms out in dramatic gesture and nearly connected with Landers' jaw. "Oh, I do beg your pardon! The detectives? Yes, but what am I to do about the service? This is terrible! I had already asked Mrs. Peebles to take over the organ—my poor wife is indisposed, a nasty summer cold, she usually plays for us—and now I find I have left my notes for my sermon at home, and what—"

"Well, I'm afraid you won't be able to use the church for a service today, if that's where the bodies are—" Higgins looked a query at Barrett, who nodded. "You'd better tell the congregation to go home."

"Oh, dear, what an upset! But I feel I must stay—my church, and while I wouldn't like to call it a desecration exactly—and who are they? Where did they come from? I never saw any of them in my life, sir! Utter strangers—in my church—and I cannot conceive how they got in, I have the only keys—" He was still agitating as Higgins and Landers went into the church.

It was rather dim in the place, the windows high up along the side walls; there were only two rows of old-fashioned bench pews with high backs, and an aisle down the middle. The only light was in the pulpit at the front of the church. Higgins looked, found a set of switches on the side wall, and flicked them all. Lights came on along the walls and overhead.

They were in the last pew on the left side facing the altar. There were three of them. A fat woman slouched head down, nearly sliding from the bench seat. A little boy about six. A little girl about three or four.

"Holy God," said Landers involuntarily. "What the hell is this?"

"Whatever it is, we want the lab," said Higgins, and went out to call them up. On the way back from the squad, past the sign in front announcing that the Reverend Harvey Macklin would be preaching on the subject of Hell, he found Macklin still clucking at McConnell and stopped.

"The church is always locked, Mr. Macklin?"

"Yes, indeed—and I have the only key. I can't understand this—those two poor children—who in the world could they be? I never saw that woman in my life, or the children—"

"Well, we'll hope to find out, sir." He went back into the church. Landers had vanished, but reappeared a couple of minutes later.

"I took a look around, There seems to be a window broken in around at the side—break looks new to me. It's nearly at ground level, I guess it goes into a basement."

They stared at the bodies, waiting for the lab men. "The damndest thing all right," said Landers. "Those kids—" They couldn't see the woman's face, but the children were quietly stretched out on the pew bench looking as if they were asleep. The little girl was pretty, with dark hair; the boy was dark too, both very fair-skinned. They were dressed in what looked like expensive clothes: the boy in a gray suit and blue shirt, the girl in a frilly white dress, blue socks and white shoes.

"Did you spot—"

"Oh, yes," said Higgins. "I just noticed it." Just outside the pew, in the aisle, stood three ordinary glass tumblers in a prim little row. They had been used; sediment showed inside.

Duke and Marx showed up in a mobile truck and took a look at the scene. "Well, you boys do turn up some lulus sometimes," said Marx. "Do you know anything about it?"

"You're going to tell us about it," said Higgins.

"Well, can but try."

"You can start with the handbag." There was a navy handbag of generous size on the bench beside the woman's body. Duke maneuvered it out into the aisle, squatted and began dusting it. He turned up half a dozen latent prints; it was synthetic leather and fairly smooth. He rummaged for tape, lifted the prints neatly, and opened the flap of the bag. Higgins and Landers squatted beside him as he upended it over a sheet of newspaper. After a moment, as if reluctantly, five coins dropped out: a quarter, a dime, and three pennies. "Damn it, they usually carry everything but the kitchen sink," muttered Duke. He held the bag open and felt gingerly inside. It had three compartments. This time he was rewarded with a handkerchief. It was just a plain white square, neither very cheap nor very expensive by the look of it. There was a zippered compartment at the back of the bag, and he pulled the zipper, held the bag upside down and shook it. A little bottle fell out. "Hah," said Duke. He got out an evidence bag and pushed the bottle into it. It was a little plastic bottle with a snap top, the kind pharmacies used for prescriptions, but if it had once borne a label it had been removed.

"Damnation," said Higgins. "Everybody carries some I.D.—"

"Except when they don't want to," said Duke. "You do turn up some lulus, George."

Mendoza came over an hour later to find the lab men still poking around and Higgins and Landers watching them.

Intrigued as usual by anything offbeat, he had forgotten all the other routine when Lake told him about this.

By then they had the woman on her back in the aisle and Duke was taking her prints. She was a very ordinary-looking woman, somewhere in the fifties probably; her face was plump and oddly motherly-looking, and her graying brown hair was uncurled, pinned in an untidy bun on top of her head. She was dressed in a plain navy-blue nylon shirt-dress, beige nylon stockings, low-heeled navy pumps, and over the dress a white cardigan sweater. Duke had just come across a pair of glasses in the pocket of that, plain tortoise-shell glasses.

"*¡Es hermoso sin pero!*" said Mendoza. "Beautiful with no buts—Alison and her true-crime classics—this is the wildest one I ever remember. Have we even one small deduction yet?"

"No I.D.," said Higgins. "Anywhere. But those glasses—send the prescription to the optical companies—"

"Forget it," said Duke, holding them up to squint through the lenses. "They're strictly dime-store. Or what used to be dime-store. Just medium-strength magnifying lenses, about six-fifty at ten thousand variety stores."

"*¡Muy agradable!*" said Mendoza. "How very nice."

"Well, there are a couple of things, Luis," said Higgins, scratching his jaw where he'd missed a few whiskers this morning. "There's a basement. There's a window broken leading into it. The minister—he hung around for quite a while before he went off—said the window wasn't broken last Sunday, and there's nothing missing. Nothing much down there anyway, the rest rooms nearer the front, and some folding chairs—odds and ends. That's probably where they got in."

"But why?" said Landers blankly. "It's like—why is a mouse when it spins? Are they her kids? Or grandchildren, more likely. And why here?"

"And how?" asked Mendoza.

"That's the other deduction," said Duke. He had the three tumblers separately packaged up in evidence bags now. "I can't tell you what until we get back to the lab, but I think it'll turn out to be one of a dozen or so varieties of, give it the lay term, sleeping pills. Phenobarb or whatever. Out of the little plastic bottle. There are paper-cup dispensers in both the rest rooms, so I think they brought the glasses with them. There's running water downstairs. She mixed up the drinks, and they sat down to die."

"But—the *kids*," said Landers. "There's no sense to it—"

"Doesn't look like much," said Duke.

"Wild and wonderful," said Mendoza. "You'll give us whatever you get. Of course her prints may be on file somewhere."

"And they may not." Marx was getting the children's prints now. "And when the minister couldn't identify them, not much chance any of the congregation could," said Higgins.

"Go through the usual channels first—the feds have got millions of prints." Mendoza lit a cigarette absently. The lab men were about finished with what they could do here; the morgue wagon was waiting outside.

Now, with what Brenda Dodson had told them, they could screen out some of the sex offenders from the records: all the Negroes, for a start. It still left quite a list of men to find.

And there was also Edward Foster. Mendoza was not particularly interested in Foster; the bodies in the church had fired his imagination. But he was conscientious at the job, and when the church had been locked behind them he took Higgins up to Hollywood and they spent an hour talking to the tenants at that apartment building where Foster had lived. On Sunday, most of them were home: ordinary working people.

They didn't find anyone who had known Foster at all. Most of them had known him by sight, by the Post Office uniform. None of them knew him personally.

A girl named Sally Pepper, who lived in the apartment opposite Foster's in the facing wing, summed it up neatly. "He didn't mingle," she said. She was a pert blonde a little like Phil Landers. "Some do and some don't. Couple of girls downstairs, Sue and Amy, we get together for sunning in the courtyard—couple of young guys share Fifteen join us now and then. Most of the other people here don't get together. That one definitely didn't. Either he was a fag or he was scared of females—I said hello to him a few times and he mumbled at me and fled. He wasn't a mingler."

"And of course that is a thought, Luis," said Higgins, back in the Ferrari. "He could have been a fag, and that kind—"

"Oh, the thought had crossed my mind, *amigo*," said Mendoza dryly.

PALLISER, in between forays after the sex nuts, had called the Bakas house twice, to be told that Phil wasn't back yet. The third time he called, at three o'clock, Phil Bakas answered the phone.

"Oh, yes, sir, Mother told me—my God, I could hardly take it in—Nick murdered! I don't know anything about it, but I'll be glad to answer any questions, help the police any way I can."

"I'll be right over," said Palliser.

This time he got inside the house, and it was a comfortable homey one. A man who would be Gregory Bakas was watching TV in the living room; there was the sound of an electric mixer going in the kitchen. Phil Bakas took him down the hall to a little den. Bakas was about Zemenides' age, not nearly so good-looking, smaller, but he had an engaging smile and friendly dark eyes.

"I couldn't believe it," he told Palliser. "Nick! Everybody liked Nick, he couldn't have had any enemies, for God's sake—"

"Most people have a few—foibles," said Palliser. "He was quite a boy for the girls, wasn't he? We're thinking he may have had some trouble over a girl—a jealous boyfriend maybe, something like that. Do you know any of the girls he'd been dating lately?"

Phil looked surprised. "Sure—Angela Leeds and more lately, Sandra Chapman. Yeah, he was like that, Sergeant

Palliser." He shrugged. "I don't think I'm a square exactly, but Nick knew I didn't—well, go at it just so hot as all that. Sure, he talked about girls some. I think if there'd been anything like that, the jealous boyfriend, I'd have heard about it. He never said a thing about any trouble. Sandra was crazy about him, and—well, foibles like you say. I used to tell him he was a louse to lead the girls on, he was ambitious, you know, he wanted to start his own business and make a million, and he wasn't about to get married before he was on the way there—he liked money even better than he liked the girls, you know. He could be kind of close with a buck. But he was so good-looking, the girls all over him, and I guess you couldn't blame him."

"Now that we hadn't heard," said Palliser. "He was all out for the money?"

"Oh, don't get me wrong," said Phil anxiously. "Nick was a perfectly honest guy—he liked money, sure, but he wouldn't do anything wrong for it. As a matter of fact, the last time I saw him—last Sunday—I told him that was the hell of a dirty trick he'd pulled on that guy, and he laughed and said it was just a joke, he'd give back the money—and he would have. Nick wouldn't—"

"What was that about? A dirty trick?"

"Oh—" Phil laughed shortly. "Well, it was a crazy thing. We really got a laugh out of it. I mean, it's the twentieth century and all—it was this fellow asked Nick if he knew a good go-between—like in the old country a hundred years back, for God's sake—you know, arrange a marriage with a nice girl with a dowry. Honest to God, I never saw Nick get such a kick out of anything—it was really funny. But when I found out he'd taken money from the guy, I told him off, it was a dirty trick. And he said it was just a joke, he'd give the money back. He would have. It was just, I mean, a little crazy—the guy having such a crazy idea—"

"And who was the fellow, do you know?" asked Palliser.

"Sure, but it wasn't anything important, I just mentioned it on account of explaining how Nick was about money. It was the waiter in a place we used to go to—Ari's up on La Cienega. He's only been here a couple of years, a real country hick I guess—Stavros his name is. But listen, Sergeant Palliser, I'd have heard about any trouble Nick had with anybody, and there just wasn't any at all—"

ANGEL WAS ENJOYING the dog show very much. It was noisy and crowded and confusion, but also instructive in a way, and it was rather exciting to be with one of the people with a dog, though Roberta was scornful about what she called the bench-show people.

"Just judging the outsides," she said. "The looks. What's important is a dog's intelligence and personality." She patted Trina's handsome head fondly.

It was the first time Angel had met Trina. "I want to look at all the little ones—she's awfully big to keep in the city, isn't she?"

Roberta laughed. "That's what I said when John broke the news that we had her. I had a fit. You never heard about it? Well, this woman from Arizona was in an accident—she breeds shepherds over there—and John was on it, and he arranged to have her great big valuable show dog boarded until she was out of the hospital—and she was so grateful she had to give us a puppy— Heavens. I was furious at the time, but it's worked out fine really. She's a very good girl— aren't you, my beautiful girl?—and you're going to show all the other dogs how smart you are—"

It was all very well to say that the inside was what counted; Angel had studied the AKC dog book earnestly. Certain breeds had certain characteristics, and you could be fairly sure of what kind of dog you were getting, with a purebred puppy.

She wandered around looking at dogs. She loved the soft-eyed spaniels, the springers and cockers—but they wanted a *little* dog, she reminded herself—and the Scotties, and the wriggling little dachshunds— She talked to people, mostly nice friendly people, and some of them bred dogs. She collected a good many business cards. She looked at cairns and silky terriers and Sealyhams and Dandie Dinmonts.

Only reasonable to consult the rest of the family—of course anything would be all right with Art, and anything at all would be "loverly" with Mark—but at the end of a couple of hours she had rather settled on a West Highland white terrier. Such a nice, smart-looking little dog it was, very cute, and of course it wouldn't need much exercise.

The obedience classes were fascinating, and Trina came through magnificently in the novice class. She only lost five points for not sitting down when she should have, and Roberta was fatuously proud of her.

But a little dog is so much easier and nicer, thought Angel.

FIVE

THE HOLE-IN-THE-WALL restaurant had only the one public room and the kitchen. Palliser told Stavros Papoulas he was taking him in to question, and Stavros glowered at him and Dimitrios said, outraged, "For God's sake why? Stavros doesn't know anything! Listen, for God's sake, you can't leave me without a waiter—the dinner crowd coming in, I can't do everything—for God's sake—"

Stavros just sat sullen beside him on the way in. At the office, everybody was out somewhere but Mendoza. There were all those witnesses from the restaurant shooting, and the sex freaks—Palliser stashed Stavros in an interrogation room, and briefed Mendoza, who was amused.

"*Vaya*, that's a funny little thing, John."

"It just occurred to me, Greeks supposed to be always interested in money."

"You can't generalize about human people. Let's see what he has to say."

Stavros was scared of cops, and he didn't like the bare little interrogation room. "I done nothing," he told them. "I don't know nothing."

"This Nicholas Zemenides," said Palliser. "You knew him better than you admitted, didn't you? We've heard about it, Stavros. You wanted to find a go-between, to arrange a marriage with a nice virtuous girl. You talked to Zemenides about it."

He looked from Palliser to Mendoza, uncertain and wary. "Come on," said Palliser mildly, "we know that. Zemenides mentioned it to a friend."

Stavros shrugged. He said carefully, "I like get good wife. It is good here, good job, but not so good make friends, I learn better the talk all the time but—like get good girl. So okay, I ask Mr. Dimitrios, he laugh at me and pat back and say is funny joke—I don't understand him— That the right way do about wife, my village. Zemenides, he is Greek too, he nice, friendly, I ask him. That is true. Is all. Nothing happen."

"Oh, now," said Palliser. "You paid him some money."

"Who tell that?" snapped Stavros. "No—no—just a little talk—"

"He said so. Did he tell you he could find the go-between for you? And you gave him money for it? He told somebody about it, you know."

There was sudden panic in Stavros' eyes. He was a weedy dark little man, he couldn't be more than twenty-three or twenty-four. He had a beak of a nose and the rest of his face ran away to a narrow weak jaw. His eyes moved nervously.

"He did not tell anything. Just customer at the restaurant. All I know."

"Then why did you give him money?" asked Palliser. "We know you did."

"I—I—I—he said—he tells—but the man he know is gone away, it is no good."

"The go-between?" asked Mendoza.

"Is right. Yes. No good. All off. Is all I know."

"No," said Palliser. "He told this friend of his he'd played a joke on you, and he meant to give you back the money. Did he? When did you see him—the last time you saw Zemenides, when was it?"

"Give back money?" said Stavros loudly, incredulously. "It's a lie! I see—I see at restaurant. One week today. Is all!"

"He told this friend about the joke, and that he was going to give back the money. How much money? He was at the restaurant last Sunday?—did he say anything about it to you then?"

Quite suddenly and unexpectedly Stavros fell apart. "You know all, police always know all, but you don' know what big fool he make me—how he say to me— He was only a big, big thief! I think he is nice good fellow, and he make me a fool!'' Stavros was standing up shouting at them, his face dark with fury. ''So you know—I tell you what don' know—this dirty big thief—yes, yes, I am stupid, I ask, and he laugh and say yes, he find such a one, must be somewhere such man, he do favor for me—he say next time will cost money, and I believe—always it cost money, I give to— two hundred dollar I give him, long time to save up! He writes down where he live, I go there on bus and give the money—and nothing happen, no go-between, and I ask—I ask and ask and ask—and that night in restaurant, I tell him he is thief, I want money back—he just laugh at me!''

He bent over the little square table, pounded on it with one fist. ''You hear? He laugh at me—he go away laughing—and when restaurant is close I go there, where he live, I say must have money—and he tell me I'm stupid, I'm too stupid to be living, aren't no such people in America— But way it always happen, my village! He say this America— don't I know?—and he just play big joke on me, pretend find such a one—joke, a joke, he say! My money is joke! He say take easy—I take easy when he steal my money, my two hundred dollar? I am very goddamn mad, I want kill, I forget how he big and me not so big, I put my hands out—so— and comes a thing in my hand, I hit him with, I hit him hard and he fall down—I see blood on him and I'm glad, I'm happy—for my two hundred dollar I show him joke!''

''Well, I'll be damned,'' said Palliser.

''I am so mad at this thief, I don' even look for money— should have looked for money and took away—but I'm glad I kill this thief! I do it again if he be back alive! Bad to steal man's money, but make big fool of honest man is worse to do, and I don' care—I don' care what do to me!'' shouted Stavros wildly. ''Man got to keep honor—got to feel, show big thief not such a fool!''

They left him sitting there while they exchanged brief comment. ''I just, for God's sake, thought he might have something to add about Zemenides' general character. Of all the idiotic things—''

"And it remains to be seen," said Mendoza amusedly, "whether he'll sign a confession after he's calmed down and thought it over." It was nearly six o'clock.

"I'll always wonder whether Zemenides really meant to give back the money."

"He seems to have been fond of it. *A poco pan, tomar primero*. Every man for himself. We'll never know that, John."

Palliser took Stavros over to the jail on North Broadway and booked him in while Mendoza started the machinery on the warrant. Let somebody else, tomorrow, type up that confession and get him to sign it, if he hadn't thought better of it by then. Tomorrow was Palliser's day off.

He went home, to hear all about Trina's triumph at the dog show.

THE FIRST THING Mendoza did on Monday was to visit Lieutenant Carey down in Missing Persons. Carey was just as intrigued as he was, but nowhere on his lists was any female sounding remotely like the motherly-looking lady in the church. "Now that is a damned queer one all right," said Carey. "But they hadn't been dead long, you say—it could be she, or they, will get reported. When somebody gets back from vacation, something like that. You never know."

"And when the hell the lab will give us anything—"

"They do take their time," agreed Carey. "Well, I'll keep my eyes open and if any possibility shows up I'll let you know. You can query NCIC, of course."

But NCIC, that clearing house for information country wide, had its computers stuffed only with information on criminal activities, and Mendoza doubted that the lady in the church had been a pro criminal.

Everybody was busy; there were all those witnesses to the Saturday night shooting in the restaurant still to clear away, as well as the sex offenders. Grace and Galeano were talking to the witnesses, taking statements. At ten-thirty three men came in and said the detective had told them to come in and give descriptions of what that guy stole—they had lost watches, rings to the drunken heister. Landers had just brought in a suspect, and took the descriptions, and Mendoza sat in on the questioning, but it was inconclusive.

He had the right record, and he couldn't produce any alibis—"Who the hell remembers where they were a week ago Friday?" he asked—but he was scruffily dressed in jeans and a dirty plaid shirt, and his voice was rough; he didn't add up to Brenda's description of the polite sharp dresser.

After that a detective from Hollenbeck precinct dropped by to pass on a little news. "We just made the guy on that bank job," he told Mendoza. "The security guard that got shot up got out of the hospital yesterday. I've just had him down in R. and I. looking at mug shots. He made him. We'll be getting out flyers and an A.P.B. He's an ex-con—done other bank jobs—by the name of Chester Spooner. Just hope we can pick him up, his pedigree is tagged trigger-happy."

Mendoza agreed automatically. Time was when the FBI handled all the bank robberies, superseding the local law; now they were too busy elsewhere, or too uninterested, and it was strictly the local lawmen's responsibility.

Hackett had gone over to the jail with the typed confession for Stavros Papoulas to sign; he hadn't come back yet, and Mendoza wondered if Stavros had had second thoughts. But Hackett came in as the Hollenbeck man left, and Stavros had signed it. He got it ready to send down to the D.A.'s office. About then Glasser came in with another possible to question, so Hackett went to sit in on that.

And Mendoza had been rereading Conway's report, and ruminating, on that theater heist. He went out to lunch a little early, and headed for the Ahmanson Theatre afterward. It wasn't until he got there, to the complex of new modern building—theaters, restaurants, shops—that it struck him that the theater would be dark on Mondays. The parking lot was nearly empty. He looked around at the buildings with the sudden feeling of being disoriented in time and space. Which was absurd because he'd been here before, he'd taken Alison to a couple of shows here, the odd concert at the Dorothy Chandler Pavilion. But when he was just another Mex kid running these streets in the oldest part of L.A., these blocks had been grimy and run-down, full of dirty old warehouses and empty stores.

There might, on Monday, be a cleaning crew at the theater, who could tell him where to find the manager. He walked up there, and one set of double doors was open; there was a janitorial crew busy. The man running a vacuum cleaner in the lobby shut it off long enough to tell him that he thought the manager was there.

Mendoza walked down to the labeled door, tapped on it, went in and introduced himself.

"Sit down, Lieutenant," said Elliott. "I suppose you haven't picked up those jokers? Well, of course we couldn't give you any kind of description, except the general size—both about five-ten, not fat or thin. They got away with forty-eight hundred and forty-two dollars, by the way, only about two hundred of it in checks."

"Very pretty," said Mendoza. "They had it planned out very nice and neat, by what you tell us. This wasn't the average heist, Mr. Elliott. The average heister wouldn't, probably, realize that there'd be so much cash on hand at a legitimate theater. Certainly he wouldn't know where the cash would be when. I think the average heister would have gone for the box office, if he'd thought of heisting a theater at all. It looks to me as if this pair knew something about how the theater is operated. This one, or any theater—is the routine about the same, most places?"

Elliott said, "I'd think so—when I was managing the Pantages I kept roughly the same schedule, it's the routine indicated, if you take me."

"Mmh," said Mendoza. "You give the people leeway, coming in late, and then shut the doors."

"Sure. Nine o'clock."

"The curtain goes up at eight-fifteen. The box office closes at eight-thirty, and the lobby doors are shut at nine—locked?"

"Bolted."

"And before the curtain is up, there'd be four ushers around the lobby, when they weren't showing people to their seats. After the curtain is up, the doors closed to the auditorium, two of them are in there?"

"That's right. It's a kind of formality—just in case. Once in a while you get somebody taken sick, or a woman fainting."

"So between eight-fifteen and nine the other two ushers are around the lobby—guiding latecomers in, just standing around. What do they do after that?"

Elliott shrugged. "Whatever they please, until the end of the show when they open the lobby doors to let people out. They can go in and watch the show if they want. Sometimes they change off with the other two."

"So what it comes to," said Mendoza, "is that up to eight-fifteen there are four ushers wandering around, and between then and nine o'clock only two, and at nine the doors are bolted. And your box-office girl—"

"Joy Fancher."

"—Brings the take into your office some time between, say, eight-forty and eight-fifty."

"On the nose."

"It was timed by somebody who knew the routine," said Mendoza. "Former employee? Here or at some other theater?"

"I'm bound to say I'd started thinking along the same line myself," said Elliott slowly.

"What employees have you got here, besides the ushers?"

"Well, my God, damn few. That's possible, but—" Elliott looked perplexed. "I take it you're not thinking of the cast? I don't suppose they'd know how the money is handled, at that. We never had a check stand here—a little old-fashioned these days of casual clothes, in California. The stagehands—hell, Lieutenant, they come and go by the stage door, they wouldn't know how the money's handled. Wouldn't have occasion to be out in front. And the janitor crew's only here in the daytime, long before the box office opens."

"Have you had much turnover in ushers?" asked Mendoza.

Elliott said thoughtfully, "Eddy and Don have been here a couple of years. All the rest are newer. It's the sort of part-time job young fellows take for a little extra money, you know—we get a lot of the college kids, and the young people hoping to break into show business. I've been here since the theater opened, and in that time we've had quite a little turnover in ushers, sure."

"Have you got records of all the names?"

Elliott laughed sharply. "Good God, man, the government's turned us all into record clerks these days, hasn't it? Have to keep all the paperwork filed—sure, I can go into the back records and look out some names for you."

"Would you do that, please? Maybe it's a long shot, but it's a possibility."

"I think so too. I'll look up some names for you, Lieutenant. I'd been thinking along the same line."

Mendoza went back to the office and called the lab to see if they'd got anything on those bodies yet. "In twenty-four hours?" said Marx. "Preserve patience, Lieutenant."

ALISON HAD an appointment at the beauty shop at two o'clock. When she came out, on her way back to the parking lot she passed a travel agency, and on impulse went in. A lone clerk was at the counter, a plump young blond man in beautifully tailored sports clothes. "Something I can help you with, ma'am?"

"Well, I haven't any really definite ideas, I'd just like to see some brochures—tours or cruises—"

"Oh, certainly we can offer a number of packaged tours of all types, that's really the most pleasurable way to travel if you don't speak another language. We have one very interesting new tour just arranged, something unusual, the first one starting in August. Sixteen days—fly to Berlin from New York, two days in Warsaw, two in Riga, and six in Moscow, with guides to—"

"Moscow?" said Alison. "Why do all of you want to send everybody to visit the Communists?"

His smile didn't falter, "Since the travel restrictions have been lifted, quite a lot of people find it interesting to see something of nations so different from ours—"

"All they want is money from the tourists," said Alison, "as if the government didn't give them enough as it is— selling them grain at two percent interest or something, it's ridiculous, and I think everybody in Washington is lunatic."

"Well, if you could give me some idea where you'd like to go, ma'am—"

"It's really where I might persuade my husband to go," said Alison. She gathered up a handful of brochures. "I'll just look these over, thanks."

She drove home wondering if there was an atlas in the house. As the gates politely opened and shut for her, and she drove on up the hill, she saw that the twins were out on the ponies, with Ken Kearney standing by to supervise. They all waved at her. And that, of course, was another thing. A horse, said Kearney. The twins had been persuaded to ride around the pony track by the corral until next year, but then, Kearney said, a horse—just a quiet old nag—so he could take them on the bridle trails up in the hills. More expense—and more hay.

She headed for the back door from the garage. Luisa
Mary was staggering uncertainly around the back lawn, with
Cedric in anxious pursuit—he was very good with the children—and Mairí was sitting in a lawn chair knitting. Alison
sat down in the other chair and lit a cigarette moodily.

"Do you suppose he'd like the West Indies?"

Mairí looked at her over the tops of her spectacles.
"You'd best go to the British Isles, *achara*. You'd like to see
the Highlands, it's the best time with the heather in bloom,
and I could give you the address of my cousin Jennie in In-
verness."

"Everybody goes to Britain, it's rather ordinary," said
Alison.

MENDOZA WAS SITTING at his desk absently practicing the
crooked poker deals, at four o'clock, when Grace looked in
the door. "Everybody else busy with those witnesses from
Saturday night. I think I've got a hot one, Lieutenant. You
like to sit in?"

Mendoza abandoned the cards and followed him down
toward the interrogation rooms. "Who is he?"

Grace passed over the Xerox copy from records and
Mendoza scanned it rapidly. "He sounds hot all right. I like
him." Alfonso Peralta, a record of child molestation as a
juvenile, attempted rape of a twelve-year-old. He had served
three years at a minimum-security prison and was just off
parole. He was twenty-six, five-ten, black and brown, a
hundred and forty.

"You'll like him better when you see him," said Grace,
and opened the door of the interrogation room.

"I see what you mean," said Mendoza. Peralta was a thin
dark fellow with a sharp-featured face, slick black hair,
restless eyes; he was clean-shaven. And he was very nattily
well-dressed, not expensive clothes but coordinated and
cared for: light brown slacks, beige and brown sports shirt,
leather bolo tie, polished brown loafers. He might be a
model for Brenda's man "all dressed up."

He was annoyed at being brought in. "I'm perfectly clean," he told them. "I haven't been doing anything—my P.A. officer got me a good job, I been clean since I got out. You can't put nothing on me."

"We just want the answers to a few questions."

"For a start," said Grace, "tell us where you were about noon last Thursday."

"I'd have to think. One day's like another, Jesus, I don't know—I'd prob'ly just got up."

"Where do you work?" asked Mendoza.

"Twenny-four-hour restaurant up Wilshire, Denny's, I'm short-order cook midnight to six."

"So you're free to roam around afternoons," said Grace. "Where were you Thursday? Can anybody say you were home at noon?"

"No, acourse not, I don't usually go out till about two, I get up and eat breakfast maybe noon or half past—oh, I remember now, Thursday I dropped into a pool hall and met some guys I know, shot a few games."

"When to when?" asked Grace.

"Jesus, I don't—two-thirty to about six. Maybe. I went home about six to have dinner."

"Not good enough," said Grace. "That gave you time to pick up the little girl and have your fun with her."

"Jesus, I never did nothing like—listen, they made me go see a headshrinker in the joint, I got over all that crap, I wouldn't do nothing like that—"

"What about a week ago Friday?" asked Mendoza coldly.

"Hell, how'd I remember, I suppose I got up the usual time, maybe took in a movie—yeah, I guess that was the day I went to a movie—"

"Which movie?" asked Grace.

"I don't remember the name, God's sake, it was a place down on Main runs Mexican movies."

It went on like that, they kept prodding him, and got nothing more definite. It was getting on to the end of shift, and finally they let him go. "He lives in an old apartment on Virgil," said Grace, flicking his lighter. "Kind of place everybody's out all day—working people. Carports in back."

"Has he got a car?"

"Beat-up old Dodge sedan, off-white."

"Mmh," said Mendoza. "Off-white. At first glance, at a distance, somebody might call that tan."

"Um-hum," said Grace, brushing his moustache. "He could be, he couldn't be. Even if we place him at the pool hall, he had time for Brenda first. We'd never place him at the movie."

"And he's not the type to come apart very easy. We can see his former P.A. officer, see what he thinks. We'll keep him in mind, Jase. *¡Condenación!* The hospital, the parents, would never let us take him to show Brenda—and you couldn't rely on an identification from a child that age. Peralta is just one to keep in mind. Bring him in again to question—keep prodding at him. Let's go home and forget the job overnight, *compadre*."

On his way up the hill he noticed that Kearney must have planted his permanent pasture, whatever that might be. Where the ground had been turned and the brown underbrush cleared away, a faint tinge of green was just beginning to show.

He went in the back door, and El Señor was sitting folded up on top of the refrigerator. He gave Mendoza a sinister look out of his Siamese-in-reverse mask. In the kitchen, Mairí smiled at him from the stove. He went looking for Alison, and found her in the living room with the other three cats on her lap under a mass of travel brochures, and the baby crawling at her feet.

"Hello, *querido*. Would you like to see all the castles on the Rhine?"

"No," said Mendoza. "I don't like beer." Luisa achieved a standing posture and grabbed at Bast's tail, and he bent to pick her up. "You're always hiding this one from me, tucked in bed when I get home—"

"Not always, darling, but she ought to be in bed now—"

Luisa crowed delightedly as he swung her up. Her hair was getting redder every day and it was going to be curly.

"Where are the other monsters?"

"Out chasing the sheep, but they'll have seen you drive in—" The back door slammed and the twins erupted down the hall shouting.

Forget the job overnight, he said—but some of the jobs—when there were two little girls to remind you—weren't easy to forget.

ON TUESDAY MORNING, with Grace off, they started out at the routine again. Galeano hadn't seen all the witnesses from the restaurant yet. Carey called about nine o'clock.

"Your mysterious bodies fascinate me, Mendoza. I've been spending some of the city's money calling around to see if anybody like your grandmother is on anybody's missing list. San Francisco doesn't want her, nor San Diego, nor Sacramento, nor Phoenix. I'm working my way east."

"Well, it's a notion," said Mendoza.

"When nobody's reported them here it occurred to me. Kids that young aren't missing long before they get reported, as a rule. And when nobody's called us in a panic to say grandma's vanished with little Johnny and Susie, they could have come from a distance."

"They could have come from Timbuctoo," said Mendoza, "but why that church? I can't even start to build a picture on it."

"Well, I'll keep on asking. The number of people who do go missing without a trace in the average year—and not every police department's got a missing bureau—no one office could ever keep up. But the grandmother and the kids is something damn strange, and you'd think they'd be on file somewhere."

"Especially as they weren't derelicts. Good clothes. Only maybe not grandmother—she wasn't wearing a wedding ring."

"Well, I'll go on asking around."

"Muchas gracias."

Ten minutes later Duke called to say none of the prints from the bodies were in their records—they hadn't expected to find the children's, of course—and he had sent them on to the FBI.

Half an hour after that Elliott came in with a list of nineteen names. "I don't know if this is going to be any use to you at all, Lieutenant. I've got no idea where any of them might be now. And the first ones go back eight years. I remember the last two here, Bob Helfert and Douglas Thorpe—they were both going to L.A.C.C., quit the job when they graduated. And I don't know what courses they were taking, what they might be doing now. Those addresses might be out of date, I suppose, and the rest a damn sight more so."

"Thanks very much," said Mendoza. "It might just give us a lead."

"I hope to God. When I think—oh, we're insured, of course, but it makes me madder the more I think about it— just walk in like that, and Saturday night, my God—I don't remember much about any of these fellows. We usually get good types, but these days you never know who might go off the rails. Good luck on it, anyway."

When he'd gone out Mendoza looked over the list. It might be worth a little casting around. That had been a slickly planned job.

He took down his hat and went out to find the address where Bob Helfert had lived two years ago when he graduated from L.A.C.C.

PALLISER GOT BACK to the office at a little after two. He'd had an abortive morning with the sex offenders, and was feeling tired. Lake said it was being a quiet day, nothing new

down. Hackett and Higgins were talking to one of the pos-
sibles in one of the interrogation rooms. He sat down to take
a little breather, and reflected that at least Stavros had signed
that confession.

They'd be spending a little time in court, necessarily.
Fillmore would probably be arraigned on Thursday, Stavros some time next week. That had been a funny one.

Amanda, he thought. Celia. Jennifer. Robin thinking
about names. In case it was a girl. Saying either Brian or
Kenneth if it was another boy. None of those really raised
enthusiasm in him.

He finished his cigarette and supposed he'd better get
back to work. He had four men still to look for, and this
kind of thing was damned tedious, the way people moved
around leaving no records—the ones like these men were
often rootless and not given to the steady jobs.

Lake looked in and said, "I spoke too soon. You've got
a new body."

Palliser felt almost relieved about it. At least he could
switch over from the sex freaks.

The address was on Fourteenth. The squad was sitting in
front and a big well-dressed civilian was talking to the uniformed man on the sidewalk. "So what's the word?" asked
Palliser, coming up.

"This is Mr. Carr, sergeant. The body's been here a little
while."

"Are you telling me?" said Carr. "Sweet Jesus, to walk
in on a thing like that—" He was about forty, with a hearty
voice and a genial smile. Automatically he reached into his
breast pocket and handed Palliser a business card. It said
Carr and Leonard Realtors, with an address on Sunset
Boulevard. "My God. I was just telling the officer, we own
this dump, strictly speculation for the land value, you understand. I think we'll see the high-rises, offices go up over
on Alvarado, Pico, and they'll need space for parking lots.
Easy enough to tear down the rat-traps like these places—we
own half this block."

"Yes, sir. Where's the body?"

"We've got the damned places rented while we sit on 'em," said Carr, "and we just got an eviction notice for the tenants here. A Mr. And Mrs. Engel, I don't know anything about 'em except that they've been here six months and they're three months behind with the rent. So we get the eviction notice, and I come down to serve it, and my God, they've skipped, the place is empty and they've left a dead body in the garage! The place is a mess. No, my God, I never saw the man before, no idea who he is."

Palliser went up the drive; neither of the other two offered to accompany him. The house was an old frame place, ramshackle; the driveway cement was cracked and broken. It was a single garage, also frame, with old-fashioned double doors; one panel was open. He went in; it was dark after the bright sun outdoors and he shoved the other panel open.

The body was lying in the middle of the dirt floor. The garage was bare, no workbench or tools. The body was that of a white male, and it had indeed been here some time. If it had been July or August the neighbors would have been complaining; as it was, with the door shut and no window, the scent of decay hadn't carried far.

Palliser looked at the body, which bore no marks to say how it had got to be a body, and suddenly something clicked in his mind and he thought, *Quinlan*. That dealer Narco thought might have got murdered. The fellow with the tattoo. And possibly faked identification.

The descriptions conformed generally. The body was that of a young man about Quinlan's age and size—five-ten, medium built, with brown hair. And by God, there was a thick bandage on its left forearm.

He felt a little excited. If it was, Narco would want it all tied up from A to Z, all the lab evidence. He went out to the squad and called the lab. He thanked Carr, and Carr drove off in a new silver Lincoln, and the squad went back on tour. A mobile lab truck came out and the man in it started to take photographs.

"I want that bandage off," said Palliser. "Would you say he'd been dead about two weeks?" If Quinlan had been murdered, Narco said it would have been a week ago last Thursday.

"Somewhere around there," said the lab man, wrinkling his nose. "Okay, I've got his prints, you can go over him."

Palliser felt in the pockets first; the body was wearing only a shirt and slacks. He came up with an old leather billfold. There wasn't much in it: three single dollar bills; but it did contain exactly the kind of rudimentary identification that the Narco men had expected. A library card, looking fairly new, and a standard I.D. form. Both bore the name of Rodney Smith, and on the form, where there was a space below the *who to notify in emergency*, a scrawl said *Joseph Smith Chicago Ill*.

He tackled the bandage. It was stiff and didn't want to come loose, but he wrestled it off at last, and saw that it had covered a long deep gash in the upper forearm. Where somebody had cut out that tattoo?

"Okay, let him go," he said, standing up. The morgue wagon was already there.

He went back to the office and called Narco, but Callaghan and Goldberg were both out somewhere and the desk sergeant didn't seem to know much about Quinlan.

IT WAS CONWAY'S NIGHT OFF, and Piggott and Schenke were sitting on night watch alone. They knew each other so well that there wasn't much to talk about any more; Schenke had a paperback and Piggott was thinking about real-estate prices. They should have looked for a house last year, but had put it off, and now the prices were through the ceiling, and with the baby coming—an apartment no place to raise children. His car needed a tune-up, and he also needed a new suit. He decided to leave it all in the Lord's hands, and put up a few extra prayers on it. About all they could do.

They got a call at nine-thirty, which was early for a weeknight. The address was down on Twenty-Seventh, so they both went on it. That was all solid black down there, not anywhere near a slum exactly but old, with rents cheap for the inner city and a very mixed population, welfare people, respectable people in low-paying jobs, and a lot in between.

It was an ancient four-family apartment, and the squad-car man was black too. There were people out, both sides, attracted by the squad. "It's the left unit upstairs," said the man in uniform. He was very black, with thin Semitic features. "Maybe you'll want to talk to the lady in the squad first. She found the body. Mrs. Bertha Jolly."

They got into the front seat and put on the roof light and Schenke told her who they were. "Oh—oh—oh!" she said. "Somebody gonna be in a real mess of trouble! Somebody gonna get it!" If she hadn't been so upset, her name might have suited her; she was a fat, brown, elderly woman with several chins. She had on a wrinkled pink pantsuit, and she rocked back and forth. "Somebody gonna get it, stick a knife in Mabel Otis!"

"You knew her?" asked Schenke.

"Sure I know Mabel. Ever'body around here know Mabel—most ever'body be scared hurt Mabel—oh—oh—oh! Just go up watch our reg'lar Tuesday night show on the TV—we ain't got a TV, I useta watch with Mabel—an' see her there astarin' up at me dead! Knife in her—poor Mabel—I don't know anybody do that to her! And somebody really gonna catch it now!"

"Do you live here? Downstairs, I see. All right, did you see her today?"

"'S afternoon—saw her go out to market," she nodded violently. "Must be after she come back—"

They might have some more questions after they saw the body. They went in and climbed dusty uncarpeted stairs. Upstairs there was a square landing and two doors opposite each other; both were open. The building was silent, apparently everybody was down in the street.

The living room of the lefthand apartment was crowded with furniture, too much furniture, chairs and tables and footstools, and there were a lot of pictures on the walls. The bedroom was the same, a high double bed, more chairs and tables. Everything looked clean enough. The body was in the kitchen.

She'd been a scrawny little plucked hen of a black woman, and she looked very small in death. She was lying on her back with her feet pointing toward the door to the living room, and the handle of an ordinary kitchen knife stuck out of her lower chest. She had bled very little; her white blouse and yellow skirt weren't stained much. She stared blindly up at the ceiling and one hand looked to be reaching for the knife, to pull it out.

On the counter by the sink was a little heap of cut-up raw potato, and on the gas stove was a frying pan with a ground-beef patty in it ready for cooking.

Piggott sniffed. "She was getting ready to fix dinner when somebody came in."

"What it looks like." They went downstairs again, and used the radio in the squad to call the lab. Dubois, the uniformed man, was circulating in the crowd.

"Now, Mrs. Jolly," said Schenke, twisting around in the driver's seat. "The dead woman was Mabel Otis. Did she live alone?"

"Yessir, since her man die about ten years back. Her daughter, she moved away to San Diego. But ever'body know Mabel, she got lots o' friends."

"Did she have a job?"

"She been retired about five years, she got the Social Security money. She useta go out do housework for people, real rich people like up Beverly Hills. She useta have her own car. But the people at that license place said she can't drive no more, eyes goin' bad on her."

"When you found her, was the door unlocked or just open?"

"It was open. That scared me, wasn't like Mabel, she hadda lot o' nice things people had give her, people she useta work for, an' there are burglars all over."

"You live alone here? Do you—"

"Nossir, nossir, my husband Artie he works nights at the railroad. Oh-oh, he ain't gonna believe this—"

"What about the people in the other upstairs apartment?"

"Mr. and Mis' Toomey—they around somewhere, I seen—"

Piggott and Schenke got out of the squad, and Dubois came up with a man and woman behind him. "I figured you'd want to talk to the Toomeys about now."

"You bucking for the front office," said Schenke amiably, "and I figure you'll make it."

Dubois laughed silently. The man and woman hung back timidly. "They won't be much help to you," said Dubois. "They both work all day—him at a gas station, her in a convalescent home—and they both get home about six. They say Mrs. Otis' door was shut when they left this morning and open when they came home. They thought she was just airing out the place." He grinned at them. "But I've been hearing this and that—I've got a little advantage over you gents right here, you know. Maybe you'll get some help from the spirits on this one. Evidently she had a reputation as a witch-woman—oh, a good witch—she could put the conjure on people and tell fortunes and cast spells for good luck."

"Oh, for God's sake," said Schenke.

"Maybe," said Dubois, "somebody didn't like the fortune she told him."

"I TOLD YOU, any kind's all right with me," Hackett had said to Angel.

"Yes, on the whole you're a very satisfactory husband," said Angel. "But she's going to be a family dog after all and we all ought to have a choice."

"She?"

"I think so, they're supposed to be better watchdogs, and more affectionate. We can have her fixed—"

Sheila was in bed and Angel hadn't noticed that Mark was listening. He looked up from his book. "Is something gonna be wrong with the puppy, Mama?"

"No, no," said Angel hastily. "Now, you both look at all the pictures and say which you like best."

But as she had thought, Hackett said amiably any of them would be fine. "Yes, that's a cute one, the one you like. Looks like a nice little dog."

Mark thought they were all loverly. So this morning Angel had looked through the business cards she'd collected at the dog show, and there were two kennels which bred West Highland white terriers, and she called them both. Mrs. Mackail at the Bonnie Doon Kennels wouldn't have any puppies until next spring. Mrs. Haverkamp at the Briar Brae Kennels said she had a brand-new litter of four. Two boys and two girls. They'd be ready to leave home in eight or nine weeks.

"Oh, fine," said Angel. "We'd like one of the girls. How much are they?"

"Well, these are only pet quality stock. A hundred and fifty."

Angel gulped. Only. Well, she didn't really need that new vacuum, and there was always spaghetti once a week.

"That's fine," she said. "About the first week in August? Could we come and see them?"

"Oh, certainly, Mrs. Hackett, I'd be happy to—you take the Golden State freeway to Sunland Boulevard—"

ON WEDNESDAY MORNING, with Hackett off, Mendoza read Piggott's report on the new one with a few cynical comments to Higgins, passed it over. Galeano had one more witness to interview from the restaurant. "Somebody had better do a little follow-up on the witch-woman," said Mendoza. "How many names out of the sex records are left?"

"I haven't counted," said Higgins. "We divided them up."

"And those ushers—" Mendoza flicked his lighter. The phone shrilled on his desk as Higgins drifted out, and he picked it up. "Mendoza."

"Well, Luis," said Captain Fletcher of Traffic, "my apologies. Sometimes we're a little obtuse."

"What have you done to me?"

"You've had an APB out on a car—a four-door Chevy," and he added the plate number.

"*¡Caray!*" said Mendoza. Edward Foster's car had gone completely out of his mind. Foster, the colorless loner. "Have you got it?"

"One of the beat men happened to wander into the garage and noticed it. It was tagged as overparked and towed in."

"From where, when?"

"Well, I looked up the ticket for you. It was parked overtime on Echo Park Avenue—that's a two-hour zone—the thirteen hundred block. It got towed in last Friday night, and nobody's showed up to redeem it. We sent out the usual notice to tell the owner where it was."

"Of course. By the Post Office. And of course the man's dead, so he didn't come after it. Well, we want the lab to look it over."

"I'll tell the garage."

Mendoza called the lab, swiveled around to look at the view out the window, and thought about Edward Foster. Foster, the anonymous little man, at his dull job of delivering other peoples' letters—coming home that Friday night, changing out of his uniform, going out again—where? Echo Park Avenue. Foster, a fag? That kind came in for the quarrels, the irrational jealousy, sometimes the violence. But something might show up in the car.

PALLISER FINALLY got hold of Goldberg on Wednesday morning, and Goldberg said, "For God's sake, neither Pat nor I ever laid eyes on Quinlan. You think this is a possible? By God! I'd better get hold of one of the Hollywood boys. My God, if it is him and we could build any kind of charge on Crossland—I'll get back to you!"

One of the Hollywood detectives met Palliser at the morgue at eleven-thirty. He took one look at the corpse in the cold tray and said succinctly, "That's not him. Nothing like Quinlan. I tailed him off and on for a couple of months, and that's not him."

SIX

Mendoza had just come in on Wednesday morning when Duke followed him and laid a manila envelope on his desk. "Well, we haven't done you much good, but we can't make bricks without straw." He strewed the contents of the envelope on the blotter. "First of all, there's no smell of any identification."

"Damnation."

"Yes. Sorry. I told you the woman's prints weren't on file with us—the feds didn't know her either."

"Just a minute." Mendoza looked into the outer office and beckoned Higgins and Landers in. "Finally, the lab report on the bodies in the church." They gathered round to listen interestedly.

"There were a thousand prints in the church," said Duke, pulling up a chair and lighting a cigarette, "but I would suppose all belonging to the congregation, and God knows you never can guess what's going to be important, but we've made a few deductions. You didn't think the congregation had anything to do with the bodies. Have you had the autopsy report yet?"

"Probably some time today."

"Well, we can tell you what it'll probably say about the cause of death," said Duke. "The sediment in those three tumblers analyzed as a hefty dose—the mathematics are in the report—of a prescriptive sleeping tablet—in tablet form, I mean. That little bottle held enough residue that we can guess a full supply, that is, the normal prescriptive dose, had been crushed into powder and contained in that. The woman's prints were on all three tumblers. Her prints were also on the basement window that was broken in at the side of the church. There was just a flimsy catch inside, and on that cardigan she was wearing we picked up eight little shards of glass that match the glass in the window."

"Crime stories," said Mendoza.

"Yeah, almost everybody's heard how you wrap something around your arm to break a window. This is where we start to fail you," said Duke. "That is about the story. All the clothes were nice and clean, Robinson labels in the kids', Bullocks' in the woman's. Her shoes are from Leeds. She wasn't wearing any jewelry at all. Those glasses in her pocket, as I said, from any variety store. The glass tumblers were made by Libby, on sale at forty thousand places nationwide."

"Oh, for the love of God," said Higgins. "Nothing?"

Mendoza just shut his eyes.

"There it is." Duke was apologetic. "Bricks without straw. We got some good facial close-ups in case you want to put out flyers."

"Maybe a little shortcut to get the papers to run them," said Mendoza. "Somebody's got to know them, unless they landed from a flying saucer, damn it."

"Well, it's your baby," said Duke. "Sorry." He put out his cigarette and went away.

"My God," said Higgins.

"No se puede pedir peras al olmo," said Mendoza. "You can't expect impossibilities. Yes, it's damned annoying, but nothing to be done about it."

"Well, we've got other jobs on hand," said Higgins, and he and Landers went out.

Mendoza read over the lab report. Twenty minutes later Lake came in with the autopsy report, and that was, if possible, even less use. They had all died of a massive overdose of the phenobarbital-based prescriptive medication. They had all been normal healthy physical specimens. The estimated times of death, between nine P.M. to midnight on Saturday night. All three of them had had a meal approximately four to six hours before death. All the rest of the doubletalk was just redundant.

"¡*Válgame Dios!*" said Mendoza. He took up the phone and asked Lake to get him the coroner's office. Bainbridge wasn't in, but he wanted the doctor who had done the autopsies, Dr. Craig; ten minutes later somebody located him and he came on the phone.

"Oh, those," he said. "I heard something about it from the morgue. Hell of a funny thing."

"The understatement of the week. What I'd like to know is, how long did they take to die? From the time they got the overdose?"

Craig ruminated. "It'd take a longer time for the adult, of course. The children would have been unconscious within about twenty minutes and dead in a couple of hours. The woman, probably unconscious within an hour and dead in about three. That's a rough guess."

"Thanks very much." Mendoza put the phone down, swiveled around to look at the view over the Hollywood hills, and thought about that. You could build a tentative sort of picture. They came—on foot?—from somewhere, after they had had a meal at around four or five o'clock. Or earlier? They got into the church sometime between seven and eight. But echo answered why.

There were also those ushers.... He had found Helfer's mother at that address, and Helfer was now working at a brokerage in Santa Monica and doing very well. He had found Thorpe's uncle at the second address, and Thorpe had got married last year and moved to Fresno. All the other addresses dated much farther back, but they could try to follow them up.

Foster—the lab might turn up something on that car.

He decided they had better get the media to run the close-ups, facial shots of the bodies in the church. He leafed over the glossy prints. Sometimes a dead body was drastically changed from what it had looked like in life, but these looked quite peaceful and should be recognizable. A queer pang struck him for the photographs of the little girl: a younger Terry, dark hair and Alison's hazel-green eyes. If they were local, from anywhere around the area, somebody should know them. "Hell," he said to himself. Not everybody looked at newspapers. Busy careless people switching on the TV to find out what was happening out in the world. And the TV anchormen were a little nervous about some things these days, with all the furor—those various religious organizations—over blood and sex and violence on the tube. They might balk at showing pictures of corpses on the six o'clock news. And some city editors could be highhanded about obliging the police.

He looked at the clock. It was a quarter past ten. The *Times* would be made up overnight, so they could get the pictures in tomorrow if they would. The *Herald* would be making up the evening edition now: too late for that. But the sooner he got on it, the sooner it would be done. He took down his hat and started out to be persuasive to editors.

"WELL, SHE WAS IN about three o'clock," said Mrs. Washburn. "She just got a few things, a pound of hamburger and some crackers and a dozen eggs and some milk." She shook her head. "She said she was feeling sort of poorly, hadn't been out all day and was going right home to take a nap. Of course we knew Mabel Otis for years, it's a terrible thing what happened to her, there's so much crime now—"

The Washburns owned this small independent market on Adams Boulevard. They were staid, respectable people in middle age. Mrs. Retta Washburn regarded Higgins and Landers with troubled eyes; she was small and thin and medium black. "She said she'd had a letter from her daughter in San Diego. She was just like she always was, not—like you said—as if she'd had a threat or any trouble, anything like that. My, I'm glad we live farther uptown, little better section, but anybody might get killed nowadays, anywhere. Everybody says, what I heard, she left her door open and somebody just walked in—Bertha Jolly said nothing got

stolen but it was around dinnertime and maybe whoever it
was got scared by the Toomeys coming home. Nobody saw
anything at all, I guess.''

"That's so," said Landers. "It looks as if she was getting her dinner when it happened, and Mrs. Jolly says she
usually had that around six o'clock.'' The Jollys had been
having dinner between five-thirty and six, and the people in
the other downstairs apartment, a couple named Cox,
hadn't come home yet.

She smiled at him a little shyly. "You know, excuse me,
but you don't look old enough to be a real detective, sir.''

"We've heard around that Mrs. Otis was supposed to be
some sort of witch," said Higgins ingenuously.

"That so?"

"Oh—" she laughed a little nervously—"I don't take
stock in such things. People said so. I know a woman
claimed she cured her headaches—well, Mrs. Otis was a
smart old lady and I suppose it's sort of the way Christian
Scientists believe, people get what they expect and if you
believe in witches and spells and all—"

"Did she tell fortunes for people?" asked Landers.
"Charge for it?"

"Oh, dear," said Mrs. Washburn. "Yes, I guess she did.
I know you're not supposed to, it's against the law, but I
heard some talk—she'd read the cards for you, and she was
supposed to be good at telling the future—it's all claptrap,
I don't put stock in such foolishness. But the poor soul
didn't deserve to get stabbed like that, it's awful." There
were a few people in the little market, her husband waiting
on them. They thanked her and went out to the street.

"No witnesses at all," said Landers. "Of course the lab
may turn something. But one thing, George—a lot of people around here seem convinced the old lady had supernat-
ural powers of some kind, they'd have been afraid to tackle
her—she might have called down a jinx."

"What," said Higgins, "from the other side of the veil?"
He laughed shortly, hunching his wide shoulders. "Too

many mindless young punks around, on the dope or not, who don't believe in a damned thing but what they can touch. That's how it shapes up, one or more of that kind straying in, finding the door unlocked or open, and going in to pick up what they could. She couldn't have put up much of a fight, or made much noise. Doing what comes naturally—the murder was just accidental when they found her there. To shut her up. And before they could ransack the place the couple across the hall came home and scared them off. How many times has it happened?''

"I know, I know,'' said Landers. "Unless the lab turns something—''

It was after twelve. At the end of June the days were starting to get warmer, hinting of the long fierce summer to come. Why anybody lived in this climate—

They went out to Federico's on North Broadway for lunch, and back to the office to write a follow-up report on Mabel Otis. "Well, where have you been?'' asked Lake. "You better chase right out again—there was a bank job went down half an hour ago, and everybody else is out on it.''

"Oh, my God,'' said Higgins. "All we needed!''

"It's a Security-Pacific on Beverly.''

"LISTEN, WHAT WAS I supposed to do?'' said the security guard to Palliser. He was a bulky elderly man named Casey, with a bulldog face. "I never noticed the guy at all until the girl started to scream—I was over by the side door, it'd been a quiet morning, not much business, and I jumped three feet when she sounded off. Naturally I looked at her, she's pointing and yelling robber, and by then all I saw was the door shutting—I ran out, but how in hell did I know who to look for? By the time I got back in the girl had fainted, she's the newest teller, Doris Hammer—and everything's in an uproar, Mr. Flock out of his office and the other tellers around the girl. She didn't come out of the faint for fifteen minutes, and by the time she can say anything the guy's long gone, for God's sake. I don't think anybody knows yet how much he got.''

Grace, Galeano, Glasser were talking to the other tellers, the bank manager Flock. The teller at the window next to Doris Hammer's said to Galeano, ''Well, I didn't have a customer, I saw somebody come up to Doris but I didn't notice him, why should I? I heard him say something to her but not what, it's about ten feet away and there's the background music—I couldn't tell you a thing about him, except that I've got the impression he was fairly big. I nearly fainted myself when Doris started to scream, she was yelling about a robber and pointing at the door, and then she fainted and naturally I rushed over to her—''

They were hearing much the same from most of the people who had been in the bank. It had been the noon hour, with three of the tellers out to lunch, also the assistant manager, and Flock had been in his office.

He said irritably to Glasser, ''I was on the phone to Mr. Nagel in the loan department, I never heard all the commotion—I came out on my way to lunch, and found the place in an uproar, and everybody running around in a panic—I don't know who had the sense to call the police—''

It was Mrs. Caroline Price at the New Accounts desk who had called the police, while the guard carried Doris Hammer to the ladies' room and the other girls tried to bring her out of the faint.

''I never saw him at all,'' Mrs. Price said. She was a brisk efficient gray-haired woman. ''I had my back to the door, and he was gone by the time I turned around when Doris began to scream. I couldn't say what he looked like.''

Oddly enough, they got more from a couple of the customers. The man sitting across from Mrs. Price at her desk, facing the front door, was Joseph Headly, an insurance executive just transferred to the west coast. ''When the girl yelled,'' he told Grace, ''naturally I looked where she was pointing, and I saw the man just going out the door. He was big and young by the way he moved—about six feet, I'd say, big shoulders. I couldn't say anything about his clothes. I didn't see a gun. I just saw the side of his face, enough to say he didn't have a moustache or beard. He was blond—kind of medium short hair.''

And the woman being waited on at the teller's cage next to Doris Hammer's agreed with that. She had seen him come up to the window, as she was waiting for a check to be cashed, and she said, ''I didn't really look at him, no reason to, but he was sort of tall, and more blond than dark, I couldn't say much about his face but he didn't have a beard, I know that.''

Mendoza and Wanda were talking to Doris in the ladies' room. She was still half lying on the couch there, pathetically sniffing into a handkerchief. She was a fairly featherheaded little blonde about twenty-two, and she was upset and shivering and tearful.

''Ever since I got the promotion I've worried about getting robbed, I wondered how it'd feel—and then it happens! I never expected it—he came up, no, of course I'd never seen him before—he just looked like an ordinary young guy, and then I *saw the gun*, and I just sort of went all over numb—I guess I wasn't really scared until afterward—but I couldn't make a *sound*, I just couldn't take my eyes off the gun, I never saw a gun that close—''

''Did he say anything?'' asked Wanda.

''Yes, sure, he asked for money and I just grabbed it up from the drawer and shoved it at him—I couldn't believe it was happening—and it wasn't till he nearly got to the door I sort of unfroze and started screaming—I don't *know* what he looked like, I was looking at the gun—he was sort of blond I guess but I don't really remember his face, honestly I didn't *believe* it was happening, I hardly looked at him before I saw the gun—''

''Exactly what did he say to you?'' asked Mendoza.

''Oh!'' exclaimed Doris. ''I'll never forget it, it's sort of burned right into my mind! He said, 'All right, dollybird, you know what I'm after, hand over the dibs!' And I just grabbed up all the money from the drawer and shoved it at him—oh, I don't *know* what he did with it, a paper bag or what, I was scared then and—''

But Mendoza's mind had made a sudden jump, and he thought, by God, that bank job in Hollenbeck precinct! Could this tie up? He hadn't paid much attention to what the Hollenbeck man had said, but there'd been a Xerox copy out of records, he didn't remember the name—

He thanked Doris and took Wanda out. The other men had got the gist of what everybody had to say by then, and they got back to the office at a little after four-thirty. They'd be having all these people in to make formal statements, and it was going to give them the hell of a lot of paperwork.

He haled everybody into his office and told Lake to get him Hollenbeck. He got, eventually, a sharp-sounding Sergeant Garcia, and asked about the bank job, switching on the phone amplifier. The heavy voice boomed out into the room with startling suddenness.

''—Right, Chester Spooner. The security guard made a mug shot on Monday. He hit a bank on Lorena Street a week ago, but he didn't get anything—the guard spotted the gun, and was heading for him, and yelled, before the teller could hand over. They had a running gunfight out the door, but the guard didn't think he hit him—he got a slug in the side, lost some blood. It was an old S. and W. .38. He got clean away, and we don't know what he's driving, there's no car registered to him in that name. We've got flyers out—haven't you seen one?''

''They'll be down in Traffic for distribution to the beat men. What's the description?''

''Oh, sure. He's six feet, husky, clean shaven, blond hair, twenty-six. He did time up to last year in a federal prison for a bank job in Tucson, he jumped parole in March.''

''Well, I think he could be our boy on a new job here, that sounds close to what we've got. If he didn't get any loot on your job, it figures that he'd pull another one this soon. In fact, I'll go out on a limb and add our job to the flyer. Thanks much, Garcia." He put the phone down and looked around. "Anybody object?"

"He sounds damn close, Luis. Somebody'd better go downstairs and pick up some of those flyers."

Landers went down to Traffic after those, and Palliser said, "Could any of those witnesses make a positive identification?"

"We'll be finding out," said Mendoza sardonically. When Landers came back with a little stack of flyers on Spooner, they looked at his mug shot with interest. It was rather a distinctive face, with a full-lipped slack mouth, eyes wide apart, prominent ears. Galeano said, "I'd think anybody who'd seen him would remember him." Glasser agreed.

Wanda was still feeling annoyed with Doris. "That bird-brained little idiot," she said. "If she'd kept her head she could finger him easier than anybody else, but what do you want to bet she'll look at this and say, Oh, I don't *know*."

Mendoza got up and stretched. "*Mañana será otro día*— tomorrow is also a day. And we'll be busy."

AT THE CENTRAL DESK down in the lobby of Parker Center, half an hour later, the desk sergeant said politely, "A murder, sir?"

The tall young man in the Post Office uniform said doubtfully, "Well, I guess so by what I heard—I only heard about it today, of course with so many people at the Terminal Annex and all pretty busy— Somebody said he was killed, it wasn't just an accident. And maybe I know something the police ought to hear, only I don't know where to go."

"If it's about a homicide, you want Robbery-Homicide upstairs, but the day watch is off now. The night watch comes on at eight."

"Oh, hell," said the other man. "I got a date with Gladys, and I got to be at work at seven. I suppose I could come in on my day off. How do I get to this place?" The sergeant told him which floor, and he turned and drifted out the wide double front door.

THURSDAY WAS going to be busy. They had all those people coming in to make statements, and it took time to listen to them, do the typing. That would take up a good part of the day.

Headly looked at the flyer and said soberly, "That could very well be the man," and the woman who had been at the next teller's cage agreed less positively. As Wanda had predicted, Doris looked at it and said, "I don't *know*," and burst into tears.

It was, of course, Higgins' day off.

Fillmore was due to be arraigned at eleven tomorrow morning, Stavros Papoulas next Monday. Somebody would have to cover both dates. If they got any leads on Otis it would be from the lab; wait for that.

At eleven-thirty Scarne called and talked to Mendoza. "This car—Foster's Chevy. We picked up a lot of latents in it, but they're all his. And that's about it."

"Wasn't there anything in it at all?"

"Not much. Nothing in the trunk but the spare. Registration all correct in the glove compartment, and a County Guide. It's pretty clean, been well taken care of. We've still got a few latents to process, I'll let you know if we find any that don't belong to him, but it doesn't look likely."

"So thank you for nothing," said Mendoza.

AT LEAST THOSE CLOSE-UPS of the bodies in the church would be run in the second edition of the *Times* today. The editor had been upstage about getting them in the edition already made up.

They got rid of the last witness at three-thirty, and Landers remarked lackadaisically that he supposed somebody ought to write a follow-up report on Otis, not that there was much to go in it. He didn't make any move to start one.

They sat around for a while relaxing after the busy spate of work. Ten minutes later Mendoza ambled down the hall to the coffee machine, and on his way back he heard Lake's voice rise a little at the switchboard, and stopped to listen.

"Now look, ma'am, I can't understand you—please try to be calm and talk slower. All right, your name is Mrs. Glidden? I've got that. Now, what's it about? Did we find who? I don't get what you— Dead bodies? Please, Mrs. Glidden, calm down and— Who are Mr. and Mrs. Norbury? I can't understand you, ma'am—I'm sorry, please say that again—"

Mendoza set his coffee down on Lake's desk.

"A church? What church?"

Mendoza tapped his shoulder and Lake looked around. "Call relayed from the downstairs desk. Do you suppose—"

Mendoza took the phone from him and said into it loudly, "Mrs. Glidden! This is Lieutenant Mendoza. Do you know something about bodies in a church?"

The female voice at the other end of the line was nearly incoherent, alternately faint and shrill. "Oh, it's terrible, it's just awful, I can't believe—only got the letter today and— she was going to kill the children—kill the *children*—got to find out— And the Reverend Cloud died twenty years ago, she knew that—got to call Mr. and Mrs. Norbury—"

He said, sharp and cold, "Mrs. Glidden! Where are you? Where are you calling from?"

"P-P-Pomona—"

"What's the address? Just speak slowly and tell me the street and number." He got it out of her finally—Balboa Avenue, "Now listen to me. You just wait there, and a police car will come to pick you up—do you understand? A police officer will come to bring you in with the letter. Do you under—" The phone clicked at the other end and the dial tone hummed. He called down to Traffic, got the watch commander to send a car out there. Hackett, Landers and Palliser had come out to the hall. "I'd better call Alison,"

said Mendoza. "I have a hunch I'll be doing some overtime."

"Me too," said Hackett. "If we're going to break that
one, I'd like to hear about it."

"And me," said Landers inelegantly. He took ten minutes to run down to the R. and I. office to tell Phil. She was
at the outer desk talking to Captain Goldberg of Narco; she
didn't look much plumper in her uniform yet. "I'll pick up
a sandwich on the way home," he told her. "Don't fuss."

He had just got back to the office when two big men came
rushing in past Lake's desk and erupted into the detective
office like twin tornados. "What the holy hell is going on
here? Thought you were supposed to be such smart-assed
cops—" One of them was waving a copy of the *Times*.
"Why in the goddamn hell haven't you contacted us the
minute you—"

"Oh, my God—the kids—those poor damned kids,
Bob—but there's no goddamned sense to it—"

"And just who in hell are you?" said Mendoza coldly.

They dug out badges, and Hackett said resignedly, "feds.
We might have known."

"All right," said Mendoza, "what the hell's bothering
you? The photographs—good—what do you know about
them? Do you know who they are?"

"For Christ's sake—for *Christ's* sake—" The biggest man
sat down suddenly in Palliser's desk chair and let out a long
whoosh. "My sweet Jesus Christ, we read it as a snatch,
we've been sitting on a phone tap, waiting for a ransom
note, since last Saturday night, damn it! Norbury's father
is president of General Oil, they've got all the money there
is—"

THEY TOLD THE STORY, when they calmed down, concise
and crisp. "The Norburys were out all Saturday afternoon
playing golf, dinner at the country club later. It was the
maid's day off—there's one live-in maid, the gardener

come on Tuesdays. The only people at home were the kids and their nurse—they call her a nanny—"

"She'd been with them five years, since the little boy was a baby. They said she's absolutely reliable, great with the kids, they'd trust her to the ends of the earth—Miss Miller, Evelyn Miller. When they found her and the kids gone, they weren't worried at first, didn't think anything was wrong, maybe they'd gone for a little ride. But then it got past the little girl's bedtime, and they knew Miller wouldn't keep her out—it's a great big place at the end of a dead-end street, only one other house down the hill and those people are in Europe. Nobody around to see anything that might have happened. That was when they looked to see if Miller's car was there, she lives in too, and it was, and then they got scared. Norbury called us right away. Anybody with that kind of money would think of a snatch right off. So did we. There wasn't a sign of any disturbance, and of course the first thing we said was, the nurse, and they said that was impossible—they knew her too well, she'd never do it. She'd been snatched too, which was crazy, but the more we thought about it—it was a practical idea, take her along to keep the kids quiet—my dear Christ, we've been thinking that maybe this was one where it'd all come out okay, the kids being taken care of—but how in the hell, how in the goddamned hell did they end up like this?" The fed rattled the *Times*.

"We set up the phone tap, we've been sitting on it round the clock—those poor goddamned people are out of their minds with worry over the kids—cute kids, Jerry and Linda—when I opened the paper and saw this—Jesus, why did anything like this happen?"

"They spooked!" said the other one savagely. "You know it's the only answer—a bunch of goddamned amateurs, and something spooked them—when there wasn't a ransom demand in twenty-four hours, you know we were nervous about that— But why in *hell*—"

"We may find out shortly," said Mendoza. "Damnation, rush-hour traffic on the freeway—why in hell didn't I tell Traffic to use the siren?" He looked at Wanda, silent at her desk next to Glasser's. "This woman may go to pieces on us, the way she sounded—you'd better hang around."

The squad-car man brought her in at five-forty-five. He looked shaken. He said to nobody in particular, "That was quite a trip. I kept thinking she was going to pass out on me."

Wanda came over at once. But the woman was now past incoherence and incipient hysteria. She just looked numb and miserable. She was a fat woman about sixty years old, with rather wild gray hair and rimless glasses over faded blue eyes. She just stood there until Wanda urged her into a chair. She stared around at all the men gathered close, looming big sandy Hackett, dapper Mendoza, handsome Palliser, thin dark Landers, and the two big FBI men. She didn't look frightened or nervous or tearful.

"I only got the letter today," she said in a flat dull voice. "As soon as I read it I knew—I knew—I had to call the police. It was—another time—I missed Bert. Bert would have known—just what to do—but of course he's dead. My husband. I hadn't—I hadn't seen Evelyn—in the last couple of months. I don't drive. I thought—the last few times she came to see me—she was talking a little queer—about sinners and hypocrites—and quoting the Bible—but Evelyn's always been awfully religious. More than me. And, oh, my dear God, those Norburys have been so good to her—so good to her—such a wonderful salary—and her own room in that beautiful big mansion—and she always said she loved those children—as if they were her own—"

She was shaking her head blindly back and forth. "I just don't understand why. Because she never got married? I don't understand, it's too horrible to think about—the Reverend Cloud died years ago, somebody I knew told me, I don't remember who—we lived down there on Grandview Avenue when Evelyn and I were youngsters, and we went to that Church then—the Calvary Bible Church, I hadn't thought of it in years—Mama always liked us to go to Sunday school—Evelyn knew he was dead. I told her. Dear God, she was clean out of her mind, she was as crazy as old Aunt Harriet—''

She stopped talking, and then she said in a kind of wail, "And the Post Office—I should have had that letter on Monday! I should have—''

"Mrs. Glidden," said Wanda gently, "may we have the letter, please?"

She had worn a brown handbag over her arm. She opened it and took out an envelope and handed it to Wanda. She asked huskily, "Did she—do it? She did—didn't she?" She didn't seem to expect an answer. Wanda gave the letter to Mendoza.

It was written on cheap thin paper out of a dime-store tablet. The writing was small and firm, surprisingly legible.

Dear Edna,

By the time you read this I will be safe in Heaven with the Lord, and my two innocent darlings Jerry and Linda. I have been getting Messages from the angels for some time and they tell me what I have seen for myself and suspect but the angels know the truth and tell me. These people are wicked and evil sinners, they drink strong liquors and smoke the vile cigarettes and indulge in all the vices of the body, and people come to this house who are evil also fornicators and adulterers with their divorces. The angels tell me I would be wicked too not to try to save my two innocent darlings for the Lord's sake and His blessed work before they are corrupted and set in wicked ways by their evil parents, they could not help but become wicked too. They will be better off to fly straight to Heaven in their sweet innocence and I have thought and thought about the best way to take them so they will not be scared. I have thought and prayed about this and the angels have told

me how to do it. They say take nothing for the journey
so all worldly things must be left. I will take only
money for the bus. I will mail this on the way. I will
take them to the old church where I first found the
Lord and was saved, and the Reverend Cloud will know
what to do when he finds us there. I will tell my darlings we are going on a visit and they trust me and will
not be scared. I will take them on Saturday after supper at five and the church is always unlocked of course.
The angels have told me how to take that wicked woman's medicine and she will think the maid forgot to get
more. It must be Saturday and so we will all fly straight
to Heaven and when the Reverend Cloud comes to
conduct the service on Sunday he will find us. I know
this is the best way for the angels have told me. Good-
bye Edna we will meet again in Heaven.

She had signed her full name firmly, Evelyn Jean Miller.

"My God," said Hackett very quietly as Mendoza's voice
stopped. The two FBI men looked at each other sickly.

Religious mania. The easy glib term for it.

Into the silence Mendoza said, "We'll have to see them,
you know."

"Christ," said the biggest fed. "I brought the paper with
me—they've been staying in, on orders, they won't have
seen— They've been out of their minds. Good people,
Mendoza. Not the jet-set people. The drink before dinner.
The quiet parties."

"I don't doubt it."

"They loved those kids. Just had—the nanny—because
they could afford it."

"Yes. We'd better go and see them," said Mendoza.

It was another job police came in for, among other dirty
and unpleasant jobs. Something that had to be done by
somebody.

They went out to Bel-Air, to the mansion in its pleasant
landscaped grounds, and saw the Norburys. They had to call

an ambulance for her, and she went down to emergency in shock. Norbury came back to the morgue and identified the bodies before he went to pieces.

Mendoza got home at eleven-thirty. The house was silent and dark all about him, and it felt even bigger in the dark. He bolted the front door and switched on the hall light to climb the stairs. Upstairs, there was faint moonlight coming in the balcony windows along the upper hall. He opened the door to the master bedroom and found Alison nearly asleep, sitting up in bed, her red head sagging against the pillows and *The Art of Murder* open on her lap. Bast, Nefertite, and Sheba were asleep on the foot of the bed, and El Señor gave him a dirty look from the top of the armoire.

"Oh—Luis." Alison sat up with a jerk. "Well, you are late—and you look tired, *mi amor.* Did something break?"

"With a vengeance," said Mendoza.

HE HAD A RESTLESS NIGHT; it wasn't often that he couldn't sleep, and long ago he had learned to shelve the sordid and ugly things that were part of the job, out of working hours. But he didn't sleep much, and got up feeling jaded.

"For heaven's sake, you're the Lieutenant," said Alison. "You can make up the overtime and go in later, *querido.*"

"No, no—you never know when we'll get another spate of work, new things going down. No, I don't want any breakfast—I'll pick up something later, and coffee at the office."

"You've turned into a workaholic, that's all. Why I say you need a vacation. A nice long vacation—you've got weeks coming to you. Only," said Alison absently, "it would hardly be a vacation to visit the Communists."

"*¿Cómo dice?*"

"Never mind. Those travel agents—a couple of weeks on a cruise liner, you'd be feeling ten years younger. And you needn't think you can go on saying no. We're going somewhere."

"I won't argue about it now." He kissed her good-bye. As he drove down the hill toward the gates, the Five Graces baaed at him amiably from the roadside.

Friday did not start out any better than yesterday had. He had just sat down at his desk with a cup of black coffee when Carey got through to him.

"No," said Mendoza when he heard his voice.

"Oh, yes," said Carey grimly. "There's another little girl missing." Usually they gave a missing report twenty-four hours, to see whether the wanderer would turn up, but not in the case of children. "Roughly the same area—Edgeware Road. Margaret Gonzales. Summer, the kids loose, they get a little more leeway, but she would have been home for dinner. She's ten. I've been chewing this one over, I told the desk to call me if there was another one, so I was out on it last night. They're a decent family, three kids—Gonzales has his own barbershop downtown. They say she'd normally have been home about four to help her mother with dinner. She was supposed to be at a girl friend's, with some other kids, but they tell us she left about two o'clock."

"Hell and damnation," said Mendoza.

"So we sit back and wait—for her to be found like Brenda—or Rosalie?" Carey swore roughly. "What the hell else can we do?"

"We can," said Mendoza, "go pick up Alfonso Peralta and lean on him. ¡Válgame Dios! No legal reason to get a search warrant for his apartment, his car—the damned judges so careful of suspects' rights—"

He collected Grace and they went out to find Peralta. They found more than they had bargained for. Grace was looking a good deal less amiable than usual; but he had a nice little girl at home too, Celia Ann.

It was, as he had said, an old sleazy apartment building with a row of carports in back. Peralta's apartment was upstairs in front, and as they came up to the door they heard voices beyond it—men's voices. Grace rapped smartly.

"And what the hell do you want now?" asked Peralta. He wore a day's growth of beard and his shirt was open to the waist. Behind him, the little living room was in wild disorder. A card table and chairs stood in the middle of the room, there were overflowing ashtrays and a few beer bottles scattered around, and there were four other men there, on their feet, stretching and yawning. They were all rather bleary-eyed and sweaty, but nobody was even high. They looked at Mendoza and Grace, spruce and fresh, curiously. They were all around Peralta's age except one, a man about forty.

"*¡Diez millón demonios!*" said Mendoza, foreseeing the outcome of this.

"You've been having a party, Alfonso?" asked Grace.

"What's it to you? So I've been throwing a party. It was my night off. You're used to sleeping days, you don't sleep good at night. We been having a poker session."

"Session's right," said the older man. "Since two o'clock yesterday afternoon, God's sake. My wife'll murder me." He scratched and yawned. "I'm ready to go home, Al. Not so young as the rest of you."

"You've all been here since then?" asked Grace.

"'S right. Quite a session. Joe here's been hot as a pistol, Marilyn's gonna bitch at me for a week."

"Mr. Gorman's the manager here," said Peralta maliciously.

Without another word Mendoza and Grace turned and went downstairs. Those fellows up there might not be the most genteel citizens around, but there were four of them; and one of them the apartment manager, a man with a job to keep. Quite conceivably four men might alibi a fifth for a heist, a burglary, or a date with somebody's wife; but the minute they found out what this alibi was for, they'd cease and desist. So it was a real solid alibi, and Peralta was in the clear.

"On this," said Grace resentfully. "He could still be our boy on the others."

"*Possible.* In a city this size, more than one sex freak running around, Jase. But—" Mendoza brushed his moustache back and forth—"rather a tight little general area to hold two. I don't know."

ABOUT ELEVEN O'CLOCK Lake buzzed him and said, "I think you'll want to see this guy. He says he has some information on something."

"All right, push him in." Mendoza was sitting looking out the window; every time the phone rang he expected it to be Carey.

The man who came in was in the middle twenties, a nondescript sandy-haired fellow, very tall and thin. He was wearing nondescript sports clothes. He said, "This where I'm supposed to be? Lieutenant Mendoza?"

"That's right. You've got some information? Sit down and tell me what it's about." Mendoza offered him a cigarette.

"Well, I don't know," he said. "It just seemed funny. And I kind of worried about it, my day off's not till Monday, and I asked Mr. Early and he said if I knew anything I ought to tell the police and they wouldn't dock me." The name rang a small bell in Mendoza's mind, but he couldn't place it immediately. "I ought to say, my name's Dow— Jerome Dow—and I work for the Post Office. At the Terminal Annex."

"Oh, yes," said Mendoza, sitting up. "Did you know Edward Foster?"

"I don't know," said Dow simply. "I didn't know the name, probably saw him around. There are the hell of a lot of carriers at the Annex, it gets kind of hectic. Mornings. I'm on a route with a lot of office buildings and that's murder, takes the hell of a lot of time. But you see, I just heard yesterday that some carrier named Foster had got killed— mugged or something—and I remembered this, and it was funny. I don't know if it's anything to do with that, but it struck me as damned funny. I went to tell Mr. Early about it when it happened, but he was busy, there was a postal inspector with him." Dow sighed and looked mournfully at his cigarette. "I told Gladys about it last night and she says I'm overconscientious."

"And what was the funny thing, Mr. Dow?" Mendoza kept expecting the phone to ring.

"Well, when I heard about this Foster getting killed some way—it was funny," said Dow. "I mean, how could it happen? It was a week ago Saturday. I came to work a little early, Saturday's a heavy day and there'd be a lot of sorting. And there in the parking lot, right up against the door, was a cart. And it was half full of mail. Which was crazy at that hour. And Foster's—"

"A cart."

"Yeah, you know, the carts we got on wheels to carry the mail. They're kept in the sorting room, we each get one assigned. You come in, collect your mail from the chutes to upstairs, sort it by blocks and buildings, load it in the cart and start out delivering. End of the route, you drive back to the Annex and turn in the cart and go home. That damn cart, it hadn't any business to be in the parking lot at five to seven in the morning. And you see, Lieutenant, that was the name on it."

"The name?"

"Edward Foster. We all get carts assigned to us. Names kind of stenciled onto the canvas part. And the damn cart was half filled with mail. It was funny."

Mendoza sat up and said, "The car! For God's sake, the— You use your cars, your own cars, to deliver the mail?"

Dow looked surprised. "Well, just to convenient spots along the route. Most routes cover quite a lot of territory, you couldn't walk it. You park somewhere and cover four or five blocks around, and move on—"

"What did you do with the cart, anything?"

"Well, full of mail the way it was, I wheeled it into the sorting room and left it," said Dow. "Like I said, I'd have told Mr. Early then but he was busy, and Mr. Lowry's away on vacation—''

''¡Bastante!'' said Mendoza. The car—for God's sake, Foster's own car—on Echo Park Avenue. His delivery route was somewhere around there. The car had been towed in that Friday night, but it had been tagged earlier, and it could have been hours earlier—morning, afternoon. ''What would have happened to it?'' he asked. ''The cart. Foster was supposed to start vacation that day.''

''Oh,'' said Dow. ''Well, there'd have been a substitute on, and he'd be using Foster's cart. I suppose he'd just locate it and think Foster had goofed off the day before. I just thought it was funny, if it was the same Foster. Gladys says I worry too much.''

Mendoza regarded him interestedly. If this said anything, it said something very queer indeed—that Edward Foster had been intercepted and strangled while he was in the middle of his mail-delivery route.

SEVEN

—Because somebody had brought the cart back to the Post Office. Foster had had the cart with him when he was killed, and—reason it out—whoever had killed him didn't know Foster's car, or he'd have left the cart there. Instead he brought it back to the Post Office, after the Annex was closed, and left it where it would be found. That was the only logical conclusion, and of all the outlandish things, a mailman murdered in the middle of delivering the mail—and it couldn't have been on the street, in broad daylight—

Mendoza thanked Dow for coming in. He followed him down the hall and looked into the detective office. There was all the necessary paperwork on Evelyn Miller, and the D.A. had wanted a conference on Fillmore: Palliser had gone down on that. The perennial heisters were always with them. Higgins was in, brooding over a report. "George, there's something very peculiar turned up on Foster. Damn it, I should have asked Traffic more about that ticket at the time." He told Higgins about the cart as they rode down in the elevator.

Traffic tickets were kept on file only for a certain time, until the fine had been paid or whatever charge was involved was cleared, or the paperwork would have filled the building. In this case Foster's car was still impounded, and they could locate the ticket. The clerk in the Traffic records office found it for them, and it had been issued by a Dane Ferguson that Friday at two P.M.

Mendoza was interested enough to call Ferguson in off tour; he was a redheaded freckle-faced young man, young enough to be a rookie. "Do you remember anything about this ticket?" Mendoza asked him.

Ferguson looked at it. "Yeah, in a general sort of way."

"A Chevy two-door, overparked there—could you say how long?"

"Well—" Ferguson scratched his head. "I'd hit that stretch of Echo Park Avenue maybe once every hour or so, cruising the beat. The way I generally do it, when the meter's red, I give it half an hour and check back before I write the parking ticket, you don't want to crowd the citizens for a dime. I know that car'd been there for awhile, I think I'd passed it maybe twice but the meter was okay until I swung by that time and saw it was red."

"But how in hell could he have been kidnapped off his mail route?" asked Higgins. "It's just wild, Luis."

"Well, I'd like to find out where he might have been."

They went over to the Terminal Annex and talked to Brian Early, who was annoyed; he was busy. The routes? Well, of course they were mapped out—there was a master plan available upstairs. "I suppose I can get you a Xerox copy," he said. "It may take a little while." When he came back twenty minutes later he handed Mendoza a photocopied map. "This is what we give the carriers when they're new on a route, until they're familiar with the area. This was Foster's route."

"Tell me something else," said Mendoza. "The carriers come in, pick up the mail—it's sorted out by routes for them?"

"Upstairs where all the machines are, yes."

"And they sort it again, before they go out. What time would most of them start actually delivering mail?"

"Well, it depends whether the mail load is light or heavy. On the average, they'd usually be leaving the station by nine-thirty."

Mendoza thanked him, and in the car Higgins said plaintively that he was starved. They went out to Federico's on North Broadway for lunch, and Mendoza was more interested in the map than his sandwich.

"Between Sunset Boulevard, down where it begins, and Temple—the other way, between Waterloo and East Kensington. Mmh. The thirteen-hundred block on Echo Park Avenue is roughly in the middle of that area. Whichever end he started first, I think that would have been his second stop—he'd park somewhere around the junction of Sunset and Alvarado if he started at that end, and spend an hour or so covering that piece of it, and park the next time about in the middle. But it doesn't matter which end he started, very roughly speaking I think he'd be parking the car there around about eleven or eleven-thirty. If we can deduce anything at all." Higgins sat back and poured more coffee.

"Look, that's still one hell of an area, Luis. How in the hell could you pin down any particular section of it? There's no way to check it. A lot of people don't get mail every day—few of them might remember, and there's no way to check the mail itself now."

"No," said Mendoza. "But—of all the damned queer things—"

Higgins swore. "I wish to hell there was something more we could do about this missing kid— God damn it, Luis, it's against all the odds, him snatching three of them off the street in broad daylight—it's not as if this was a country village, for God's sake—"

Mendoza said absently, "Maybe easier if it were, George. City people busy, not noticing things there to be noticed."

"But he's got some place to take them—we didn't get much out of Brenda about that, but— It sounds like an apartment. And in that kind of area you'd think somebody would have seen him carrying a trussed kid out of a car—"

"We know nobody did. Not so necessarily." Mendoza was still hunched over the map on the table.

"It has got to be the same bastard on all of them. Third Street and Harvard—Griffin and Darwin—Edgeware Road. It makes a kind of triangle. Damn it, Margaret Gonzales is our business in a kind of way, I'd like to poke around a little."

Mendoza said, "It's nearly twenty-four hours now, isn't it? Wait and see. She'll be turning up, George—somewhere, sometime." His tone was grim. "Maybe not soon. Rosalie wasn't dumped in that playground for at least two days after she was snatched—Brenda was found within twenty-four hours, but she was alive. She'll turn up, George. We just have to wait."

"What you mean is," said Higgins, "the longer it is, the bigger the chance that she's dead."

"Add it up yourself," said Mendoza.

HIGGINS WAS UNSATISFIED. When they came back from lunch, he got his car out of the lot and drove up to Edgeware Road, with no particular plan in mind. It was an ordinary old residential area, quiet, mixed with single houses and a few apartment buildings. There was a secondary main drag, Bellevue, crossing it. Other streets like it all around here, not exactly an affluent classy area, but decent.

He was cruising slowly down the narrow street when he spotted Lieutenant Carey standing on the porch of an old California bungalow midway down the block. On impulse he slid the car into the curb, got out and went up there.

Carey didn't look surprised to see him. He didn't introduce him, just went on talking to the woman there. It was the mother, Mrs. Gonzales, and she was distracted with worry but in tight control: not a bad-looking woman, slender and dark. There was a nice-looking boy about twelve sitting in a porch swing, not doing anything, head down.

Carey had evidently about finished talking to her. "You can't think of anywhere else she might have been going?"

She shook her head. "I thought she'd be staying at Annie Fuentes' all afternoon, most of her other friends live a lot further away, and like I told you she didn't have her purse with her, no money—she wouldn't have been going up to the stores on Bellevue, you found that out."

Carey asked the boy, "You're sure she didn't say anything to you, Danny? About where she meant to go?"

The boy said hoarsely, "I told you, sir—I never even saw her when she started for Annie's. I was with Joe and Pete Gomez all day."

"Ah, those two always squabbling," she said. "You know how brothers and sisters are—" She put a hand to her brow in an unconsciously dramatic gesture. "You've got to feel it helps, to pray. You got to believe it."

The boy said in a choking voice, "I'm real sorry now, Ma. About—fighting with Margaret—I—" He was trying hard not to cry.

Higgins followed Carey out to the street. "I just wish to God there was something we could *do*," said Carey. "Damn it, Higgins, crowded streets, people living close, you'd think somebody would have seen something—"

"What do the other girls say? Where she was?"

"They were surprised she left so early, when she didn't have to be home until dinner time. All she said was, there was some place she wanted to go, wouldn't say where or why. The Fuentes live on Calumet, she was four blocks from home, but we haven't a clue where she was heading. Damn it, damn it, two in the afternoon of a sunny June day—how in the goddamned hell could she have been snatched—"

Higgins reflected irrelevantly that this was right on the edge of that mail route of Edward Foster's. No connection, of course. He hoped to God that the girl would turn up soon, and he hoped to God she'd be alive.

MENDOZA WAS WASTING TIME, maybe trying to invite a hunch. He had left the Ferrari about where Foster had parked when he got the ticket, and wandered down Clinton Street, up Alvarado to Ynez, back to Echo Park Avenue. The streets where Foster had gone wheeling his cart, delivering the mail house to house. Vaguely he thought, *down these mean streets*— An old part of the city, humdrum, part business, part residential. Old houses and apartment buildings. He crossed and ambled down the other way, down Montrose to Laguna, up a little dead-end street called Carolyn Lane. The streets were quiet and deserted, and of course they told him nothing. Nothing at all about where or why or how Edward Foster had met death as he went prosaically about delivering mail. There was a telephone truck at one corner, a man working on the wires on the pole; he paid Mendoza no attention.

He went down Kensington to where the Hollywood freeway crossed above, and back again to Echo Park Avenue. He sat in the Ferrari and lit a cigarette, and no vague hunch came into his mind about what had happened to Edward Foster, the colorless little man. One of the queerest things that had ever turned up—he wondered if they would ever find out what had happened.

And there was Margaret Gonzales—it suddenly occurred to him—vanished away only a few blocks from here. *"¡Vaya casualidad!—¿qué es esto?"* he said to himself, and swore as the cigarette burned his fingers. He tossed it out the window.

Dios, if that X lived in this general area, could Foster have noticed something suspicious? That he could have told about, that had made him dangerous, and X realizing it? That was the Friday that Rosalie had been abducted—but later than Foster had been killed—

That was the wildest idea yet. Impossible. If that was the only hunch that was going to come to him, it meant damn all and Alison was probably right that he needed a vacation. He switched on the ignition.

ABOUT THREE O'CLOCK Friday afternoon, with Landers and Galeano the only ones in, the lab report on Mabel Otis' apartment came up. Landers read it and looked at the photographs of the crowded fussy old apartment, the scrawny little black woman dead on the kitchen floor. Galeano, at loose ends, came over to look too, and they discussed it desultorily. "If she could foretell the future you'd think she'd have foreseen her own danger and kept her door locked," said Galeano, and Landers laughed.

"True." Suddenly he spotted something on one of the photographs and looked closer. Something on the floor in the living room—it was a long shot facing the kitchen door. A little paper bag? Higgins came in just then, and Landers said, "Come here and tell me what this looks like to you." They both looked, and Galeano got out a magnifying glass.

"Paper bag from Bullocks'," said Higgins. "You can just make out the name on it. What about it?"

"That place was pretty neat, if there was too much furniture in it," said Landers. "It just strikes me—" He picked up the phone and got the lab, talked to Horder. "You remember anything about it? It shows in one of your photographs."

"Oh—yeah," said Horder after thought. "I looked at it, it was a scarf or handkerchief or something she'd evidently just bought, the sales receipt was in with it. Nothing important, I just left it."

Landers put the phone down and passed that on. "But she hadn't gone out that day—she told Mrs. Washburn she wasn't feeling well, she just went out to the market."

"So she'd bought it the day before."

Landers repeated slowly, "That place was pretty neat. I think she'd have put it away in a drawer. Nobody ransacked that place, to leave a mess. Somebody just came in and stabbed her."

"Nitpicking," said Higgins. "Or are you having a hunch?"

"I don't know—I'd just like to know more about it," said Landers abstractedly.

"Well, it's okay with me, there's nowhere else to go on it."

They went out and drove down to Twenty-seventh Street. Landers had found a letter on the kitchen table, on Wednesday, and it was from Mrs. Otis' daughter in San Diego; he had sent her a notifying wire. They found her here now, a nice-looking medium-brown woman in early middle age. Her name was Shirley Lightner, "Oh," she said to the badge, "have you found out who did it?"

"I'm afraid not. We've just got a couple of questions."

"Well, come in. I came up on the bus last night—something'll have to be done about all Mother's things, but I can't rightly pull myself together to start, somehow. My husband's coming up tomorrow to help me. I suppose most of it'll get sold, only a few things I'd want. It was an awful shock, hearing what happened to her, we'd told her she ought to move down with us now the kids are grown—any big city, the crime rate's terrible—but she liked to be independent. What was it you wanted to ask?"

Landers produced the glossy print. "Did you notice this little paper bag, Mrs. Lightner? Somewhere here?"

She thought. "Oh—yes, something Mother'd just bought, I guess, I was still feeling so upset I didn't look at it—what did I do with it?—put it in a drawer in the bedroom, I think. Do you want it?" She was surprised.

"If you don't mind."

She went into the bedroom, came back with the bag. It was an ordinary yellow paper bag with the Bullocks' logo in brown. Landers unfolded the top and reached in and brought out a square nylon scarf. It was printed all over with bright pink poodles on a blue ground, and there was a sales receipt with it. "Goodness," said Mrs. Lightner, "what in the world did Mother buy that for? It doesn't look like anything she'd want. Oh, for goodness' sake keep it, I'm sure I don't want it."

Back in the car, Higgins said again, "Nitpicking, Tom. She got it as a present for somebody."

"Not that day," said Landers.

"Well, we can't tell anything from the sales receipt, even which Bullocks' store it was—that's a big chain—"

Landers laughed suddenly. "Oh, can't we? Take a look at this."

The receipt was an ordinary rectangular slip from a cash register, with the name of the store at the bottom and the date in figures: last Tuesday. At the top was the figure 4.95, below that .49, below that 4.46, below that .27, and at the bottom a total of 4.73. "What are you getting at?" asked Higgins, looking at it.

"You're not operating on all cylinders. Read it," said Landers. "There was ten percent deducted from the purchase price before the sales tax was added."

"It was on sale."

"Maybe. But store employees get a ten percent discount on anything they buy in the store. I think it might be just worth asking about."

"Well, now," said Higgins. "It might just be."

They drove up to Bullocks' at Eighth and Hill. It was an old store, the original store, and probably due to be torn down or renovated one of these days. They had no idea whether the main accounting offices were here, but they probably couldn't tell them much more about the receipt anyway; they had no idea if this was the Bullocks' store where the scarf had been bought. It was just a little lead worth a few questions. They looked at the directory and found the department that sold scarves, gloves and handkerchiefs on the third floor, and rode up in the elevator.

Landers showed the scarf to a sales clerk, a pretty Oriental girl, and asked if it had come from here. "I don't know," she said. "We've got quite a selection. I'm only part-time, you can ask Rose." The other clerk here was a friendly black girl. She looked at the scarf and said at once, "Who could forget a thing like that?—it's hideous—I couldn't imagine why even Lil would want it—hey, did she lose it? And you found it somewhere here? But it was last Tuesday, the cleaners would—"

"You sold this to somebody you know?" asked Landers.

"Why, sure—" she looked puzzled. "Lil Hardy over in lingerie. Tuesday on her morning break."

Landers and Higgins looked at each other. A loud bell sounded. "Well, thank God," said the girl. "I'm sorry, you'll have to leave, the store's closing. If you want to catch Lil—''

WHEN ANGEL went out to the back yard at one o'clock to bring Sheila in for her nap, she found the children playing with a dog. "Where on earth did that come from?" she asked.

"It jumped over the fence and come to play with us," said Mark. "It's a loverly dog." Sheila laughed delightedly as the dog licked her face. It was a very large ungainly dog of very mixed ancestry. It had a vaguely setter-like head, but one ear was half pricked and the other dropped spaniel fashion; it was reddish brown with black mottles all over a short coat, a long plumy tail, and gangling long legs. It simpered at her, baring its teeth in a ridiculous grin, rolled over and waved its legs in the air happily, and she saw that it was a male. There was a leash law, but people were careless, and who would want such a dog—Fifty-seven varieties all right, she thought.

"Lassie!" said Sheila, trying to reach to put her arms round the dog's neck as it pranced upright. They had seen some of those reruns on TV.

"It's a boy dog, darling, it'd have to be Laddie. Come on, nap time. We'll put him out the gate and he'll go home."

"He wants to play," said Mark.

"He doesn't belong to us, Mark, he must have got out of someone's yard." She coaxed the dog over to the gate, and he leaned on her affectionately and licked her hands. When she shut the gate on him he sat down, lolling sideways on one lean hip, and whined. Angel took Sheila in.

When she went out an hour later to empty a wastebasket, the dog was chasing Mark around the yard, his long legs flying excitedly.

"He jumped over the fence again just a little while ago," said Mark apologetically.

"Heavens," said Angel.

PIGGOTT WAS OFF. Schenke and Conway had a quiet night up to ten o'clock when they had a call from Bill Moss, riding a squad round the downtown beat. "I just nailed that guy you've had the APB on," he said. "That Spooner. It was the damndest thing—I called in a Code Seven and just dropped into this McDonald's on Wilshire for a break, and there he was big as life just finishing a hamburger."

Conway laughed. "Sometimes we get the breaks."

"I've got him cuffed in the back of the squad, and he's mad as hell. What do I do with him? Do you want to talk to him?"

"Oh, leave him for the day watch," said Conway. "The warrant's out—I'll meet you at the jail."

At the main jail on North Broadway, he booked Spooner in; there'd been a gun on him, which Moss handed over. It was an old S. and W. .38, loaded. Spooner was still mad, but he was a pro and he knew the ropes; resignedly he emptied his pockets on the jailer's desk, and he didn't have much on him—forty bucks, a wristwatch, some keys. He said, "I got a car parked over there where you tagged me. Old Datsun. Be obliged if you'd drop it off at Gil's Shell station on Alvarado."

Conway dropped the gun off at the lab; Hollenbeck would want a ballistics report on it. And after that they didn't get a call until nearly midnight. It was reported as a heist, at a bar on Olive. When they got there they found a car canted up over the curb against a hydrant, a body in the street, and some excited people milling around the squad car.

"He came in with a gun and held everybody up—" That was probably the bartender, by the apron. "The customers too, and he was drunk as a lord, I was afraid the damn gun'd go off any second—the minute he went out I picked up the phone to call, and then there was this hell of a crash outside—"

The driver of the car was very shaken up. He was one of the young lawyers from the Public Defenders' office, and he'd been working late at the courthouse, been on his way to the Stack to get the Hollywood freeway home. "He walked right out in front of me, I couldn't have stopped—I was only doing about thirty—he walked right out—"

It seemed to be the big blond heister, and he was dead; the car had gone right over him. This would give the day men some more paperwork.

SATURDAY WAS LANDERS' DAY OFF, but he came in. Yesterday afternoon at Bullocks' he and Higgins had tried the lingerie department and found it was Lil Hardy's day off. They had annoyed some people up in Personnel, who wanted to go home, and got her address on Orchard Street. They were both interested enough in this unexpected development to do a little overtime, so Landers had called Phil and Higgins had called Mary, and they tried the address about eight o'clock, but she wasn't home. It was a small apartment building, but nobody knew where she was, so they left it.

Now they told Mendoza about it, and he was interested too. "You never know where you'll hit pay dirt, and that was nice deducing, Tom."

"See if we can pick her up at the store—it's open at nine-thirty, I think."

Margaret Gonzales was still missing.

Landers and Higgins got to Bullocks' as soon as it opened, rode up to the lingerie department on the third floor and asked the bored-looking elderly woman lounging at the cash register if Lil Hardy was there. She nodded at the woman across the aisle, arranging boxes of brassieres at that counter.

She was a short, plump black woman looking to be about forty-five, with an old-fashioned Afro hairdo. She was wearing a shocking-pink nylon sheath dress, stilt-heeled white sandals, and a lot of costume jewelry, dangly earrings, bracelets, rings.

Landers went over to her and produced the bag, took the scarf out of it. He had his mouth open to ask if this was hers, when she beamed at him, reached for it and said, "Oh, gee, thanks, that's mine, I didn't know where I lost it! Thought I'd never see it again—where'd you find it? I thought I put it right in my purse, but I musta dropped it in the store some place—where'd you find it?"

"That's a good question, Miss Hardy."

"Mrs.," she said automatically. "What you mean?" And then she took another look at Higgins, with *cop* written all over him; and when they produced the badges she turned a sickly gray. She wouldn't say another word while they took her out to the car and back to Parker Center. Mendoza sat in on it in the little interrogation room.

"You know where we found this, Mrs. Hardy? In Mabel Otis' apartment where you dropped it after you stabbed her," Higgins began it.

"That's not mine, I made a mistake."

"Oh, yes, it is," said Landers. "The girl in that department remembers selling it to you, last Tuesday, and the sales receipt shows your discount as an employee."

"I never seen it before."

Higgins said, "We can prove it, you know. Why did you want to stab Mrs. Otis?"

She was dumb and scared, seeing the trap closing in on her. Landers spelled it out. "We can prove when you bought it, Tuesday morning. Mrs. Otis was stabbed to death about six o'clock—" They had seen the autopsy report now—"and by ten or so when our man was taking these pictures, it was in her apartment. Did it fall out of your handbag while you were having a tussle with her? Why did you stab her? If you didn't, what were you doing there?"

She looked down at the floor, dumb. "Come on," said Higgins, "we know you were there, and if she'd been alive after you left she'd have picked that up off the floor. Why did you stab her?"

She burst out suddenly, "I didn't go there to kill her—I didn't! I was just so mad at that old cheat, she didn't know nothing at all, she was no good, just a cheat and a liar! Paid her twenty-five dollars I did and she said it bound to work, her best true-love spell, but it never did—"

"You bought a spell from her?" asked Mendoza.

She said in a despairing tone, "I'd like to get married again, I'm not so very old and I keep myself up good and all, be a good wife to any man, but I kind of had my eye on Chuck—Chuck Jacobs, he drives a delivery truck for the store—I'm not more 'n five years older, he's got no call to put names on me—" Embarrassingly she began to cry. "I heard—about that old woman—real wise woman, ever'-body said, knew how to make spells and bring wishes true and all like that. And she said, cost twenty-five dollars for her best spell, it bound to bring Chuck to me in true love—she burned a white candle and said a lot of funny things and told me just how to do, and I did it—all just like she said—the white dress and bow to the new moon over the right shoulder while I prayed true love would come to me—three times running, and he be bound to seek me out— But he never, he never—next time he laughed at me same as always, I try be nice to him, he call me silly old bitch—and I knew then he never would, and I was so mad at that old cheat and liar—

"And I didn't feel so good on Tuesday, I couldn't finish out the day, I left early and on the bus I just got to feeling madder and madder at her—and I went to ask her to give me my money back—and she laughed at me too! Let me in and she was cutting up potatoes, hardly even listened to me, and then—and then she looked at me and laughed and said best spell in the world couldn't do a miracle—and I was so mad—before I knew what I was goin' to do I grabbed that knife out of her hand—I didn't go there to kill her!" She began to cry.

Mendoza sighed and stood up. "Human nature, human nature," he said. "I'll leave you to do the paperwork on it, boys."

GALEANO AND GRACE had gone over to the jail to talk to Chester Spooner. It was a strictly routine job, because Hollenbeck had a charge on him and a second one would just carry more weight. Schenke and Conway had got an address out of him last night, and they had applied for a search warrant. They knew now that the heister at the bank on Wednesday had got away with fifteen hundred and seventy dollars. If there was a wad of cash in Spooner's pad, all to the good.

He didn't mind talking to them. He knew he was nailed on the Hollenbeck bank job. He told them he'd never have shot that guard if he hadn't fired first.

"We're not here to talk about that," said Grace. "What about that heist last Wednesday, Spooner?"

He looked blank. "I don't know what you're talking about. I never pulled a heist last Wednesday. I was at work all day."

"At work?" said Galeano incredulously.

"Yeah, that's right. I landed in this burg broke, and that heist job went all to hell, I didn't pick up a lousy damn buck. Well, hell, I got to eat like everybody else, don't I? They taught me to be a pretty damn good mechanic in the federal pen, I got a job at a garage. It's the one back of Gil's Shell station on Alvarado. I was there all Wednesday, the owner'll say. You can't pin anything on me but that damn guard, and if he hadn't fired first—"

"Oh-oh, don't tell me," said Galeano.

They found the Shell station, and talked to the owner, who was surprised and annoyed to hear about Spooner. "Best damn mechanic I ever hired," he said mournfully. But he also backed up the alibi; he and another man had been at the garage all day, and Spooner hadn't gone out to lunch until one-thirty.

"Oh, hell," said Grace.

"*UN MAL LLAMA A OTRO*," said Mendoza resignedly. "Troubles never come singly. So Spooner's not our boy on that job."

"Well, we hadn't much hard evidence at all," said Hackett. "Spooner looked like the logical answer, but now—"

"And damn it," said Mendoza, "we can't get at the bank people over the weekend—they weren't much use to us anyway. I think we've got what they had to give. That Headly was the best witness and he said he didn't see the man's face."

"All we've got, in fact," said Galeano, "is tall, blond, young, clean shaven."

"Yes," said Mendoza. "We can look over the statements again and see if anything prods us into a new idea on it. Damn that girl Doris Hammer, she was the one facing him two feet away, and if she wasn't such a nitwit she could give us more than anybody else—*¡Diez millón demonios desde infierno! Qué demonio*—"

"What the hell hit you?" asked Hackett.

Mendoza was scrabbling in the file case after those statements. "My God, just as I said that it came back to me—Doris—what she said—if that's what she did say—and I think it was just about then I'd had the bright idea about Spooner and it faded right out of my mind. All right. Here we are." He had found Doris Hammer's statement. He read it over swiftly and said, "Listen to this. 'He came up to my window and then I saw the gun. And then he said, All right, dollybird, you know what I'm after, hand over the dibs.' How does that strike all of you?"

"Dollybird," said Hackett thoughtfully. He fingered his jaw. "That's British slang, isn't it? And, dibs. But I think they're both outdated British slang, Luis. Not that I'm an expert."

"Old British movies," said Galeano, nodding. "I think so too."

"I think I'd like to check this," said Mendoza. "That empty-headed girl—*¡Ca!* She's a nitwit, but she's had four days to think it over. The trouble is, I doubt if she'd have the imagination to dream that up."

They had her home address on the statement, Edgemont Avenue in Hollywood, and he drove up there. It was a new apartment built around a pool. She lived with her parents, and her mother told him she was down at the pool.

He found her on a deck chair sipping a Coke. A nitwit she might be, but she had a luscious figure in the brief bathing suit. "Oh, I sort of remember you," she said.

"At the bank the other day. I wanted to—"

"Oh!" she said. "Oh, yes. That awful man."

"Have you remembered any more about what he looked like?"

She shook her head, "I told you, I didn't really look at him once I saw the gun. I kept looking at the gun."

"And are you absolutely sure of what he said to you?"

"Oh, I'll never forget it as long as I live! He said, All right, dollybird, you know what I'm after, hand over the dibs."

"And you understood what he meant?"

She widened her eyes on him. "Well, as soon as I saw the gun I knew he was a robber—he didn't have to *say* anything—"

"Did he have any kind of accent? A British accent?"

"Why, no," said Doris. "No, he talked just like a plain American—kind of slow. I'll never forget it as long as I live!"

PALLISER WAS THE ONLY ONE in when a messenger left a manila envelope with Farrell. It was the autopsy report on that Rodney Smith. He had died of an overdose of heroin. There was nowhere to go on that, of course. Smith might have been connected with the tenants who had skipped, or not. There were a lot of young people wandering around with no permanent homes—he could have been one of those. The address on the library card was a phony. Palliser had asked the Chicago police to check that address, but trying to find a Joseph Smith in Chicago— And if Smith had been connected with the tenants, they had skipped when they found him passed out, to vanish in the anonymous city crowds. They'd never know now about Rodney Smith.

That little girl was still missing. Higgins came in and began to type a report, swearing at the typewriter occasionally.

Farrell buzzed Palliser and said there'd been an attempted assault or something in Pershing Square, just called in by the squad. "Pershing Square!" said Palliser. "My God. When I think how that used to be a nice peaceful park—all right."

But when he got there, everybody had gone. All Faye, the squad-car man, could show him was a mess of blood on the grass, and a masterful lady. "Two kids got attacked," he said. "Well, maybe sixteen or so. Black. Some thugs jumped them, and they were both knifed—one of them looked pretty bad, I called the paramedics and they took them right in. This is Miss Truax."

She was nearly as tall as Palliser, and she had iron-gray hair, a deep firm voice, and complete control of the situation. She said, "I saw the whole thing, Officer—"

"Sergeant," said Faye.

"Oh, I beg your pardon. I am perfectly willing to testify or do whatever is necessary. It's quite disgraceful that honest citizens should be victimized, and the crime rate grows every day. Those two looked like nice boys." She gave him a smile. "I taught school for forty years and I flatter myself I can size up anyone between five and twenty at a glance." He believed her. "I saw the ringleader, the one who led the attack, very clearly—I can not only give you a description, if you'd like to try the Identikit I can draw you a picture."

"That's fine, Miss Truax. We'll certainly keep you in mind."

"Everyone else nearby," she said fiercely, "simply turning their backs and walking away! Cowards! Afraid of a little responsibility! I'll give you my address."

It might not turn out to be anything at all, but again it might, so Palliser drove out to Cedars-Sinai to ask Emergency about it. He found the paramedics still there. "One of them was D.O.A.," said the white one. "We tried, but he'd lost too much blood by the time we got to him. These senseless things. The other one's okay, just cut up a little, but he's conscious and wants to talk."

So it would be something for them to work.

He talked to the live victim, who was anxious to talk. He was very black, under the bandages, and he said his name was Sammy Keefer, and he was sixteen. He was worried about his cousin Dave—Dave Packer. "They won't tell me if he's okay. Listen, sir, can I ask you please to go tell my dad about this? He'll be worried. We were supposed to meet him in the garage, you know the garage under Pershing Square—that's why we were there. He's one of the attendants there, to take the money. Mr. Julian Keefer. Dave and I were supposed to meet him so he could take us to the party when he gets off work—Mother and Aunt Frances and my sister all drove out this morning—"

He was very worried. "Take it easy," said Palliser. "We'll see to it."

"But we should have met Dad at least an hour ago! He'll be worried. See, it's Grandpa and Grandma's fiftieth wedding anniversary, a special party—they live in Covina—and Mother and the rest of them went to fix everything for the party—Dave and I came down on the bus from Hollywood to meet Dad—"

"All right," said Palliser. "Why did those men pick on you and Dave, Sammy?"

"They weren't hardly older 'n us. I guess it was our clothes."

"Your *clothes*?"

"Yeah, see, we were all dressed up—my best suit, it's got dirt and blood all over it—Dad only bought it in March for my birthday—we were dressed up for the party, ties and everything. And both Dave and I know that kind of dude, just always lookin' for trouble—we got some like that in school, you just stay out of their way—the kind use dope and carry knives. Real tough kids. There was about four of them. They come up and started shoving us around, saying about nice pretty Sunday School boys all dressed up for dancin' school—you know, like that—I think they were all high on dope—and then the one with the moustache pulled a knife— Listen, I got to know if Dave is all right— This is just awful, spoil the whole party for Grandpa and Grandma—'' He looked up at Palliser imploringly.

And remembering Miss Truax, cravenly Palliser decided that he was a coward too. He would let the efficient impersonal hospital staff break the news.

He drove back to Pershing Square, where he found a very worried man, and it was bad enough, breaking the news to Mr. Julian Keefer.

RIDING A SQUAD CAR was a lonely sort of job, but it could also be a varied sort of job. You never knew what you were going to meet in the next eight hours, when you picked up the squad and started out on tour—the drunks, the wanted men armed and dangerous, the women about to have a baby, the overdoses, the people stoned on drugs, the heisters, the mugged honest citizens, the dead bodies, the brawls, the hit-runs or plain accidents—Bill Moss had run into them all, anything that could happen to a man riding a squad. On the whole it was a job he liked, responsibility attached to it but not too much; he didn't think he'd like being in the front office.

And they didn't have enough men, with the area they had to cover, to run two-man cars even in the inner city now. It would be nice to have some company besides the radio sometimes; but you got used to it. He liked the swing shift; he was night people. Some nights you rode around and nothing happened at all. Some nights too much happened. You never knew how it would be.

He had come on shift at four o'clock, and he'd been cruising the beat—made the rounds, picking different streets at random, keeping the eye out for any sign of trouble, listening to the radio. He hadn't had a single call.

He turned onto San Marino for the second time in three hours. It was a quiet residential street like a lot of old streets down here. But in the middle of the block he suddenly braked the squad. The headlights showed him a man up there on the sidewalk, a man staggering—

Drunk, thought Moss. The man had fallen down into the gutter. Moss got out and turned his flashlight on him, and he was covered with blood, he was unconscious, in bad shape from a beating or knifing. He was an Oriental of some kind, by what Moss could tell.

Whoever he was, he needed help. Moss radioed for the paramedics, and used his flashlight some more. There was a trail of blood from the man in the street back to the house there. It was a duplex, and the blood went up to the door on the right. It was open, Moss went in and felt for light switches; lights came on and he said, "My God!"

There were two more, on the floor of the living room. Orientals, a man and a woman. Bloody and unconscious or worse.

Moss didn't waste time. Efficiently he put in a call to Robbery-Homicide. But there wasn't anybody there. Saturday night could be busy. They were probably out on a heist.

EIGHT

THE NIGHT WATCH was out on two jobs. Rich Conway had gone to look at a body, but it was just an old near-derelict at a men's hotel on Alameda, dead of natural causes, probably alcoholism.

Piggott and Schenke were over in the manager's office of the Dorothy Chandler Pavilion. By what they were hearing from Mr. Upshaw, it was the same two heisters who had hit the Ahmanson Theatre a week ago tonight. There was substantially the same routine here. A revival of an old Broadway musical was playing, and the curtain went up at eight-thirty, when the lobby doors were shut but not bolted. The box-office girl usually brought the money to Upshaw's office about eight-forty, but tonight she was off sick and one of the ushers had been substituting. He was a willowy young man with frighteningly intelligent eyes, Gerard Gault. The heisters had walked in at eight-forty-five while he and Upshaw were just starting to check the money.

"I've got no idea how much," fumed Upshaw. "And when they left, my God, they propped a chair under the doorknob outside and we were trapped—no use shouting with all that unearthly noise from the stage—and it's the first night of the show and all the damned ushers were inside watching it! I called the police from the office and the officer let us out." There had been two of them, with the stocking masks, the two guns. Neither Upshaw nor Gault could offer any description.

"There was just one little thing I did notice," said Gault diffidently. "I don't suppose it'd be any help to you."

"What was that, Mr. Gault?"

"Well, I'm a drama student—Pasadena Playhouse—and you get in the habit of noticing accents and voices. The way people use language, you know. One of the men said to me, 'Just keep your hands down on the desk'—only he said 'don' instead of 'down.' I've only heard that once before—from a fellow who was in drama class in high school with me. The teacher was always calling him on it. He was from Pittsburgh, maybe it's a Pennsylvania usage."

SUNDAY MORNING, with two new cases gone down—and no sign of the Gonzales girl. She'd been missing since two o'clock Thursday afternoon, and the men at Robbery-Homicide didn't say it to each other but they knew she had to be dead.

Looking over the night report, Hackett said, "I suppose we'd better follow up this assault and find out who the people were at least. They all landed in emergency." He called the hospital and talked to a nurse. "Oh, those," she said. "The older man was a D.O.A. There's no identification on them at all. The other two, an older woman and a young man, have been nearly beaten to death, there are internal injuries—they're both critical and unconscious. We'd like to find out who they are, to get the records straight. They're both Chinese, evidently." Robbery-Homicide would also like to know, and Hackett and Higgins went out to the address on San Marino. The place where the people had been found was an old frame duplex, and one side of it was vacant. The other side was only a little less bare: there was the necessary furniture, beds and chairs, an ancient refrigerator and gas stove, a few clothes in closets, and that was all. Whatever had happened, it had been in the cramped little living room—blood here and there, the furniture knocked over. There wasn't a phone; there wasn't a paper of any kind in the place, at first glance; but further search turned up a business card on the mantel of the fake fireplace. *The Golden Lantern Restaurant,* it said, *Ah Tam Lock, Prop.,* and an address in that complex of new buildings around the Music Center.

They tried the house next door, and a woman opened the door to them and looked at Hackett's badge. She was short and solidly fat, with a flat face and no eyebrows.

"Did I hear anything over there last night? I certainly heard all the commotion, fire truck coming and police car— when I saw it wasn't a fire I went back to bed. What happened, were they smoking opium or something? *Know* them? Of course I don't know them, heathen riffraff, I don't like to see all these peculiar foreigners coming in by the droves, can't even talk English, sound like monkeys chattering. I never had anything to do with them—they've been here about three months, I guess. We inherited this house from my mother but I've been telling Walt we ought to sell and move to a better area—all the crime going on, and worse down here—"

"Before the police and the fire truck came," asked Higgins, "did you hear any disturbance?"

She sniffed. "Didn't hear a thing, but Walt always has the TV on pretty loud. You could ask Mr. Dempsey, he lives in the house the other side, he might have. He's a good man, heart as big as all outdoors, he's retired from the railroad, old widower, lives alone with that little German sausage dog he calls Trudy—he says to me, he's sorry for those people— Sorry! Coming here just to get on welfare if you ask me! But now I come to think, Mr. Dempsey said something about going to see his married daughter in Bakersfield—"

They tried the house on the other side, but got no answer.

"That restaurant won't be open yet," said Higgins.

"There'll be an emergency number."

The Golden Lantern Restaurant looked like a very prestige place, in the middle of that classy complex of theaters and restaurants. There were gold dragons on the double front doors. It was closed, but as Higgins bent to copy the emergency number required to be displayed, they both saw movement in there through the doors' glass panels—a man walking away from the door. Hackett rapped sharply on the door and, as the man turned and looked back, held up the badge.

After a moment the door was unlocked and the man faced them. He was a tall thin Chinese in an impeccable gray business suit and white shirt. He might be any age from thirty to fifty. He looked at the badge and said in unaccented English, "Oh, police. What can I do for you?"

Hackett explained. "We're trying to identify these people, and the card from your restaurant was the only—"

"Yes," he said. "You had better come in. I'm very sorry to hear about this. I'm the proprietor here. Yes, I know them—" he laughed shortly. "At least, I can tell you who they are." He led them down a short hall, past an elegantly decorated dining hall, to an expensively appointed little office. He sat down at the desk, and lit a cork-tipped cigarette. "That's one hell of a queer thing," he said unexpectedly. "When you think about it. They go through hell to get away from the Communists, get over here safe and get beaten up by our home-grown criminals. Damned queer. Well, I can give you the names—the young man is Chung Lo Wei. I don't know the parents at all, but I've got all their papers in my safe—Chung asked me to keep them—all the immigration forms and so on." He blew a thin stream of smoke. "There are various organizations who try to help these people—the Chinese-American Society, the Christian Oriental Association—others. They try to find jobs for them, places to live, help them get assimilated. I've found jobs for several of them, but these people posed a little problem. They've only been here four or five months—"

"Boat people," said Hackett. "Chivvied hither and yon after they got away."

Ah Tam Lock lit another cigarette. "That's right. Some of them are educated intelligent people—some of them just—" he spread his hand—"people. Chung and his parents aren't city people—no English at all when they got here.

Well, he's willing and eager to work—I gave him a job here, all the rough work, odds and ends of rough jobs. A couple of the staff speak the language—which I don't,'' and he grinned, ''but not Chung's dialect. He's been picking up English fairly well. The Society found them a place to live at cheap rent. But why in hell this should happen—my God, gentlemen, they've got nothing worth stealing. Why the thugs should break in and attack them—it's crazy.''

At least it would give them, from the immigration papers, the names—the queer-sounding names. Chung Lo Wei, Chung Yang Lo, Wu Sen.

''Let's hope the two of them left alive can eventually tell us something,'' said Higgins. ''It doesn't seem to make much sense. We'll have our lab men go over the house, see if they can pick up any known prints. At the moment it's all up in the air. Well, thanks very much, sir, we're glad to know this much anyway.''

PALLISER CALLED Miss Emily Truax when it got to be a decent hour on Sunday morning, and she agreed instantly to come in for a session with a police artist. He went to pick her up. She lived in a nice house in Monterey Park, and on the way in she explained that she hadn't been in downtown Los Angeles in years, but she'd heard that there were some good new shops around the Music Center, she'd been shopping for her sister's birthday, and was on the way back to pick up her car at the lot under Pershing Square when she witnessed the fracas. She was shocked to hear that one of the boys had died.

He settled her down with one of the artists at the lab, Sergeant Cipriano, and told her to call him when she was ready to go home. She said there was no hurry, she hadn't anything special to do today.

MENDOZA, DRIFTING IN LATE as usual on Sunday, was interested in Piggott's report. "That's a queer little thing—'don' for 'down'—don't know that I ever heard that one."

"Well, you get the different pronunciations and usages in different parts of the country," said Galeano, "even with everybody listening to the same TV anchormen. It's nothing to give us any help unless we catch up to this pair."

"I wonder, Nick." Mendoza laughed. "First the dollybird and now this. Damn it, that strikes me as a damned peculiar little thing—if he doesn't have a British accent what was he doing using the British slang?"

"He's been here long enough to lose the accent," said Galeano. "Or most of it. We did say the slang was outdated."

"I hadn't thought of that. I suppose it's possible. But this—" Mendoza ruminated, got out the list of ushers, and called Elliott at his home number; he wouldn't be at the theater yet. "How are you doing?" asked Elliott.

"You'll be interested to hear that the Dorothy Chandler Pavilion was held up last night."

"Don't tell me. Another Saturday night take. The same pair?"

"Evidently, by what we've got. I don't know if you can tell me something I'm curious about, Mr. Elliott. It's one very damn long shot, but would you remember—from this list of ushers—was one of them originally from somewhere in Pennsylvania?"

There was a long pause while Elliott thought. He said, "Wait a minute—I'm trying to remember his name. Though why in hell a home town should mean anything—"

"There was one?"

"I wouldn't remember except that he was so damn supercilious about California—he was always saying it's full of a million nuts and weirdos, the only reason to come out here was to break into bigtime show biz and make a million—" Elliott laughed. "If he did he changed his name. That kind of thing annoys me, not to sound all chauvinistic about it—if people think we're all freaks they can damn well stay home.''

"If his name's on this list, would you recognize—''

"Gurney!'' said Elliott triumphantly. "Alan Gurney. It was a few years back. I don't remember anything else about him.''

"Thank you so much.'' Mendoza looked at the list. Gurney had worked at the theater for nearly two years, up to more than three years ago. The address for him then was Atchison Street in Pasadena.

Galeano said, "Talk about long shots—you're really feeling reckless, aren't you?''

"Well, we can have a look,'' said Mendoza meekly.

They drove out to Pasadena in the Ferrari. The place was an old frame house with a small rental unit in the back, and that was the address for Gurney then. A pretty dark girl answered the door and said blankly, "Never heard of him. Lou and I've rented this place for about a year. Maybe Mrs. Engstrom would know—the front house, she owns this place.''

Mrs. Engstrom was an ample, amiable, sentimental woman with thick gray braids wound around her head. She said at once, "Oh, Alan. That was the only other time I've rented to young people, before Sally and Lou took the place—and I like young people, I'm always interested in them. Alan Gurney and Bill Hunter, they rented the back place for nearly three years, I think it was—I could look it up—both such nice young men, and Alan so good-looking—well, he wanted to get into show business, you have to be good-looking for that. He was studying acting at the Pasadena Playhouse, and Bill Hunter was going to City College. What do you want to know about Alan for?''

"We'd like to find him, just to ask a few questions,'' said Mendoza. "Do you know where he moved?''

"Well, what the police want with Alan— Let me think when it was. It was about this time of year, three years back, when it happened. When Alan's mother lost all her money—something about a trustee stealing it all—and he had to quit studying at the Playhouse. It's a pretty expensive college, you know, having such a high reputation. Poor Alan, he was so upset and disappointed, but he wouldn't go back east—he said he'd make it somehow, and he got a job at a men's store up on Colorado, he'd only been working part-time as an usher at a theater."

"Which store?" asked Mendoza.

"Kessler's, I think. Then Bill Hunter got married and moved, and Alan couldn't afford the rent alone, and he moved too. I told them both to let me hear from them, and I always get a Christmas card from Bill Hunter, but I never heard from Alan again."

"Have you got Hunter's address?"

"Surely."

It was Gaynor Avenue in Sherman Oaks. "Well, it's a nice Sunday for a drive," said Galeano. "You're not really thinking this is going to add up to anything?"

Mendoza said seriously, "Like Tom and that paper bag, Nick. You never know."

The house in Sherman Oaks was a trim stucco with pleasant landscaping. A pretty blond girl answered the door and said yes, Bill was home: took them down to a small den.

He was a sandy, unhandsome young man with a friendly manner. Mendoza explained that they were looking for Alan Gurney. "We understand you used to live together while you were both in college. You weren't ambitious for an acting career like Gurney?"

Hunter laughed. "What, with my face? No fear. I'm with Steiner and Fuller brokerage. What do you want with Alan?" He cocked his head at them. "I kept up with him—awhile—and then lost track. I wouldn't know where he is now." He waited a moment and then asked, "Police—has he got into some more trouble?"

"Had he got himself into trouble?" asked Mendoza.

"Well, I should think you'd know about it." Hunter paused, and said unhappily, "Oh, hell, I felt sorry for the

guy, but— Well, he'd been spoiled, never had to work before, and I guess he's just weak. He was working at a men's
store in Pasadena, and—well, he got into the accounts there,
took them for quite a bit, I guess, and got himself in jail.
That's the last I heard of him."

"Now that's very interesting," said Mendoza gently. "We
don't know if he's been up to anything, but we'll hope to
find out."

In the car, Galeano said, "You and your hunches!"

"Once in a while they pay off, Nick."

They drove back to Pasadena police headquarters and
asked to look at some records. Gurney had been charged
with grand theft, and as a first offender had served one year
at the men's colony at San Luis Obispo. He had been out for
eight months and was still on parole. They got hold of his
parole officer, who said he had got Gurney a job on the
janitorial crew at Pasadena City College, and he had a two-
room apartment on Raymond Street.

"Mmh, yes," said Mendoza. "A little come down from
the Pasadena Playhouse, Nick. I can see Gurney feeling a
little restless too."

ANGEL SAID FIERCELY TO THE DOG, "Go home!" The dog
wasn't wearing a collar. People—there was a leash law. The
dog, attracted by her voice, immediately jumped the fence
into the back yard, came up and leaned on her affectionately, panting. He bared his teeth and gave her a simpering
smile. "Go home, you don't belong here," said Angel. She
hoped the children were still watching cartoons on TV.
Really he was the most ridiculous-looking dog she had ever
seen, and one of the largest—his hind legs longer than the
front ones, and those ears—

He gazed up at her with melting brown eyes, and then lay
down and rolled, waving his ungainly legs coquettishly in all
directions. "You idiotic big lummox," said Angel. "Go
home!" She was taking the children out to the kennel in an

hour, to see the West Highland puppies and choose their own little girl.

If she just went inside and ignored him, he'd go away. She hoped.

BY THREE O'CLOCK Miss Truax had, with the aid of Identikit and Cipriano, produced a good picture for Palliser. The face was almost handsome, wide at the cheekbones, with a widow's peak of dark hair and the suggestion of a small moustache. He looked about eighteen or twenty; of course some teenagers would start shaving early.

She said confidently, "That's him. The one who started the attack. I saw him pull out the knife, I can testify to that. I couldn't say about the others."

Palliser thanked her and took her home, and came back to Parker Center. Sunday was just another day to cops. And by what Sammy said, this one might have been in cop trouble already. Palliser didn't feel inclined to go poring over the mug books. It was just a place to ask, he didn't really expect anything to come of it, but he went down to Juvenile and asked to see anybody who was in. He was welcomed by a Sergeant Glenn, stocky and genial, who asked, "What can we do for Robbery-Homicide, sergeant?"

Palliser handed over the artist's composite drawing. "By any millionth chance, does this ring any bells with you?"

"Why, bless my little heart," said Glenn, "it's Tony Damico. Good picture, too. He turned eighteen the other day, so now we can do something more than slap him on the wrist."

"Usual pedigree?" Palliser was gratified.

"Possession, using, attempted assault, petty theft. What in hell has he been up to that you're after him? Are you?"

"You'll be happy to know," said Palliser, "that we're going to slap a Murder Two charge on him. If you can tell us where to find him."

MENDOZA WAS ENSCONCED in his deep armchair somnolently rereading *Many Inventions*, with Alison opposite brooding over travel brochures, when the phone rang at half-past nine. And as he put the book down, he knew what it was. He went to the nearest phone in the hall; he said, "Carey."

"I always heard you had ESP," said Carey. "She's turned up. Margaret Gonzales."

"Dead."

"Dead."

"Where and when?"

"On Bellevue, about the middle of the block. A squad spotted her—she was right on the sidewalk. And the squad had cruised that block about forty minutes before, and she wasn't there then."

"Oh."

"And—Mendoza. She wasn't raped," said Carey. "Her clothes are all intact, there's no sign of rape, attempted rape, any kind of molestation."

"*¿Qué sé yo?* Now that is very damned peculiar. How was she killed—any indications?"

"It looks," said Carey, "as if she just got a blow on the head—skull fracture maybe—the doctors will tell us. There's not even any blood. You know what I thought about it?"

"Yes," said Mendoza. "That X—despite appearances—is squeamish. He wants to rape them alive. And Margaret got herself killed in the process of abduction, so he didn't—"

"Well, it's possible. With the perverts, anything is possible."

"I'll see you in the morning," said Mendoza, and put the phone down.

Alan Gurney hadn't been at his cheap apartment on Raymond, and he wanted to follow up Gurney. But this was more important.

THE NIGHT WATCH had left them two new heists, with nine witnesses to come in for statements. It was Palliser's day off.

Hackett had talked to the hospital yesterday, identifying the Chinese victims for them: not that the bare, strange names constituted much identification. Marx had taken a look at that place and said, as Hackett and Higgins had seen for themselves, that the attack had taken place right there. Furniture overturned, blood: no weapon of any kind visible. It was a forlorn hope to check for prints, probably. The pro burglars were often stupid, but anybody would have known there was nothing of remote value in that house.

Now on Monday morning he called the hospital again to check on the victims.

The nurse he got said, "The young man's still unconscious. There are broken ribs, internal injuries, a broken arm, concussion—we're still listing him as critical. The old woman's been conscious off and on, but she doesn't speak a word of English, she can't communicate at all. It's extremely difficult. We'd be obliged for a Chinese interpreter, Sergeant."

Hackett laughed, and said, "So would we, if she can give us any information. I may get back to you." He thought. The colleges were all out now, though there'd be summer sessions coming up. After a little more thought he called the big museum in Exposition Park, and talked to one of the curators there.

"Why, yes, as a matter of fact we have one staff member who speaks Chinese. Dr. Barlow. I believe he's here now—"

Barlow was intrigued, and put himself at Hackett's disposal. "But I should explain, Sergeant, that there are many Chinese dialects and some of them are as different from each other as English and German. I hope I can help you, that's all."

Hackett called the hospital again and the nurse told him the old woman's pulse was a little better and she could probably be roused. Hackett remembered suddenly that those immigration papers had listed her—the young man's mother—as forty years old. Well, what these people had been through—

He called Barlow, who said he'd meet him there. They had her in a two-bed room with a screen up. She was conscious, but obviously very weak. She looked very old: toothless, wrinkled, skeletal. She also looked frightened. She began to mutter, and Barlow said something to her in a curious sing-song tone. She stared up at him and began to chatter weakly, wildly in some gibberish unlike any language Hackett had ever heard.

After five minutes Barlow said, "I'm sorry, Sergeant. She's speaking some country dialect I'm not familiar with at all, and she evidently doesn't speak anything else."

"Damnation," said Hackett. But Ah Tam Lock had said the young man—Chung—did know some English. Hopefully when he came to he'd be able to tell them something.

MENDOZA STOOD in the middle of the sidewalk on Bellevue Avenue and looked up and down the block. "There's nothing to see," said Carey. "Just the place where the body was found, right about here. She was dumped from a car just after dark, as I read it. The squad passed here about seven-forty. It'd be dark around eight-fifteen, and the squad came by again at eight-thirty."

"Mmhm," said Mendoza. This was a secondary main drag, a block of small business. There was an independent drugstore on the corner, a cleaners' next to it, a bakery, a thrift shop, all in one building. Then, about the middle of the block where they were standing, a narrow alley ran through to the next street down. On the other side of it was another building of shops.

"He just picked a convenient place to dump her," said Carey. "All these places are closed at night, the block would be deserted."

"Don't interrupt his ESP," said Higgins dryly.

Mendoza leaned against the Ferrari and lit a cigarette. They kidded him about his hunches, and you could never depend on hunches, but if Luis Rodolfo Vicente Mendoza had any extrasensory perception, it was tied to people: he had an instinctive understanding of how human people reacted to human people. He said, "It's outside the pattern. I don't like it."

"I don't like any little girls getting killed either," said Carey.

"Vaya despacio." Mendoza stood up straight and looked up and down the block. Beyond the little alley, the first store was vacant. It had most recently housed a telephone answering service: the faded sign was still in place over the door, Quik-Answer Service. Next to it was a shoe-repair shop, on from there a woman's dress shop, next to that a small market, and on the corner a variety store.

"I told you, it looked to me as if she's been dead since Thursday. The doctors will say, but—"

"And not raped, not even touched," said Higgins. "It's funny all right."

Mendoza dropped his cigarette, stepped on it and said, "Let's follow our noses." He started up the alley.

"Where are you going?"

"It's out of the pattern. Suppose there wasn't a car?"

They followed him in silence. Forty feet up the alley, in the building to the left, was a side door. It would lead into the rear of the empty shop. Mendoza put his hand on the knob, and it turned, and the door opened inward.

"What the hell—" said Carey.

It was dim in the little room, but there was a dusty window admitting light, and they looked around. The room was about twelve by fourteen. Directly across from the outside door was the door to a bathroom; on the wall at right angles was an old porcelain sink and counter. The only furniture in the room was an old chair with a broken rear leg. In the far corner, against the wall, was a little stack of dog-eared magazines. And scattered all over that corner was a little confusion of comic books, as if they'd been stacked and upset. Mendoza went over and looked at the magazines. *Aviation Life, Motor Car, Motorcycle World, Dunebuggies.* They were all several months old. He looked at the comic books. They were all of the innocuous variety, just the crude adventure. He picked up the first one to hand and opened it, and he said, *"¡Basta ya!"* and held it out to Higgins.

Inside the front cover was the scrawled name: Dan Gonzales.

"Oh, my God, Luis," said Higgins. "My God." He handed it to Carey.

"WHY, YES, DANNY'S HERE," said his mother. "He's been sticking pretty close to home since—" Her mouth quivered. The waiting had been hard; perhaps the reality was worse. She said, "My husband's—gone to see Father Michael. About the funeral. You said—" she looked at Carey—"maybe next Thursday. Why do you want to see Danny?"

They just waited. When the boy came in, Mendoza held out a little stack of the comic books to show him. His name was in most of them. He was a nice-looking boy.

"What about it, Danny, these are yours, aren't they?" asked Mendoza.

He looked at them, and he began to cry, hopeless and desperate, and he burst out, "I'm sorry, I'm sorry, I'm sorry—it was just an accident, nobody meant to really hurt her—ole Margaret always had to go pokin' her nose—in things—find out everything—it was none of her business, we wasn't doing anything wrong—wasn't doing any harm—" His mother stared, frozen.

"You and your friends found that door was unlocked, and it was a good secret place to meet," said Mendoza softly. "To have a secret sort of club?"

He nodded, choking. "We wasn't doing—nothing wrong—ole Margaret had to— It was just—a good place—

keep all our books away from the little kids— And she had to come sneakin' around after us and find out—and she came right in—and said she'd tell on us—and we'd get put in jail for breakin' in—and we never—but she was goin' to tell—"

"Oh, my God," she said.

"—And she was sort of giggling the silly way she did— and Joe just ran at her and hit her—and she fell against the sink there—nobody meant to really hurt—"

"All right," said Mendoza. "And you were all scared, and just left her there. And—"

"Nobody meant to hurt her—I—I—I—it didn't seem she could be—"

"And last night you went back and put her out in the street so she'd be found. Just you, or all of you?"

He was sobbing steadily, "Ma and Dad—been so worried—and I knew where she was—she was—and even ole Margaret—didn't like her—just lyin' there—have to have a funeral when people—are dead—I'm sorry, I'm sorry, I'm sorry!"

"Mrs. Gonzales, where's your husband?"

She told him the name of the church faintly, and then she sat down beside the boy and put her arms around him and began to cry. Mendoza went to find the phone.

So they would still be looking for the rapist, on Rosalie and Brenda. What would happen to these kids was up to the Juvenile Court. They were basically decent kids—as Danny said, it was an accident.

Go and pick up the Gomez brothers. Do all the paperwork. Stash the kids in Juvenile Hall pending the hearing. Both Mendoza and Higgins felt tired, just thinking about it.

GRACE AND GALEANO had gone over to Pasadena to look for Alan Gurney. "And I thought he was goofing off," said Galeano. "Turning up a lead like that, just from an accent on one word—"

"Tom and the paper bag," said Grace. That one would probably follow Landers through his whole career.

The city college was about to open for the summer session, and the janitor crew was there, and busy. A big gray-haired man in the hall of the main administration building was pointed out as the boss, and Grace asked if Gurney was on.

"Sure, why? This place isn't open yet, you shouldn't—Oh-oh!" He looked at the badge, and he said, "I never did like the notion, hire an ex-con. He just took out a load of trash through that door. I'd be just as glad to see the last of him, he don't like to work too hard."

Just outside that door, where a driveway led out to the street, were two of the big city dumpsters installed in places which accumulated vast amounts of refuse. There was a man standing at one of them, the lid lifted. "Gurney?" said Galeano.

Swiftly he slammed the lid of the dumpster, and turned. He was about twenty-six, a boyishly handsome young man with wavy black hair and regular features running down to a weak chin. He looked at the badges. He said, "What do you want?" And involuntarily he cast a quick glance sideways at the dumpster.

"Just a few questions," said Grace. "Such as where you were at eight-fifty last Saturday night?"

"I was home. My P.A. officer knows I'm clean, sticking to the job and staying out of trouble. Damn you guys, make one little mistake and the fuzz come down on you forever—" but he was nervous.

"What are you so nervous about?" asked Galeano.

"I'm not nervous, for God's sake—"

"Now I wonder," said Galeano suddenly. "Saturday night—and yesterday was Sunday—I do just wonder." He went past Gurney and lifted the lid of the dumpster, and Gurney took off down the drive. Grace tore after him and collared him in a football tackle in the middle of the lawn, and Gurney caved in.

"Very nice," said Galeano. "And nice timing too. He'd just stashed it when we came up." On top of the miscellaneous trash in the dumpster was a little bundle of checks held together with a rubber band. They were all made out to the Dorothy Chandler Pavilion: the small part of the loot unusable by the heisters. "It was a good idea, Gurney, getting rid of these in a public place that accumulates the wastepaper. But these constitute some beautiful evidence."

"God damn you!" said Gurney bitterly.

THE CLERK SMILED PLEASEDLY at Alison. "Oh, yes, we have a number of packaged tours," he said. "Where did you think of going?"

"Vienna?" said Alison doubtfully. It had become almost automatic with her now, collecting all the travel brochures. But she didn't like beer either, and Luis was no waltzer.

"Oh, yes," said the clerk. "We have a very nice sixteen-day tour—first-class all the way, and excellent guides—New York to Vienna, four days there, Prague, Warsaw, and Budapest—a most interesting city—"

Alison just looked at him. "Why? Why is it that the first thing all of you think of is sending people to visit the Communists?"

He looked surprised. "Well, since travel restrictions have been lifted, many people find—"

"No," said Alison. "Don't tell me it's educational. Or like mountain climbing."

"Mountain—"

"Just because it's there."

There was a slightly uneasy silence. Alison picked up a brochure about Sweden. "Er—that is one of our most popular tours. Copenhagen, Stockholm, Helsinki, and there is an optional two-day side trip—"

"To Riga in Latvia. So I notice," said Alison.

"Well, really, ma'am, where would you like to go? We have a fourteen-day cruise through— There, I wonder if you'd be interested in one of our working cruises in the Gulf of Mexico. They're very popular, especially with young people."

"Thank you," said Alison. "What's a working cruise?"

"They're very inexpensive. On a restored genuine old sailing craft. The passengers actually help to sail the ship—what so many people enjoy is the absolute informality of it, you have no occasion for any clothes but dungarees and bathing suits and so on—meals taken on deck wherever you please, and it's all very good fun—"

Alison tried to envision Luis' expression when she told him he'd be expected to help run the sails up and down, and eat dinner on deck in dungarees, and burst out laughing. "Thank you, if I'm going on an expensive vacation I want to dress up for it, and have the best service and accommodations." After all, she thought, Denmark and Sweden might be interesting—at least that far north it would be cool, and August and September here could be hell. She put the brochures into her bag.

GURNEY WASN'T SAYING anything; he wouldn't part with the name of the pal who had joined him in those heist jobs. Galeano called his parole officer again to see if he had any ideas. All he could suggest was that Gurney had mentioned the name of a fellow at San Luis with him: a Roy Fidler. They were about the same age and had seemed to hit it off. Fidler had been in for armed robbery. If he was out—

"Thanks very much," said Galeano, and spent some of the city's money calling the men's colony at San Luis. Fidler had gone on parole three months ago. He hailed from Santa Monica originally and he was attached to the P.A. office there.

Grace sat back and lit a cigarette. "Take a bet."

"Oh, so would I." They had been busy, what with Gurney, the report to write, and other phone calls still to make; they wouldn't hear about Danny Gonzales and the Gomez boys until later.

The most recent address Juvenile had had for Tony Damico was no good; the family had moved. Palliser had put out an APB on him yesterday; it hadn't turned him up so far.

MRS. JEAN EBERHART said angrily, "The dratted thing." She poked the elevator button again. Mrs. Florence Nofziger came up and said, "Don't tell me it's on the fritz again. Damn, it's been a long day and I want to get home." They both poked the button hard as more women came down the hall.

"Not again!"

"All those stairs—"

"Better walk down than up! Think of last Wednesday morning! Four flights of stairs, and eight hours at a sewing machine at the top—"

"—And when I think of the thousands of dollars the new one cost, not six months ago—it's a sin and a shame," said Mrs. Eberhart. "The old one worked better! Henry'll have to do something, that's all. Call the people who put it in to come fix it."

"Well, it's only the last week it's been sticking, maybe it's just stiff or needs oil or something—"

The elevator finally arrived and they all piled into it. It descended ponderously, and they scrunched back to take on another load of women on the third floor.

WHEN HACKETT came in the back door and kissed Angel he said, "There's the funniest-looking mutt I ever saw out in the front yard—looks like a greyhound crossed with a camel. Running loose."

"Mhm," said Angel. She took the casserole of scalloped potatoes out of the oven. "It must belong somewhere around here, it's jumped the fence a couple of times."

"Queerest-looking hound I ever saw," said Hackett, and the children came running up, Sheila demanding to be read to. "After dinner, baby. Before bed."

About nine o'clock, when Angel went out to the kitchen to take the clean dishes out of the dishwasher and put them away, she looked out the glass door of the service-porch door.

The dog was asleep on the back porch, sprawled out with his ungainly hind legs hanging off the top step.

"Damn," said Angel.

MENDOZA HADN'T been in the office fifteen minutes on Tuesday morning when Lake called to say somebody wanted to see him. He was slightly annoyed; there was a little spate of work on hand, the fiddling detailed paperwork—the loose ends to tie up. The D.A.'s office wanted to talk to him about Lil Hardy, for some reason. There was Gurney's erstwhile pal to locate. He had an appointment at Juvenile Hall with a judge, over Danny and the Gomez boys, after lunch. Those Chinese people—that was a queer one. And the one Palliser had turned up on that knifing—

The night watch had left them two new heists, and there would be seven witnesses coming in to make statements.

The man who came into the office was middle-aged, a spare desk-type fellow with thin gray hair carefully combed over a bald spot; he was wearing a formal gray suit. "Lieutenant Mendoza? I may say that I have deliberated quite awhile before coming to see the police."

"Sit down," said Mendoza. "What do you want to see me about?"

"My name is Lowry," said the man. He sat down, lifting the knees of his trousers carefully. "It really did seem quite irrelevant. The crime rate going up, and any respectable citizen can get killed. I thought about it. Turned it over in my mind."

"The crime rate?" asked Mendoza, bemused.

"No, no." Lowry looked at him severely. "It really did seem irrelevant. After all, it was the only mark on his record. They do say, every dog allowed one bite. I thought it over very carefully at the time it happened, but I decided— in view of the fact that it was the only mark against him— that I would not ask for termination of his job. Of course it would have been easier to terminate his job than some others—he was a white man. With the blacks and Latins, it is very nearly impossible, this Affirmative Action and all the federal guidelines. But I decided not to try. And of course it must be quite irrelevant to his death."

Mendoza sat back in his desk chair. "Mr. Lowry," he said, "what in hell are you trying to tell me? About what?"

Lowry adjusted his rimless glasses. "When Mr. Early told me about it—about this carrier Foster—well, it must be irrelevant, but it is information about the man which perhaps the police should know. I thought about it all day yesterday, it was my first day at work after getting back from vacation, and the first I had heard about the man's death, and I thought perhaps you should hear about it."

"About what? You work at the Post Office," said Mendoza, suddenly remembering that Early had mentioned his name.

"Why, yes—"

"I might have known. The federal bureaucrat. What are you trying to say?"

"Lieutenant Mendoza," said Lowry, leaning forward and lowering his voice, "I must tell you that there had been a citizen's complaint against Edward Foster."

"Well, don't keep me in suspense, Mr. Lowry. What was it?"

NINE

ONE OF THE recent heist witnesses had just come in and Higgins had started to talk to him when Mendoza came into the office and lifted a finger at him. "Who else is here?—let Henry take the statement, and Wanda can hold his hand." He was looking slightly amused. "I think we have a new idea about what happened to Edward Foster. There may be nothing to it, but I really think— It was the address struck me, you know. Allison Avenue."

"What about it, and what have you got?"

"Well, it's right smack in the middle of his mail route, and he'd be walking around up there, wheeling his little cart ahead of him, somewhere around eleven-thirty to noon. He'd have parked his car on Echo Park Avenue about forty minutes before, and the meter would be safe until, say, one or one-fifteen. In the normal course of events he'd have gone back to move the car again or put in another couple of dimes. But he didn't. Oh, it fits, I think. Come on, George, let's go find out."

He told Higgins about it on the way, and after a minute Higgins began to laugh. "Well, for God's sake, Luis. I know we all complain about it, and the service is getting worse and worse, but—my God, of all the crazy things. Do you really think—"

"Well, take a look at him, hear what he has to say."

"Where does he work?"

"He's one of the maintenance crew at the Hillcrest Country Club. He'd just asked to have his mailing address changed there last week. Which is the only other thing Lowry could tell me."

They drove out there in Higgins' Pontiac, to that exclusive country club just on the edge of Beverly Hills. It was a beautiful day, but ominously warm already, July just coming up—the long hot summer ahead. The rolling green lawns sparkled in the sun; they couldn't see a soul out playing golf, but it was a weekday and the middle of the morning. Higgins parked and they went into the clubhouse, which seemed to be empty; eventually they found a man at the end of a hall past a cavernous dining room.

"We're looking for Frederick Sanborn," said Mendoza. "One of your gardeners here."

"Groundskeepers. I suppose Sanchez would know—he's the head groundskeeper—"

They found Sanchez on a terrace outside the window-wall of the dining room, looking with a professional eye over the sweeping acres of lawn, a big man in a tan jumpsuit. He asked why the police wanted Sanborn, one of his best men, wouldn't be in any trouble, didn't even drink or smoke. Well, he was up cutting a couple of acres around the fourth to seventh holes. He pointed in the general direction.

It wasn't often they got to take a walk on grass. "Nice morning," said Higgins, sniffing the fresh air. "I never saw any sense in golf, but it's nice out here—peaceful. I can see why some people enjoy coming out to a place like this after the rat race in any office."

Presently they spotted a man on a riding lawnmower ahead of them. When he turned it around, riding in big circles on the vast stretches of lawn, he saw them and Higgins beckoned him. He turned off the engine and they went up to the lawnmower. "Frederick Sanborn?" asked Mendoza.

"That's me." He was a big heavy-shouldered man, dark, about forty, with rugged features and brown hair starting to turn gray. He was very tanned, and he wore denim work clothes. Mendoza showed him the badge, and he just looked at it, expressionless.

"You know, we'd like to hear about it, Mr. Sanborn," said Mendoza. "Now I look at you, I don't think you meant to kill him, did you?"

Sanborn got down from the mower. He was just as big and wide-shouldered as Higgins. They were near one of the holes with its gay little flag marker, and there was a green-painted lawn bench over there; Sanborn walked over to it and sat down, and they followed him. He lit a cigarette and looked at it.

"I've heard the gist of it from that assistant postmaster Lowry," said Mendoza. "I can see it must have been annoying. But there's really no other answer, is there, when he disappeared from the middle of his mail-route—we can even narrow it down to within a few blocks, because of the car—and the cart being taken back—and all the rest of it." He looked at Higgins. "We should have realized that Foster would have had a second uniform."

Sanborn still hadn't said anything. He looked at the ground, and suddenly he looked angry.

"Would you like to give us your version?" asked Mendoza.

Dispassionately Sanborn said. "Hell. I should have known I wouldn't get away with it. And sure as hell I never meant to kill the man—it's been on my conscience, but I was just so damn mad—I lost my temper, which I don't do in five years. All right, I'll tell you about it. I don't suppose I should get away with it, not pay for it some way, but I was just so damn mad—" He looked at his cigarette. "You'll have to have some background."

"There's plenty of time."

He drew on the cigarette. "Flo and I bought that house about ten years ago when we got married. I still owe about fifteen thousand on it. Flo died last December—cancer—she was only thirty-nine. We didn't have any kids. All my family's back in Perth Amboy, Jersey. Seemed more sensible to go on paying on the house, I've got an equity in it, I couldn't rent a place as cheap. But the medical bills had piled up—the

insurance doesn't pay everything by the hell of a long shot.
Things have been pretty tight.

"The house. It's empty all day, and I needn't tell you
about the crime rate. I'd put grills on the windows, but last
October some bastard broke in the front door—it's dark
then before I get home, and Flo was in the hospital—so I got
one of these folding metal grills like you see on newsstands,
you know?—with a padlock. It's across the front door. The
mailbox is on the wall by the front door, and I tried it to
make sure it was okay, you could reach into the box through
the grill.

"Well, my mother'd been pretty sick back home, and my
brother Harry and his wife Alice had been writing me even
oftener than usual—at least once a week—" He lit another
cigarette. "I can't say I get a lot of mail, but there's the
family, Flo's brother in Sacramento, couple of old Army
buddies—besides all the regular bills and junk mail. And I
stopped getting any. Flo used to take care of all the bills, and
when I realized all of a sudden I hadn't had an electric bill,
gas bill, in a while, I remembered seeing something in the
paper about those companies wanting to change to billing
every two months instead, I figured that was why. I should
say—I told you money was tight, I was paying on the med-
cal bills—I'd had the phone taken out. There's a base
charge, and I don't use the phone much, it was one less
thing. But I was worried as hell about the family, because I
wasn't hearing from them. And I never got the bill for the
house payment from the bank—the mail service is lousy,
and I thought it could've got lost—anyway, I went on sending the checks in, but I didn't have the statements to go
along, with the account number and all. And I don't hear
from Harry or Alice or anybody, nothing in the box day af-
er day, and I think, for God's sake, all the mail can't be
getting lost, I write Harry and Alice, what's going on, why
haven't I heard, and how's Mother—and time goes on,
there's nothing, I finally send a wire and ask what's wrong.
Nothing. I don't get a thing. No bills, no letters, nothing.

"Well, look. I work six days a week, I can't get to the electric company, the gas company, so easy. And by now I'm damn worried about the family, about Mother. I take a morning off and go to the Post Office and complain, I'm not getting any mail and where is it? Snippy little black girl says they can't deliver mail to anybody if there isn't any to deliver. I say the family's got to have been writing, she says how do I know, they deliver all the mail comes in. Well, I did what I should have done weeks before, I go to a public phone and call Harry. It cost me fifteen bucks. Wouldn't think about sticking him for it, things have been bad for them too, he's got laid off and there was Mother in the hospital— They're worried as hell about me, because they've been writing and by what I write them I'm not getting their letters. So back I go to the Post Office and raise hell. I get another clerk, she says they don't lose mail often but it gets delayed sometimes. By three months? I say. I say like hell, I want to see somebody higher up—" Sanborn sighed, dropped his cigarette. "I see this assistant postmaster and he gives me the doubletalk, all the mail gets delivered, these new machines cause delays occasionally—I don't think he really listened to me, how I knew there was mail that hadn't been delivered. They're always right, they always know, I'm just a stupid citizen who doesn't know what he's talking about.

"I couldn't afford many phone calls, neither could Harry. You can't phone somebody at a public phone in an emergency. When Mother died at the end of April they sent me a wire, but Western Union doesn't delivery any more, uses the phone and sends a copy by mail. I never got it. I never knew till I phoned Harry two weeks later. God, I'd have got back to the funeral somehow—"

He looked out over the view of the beautiful green acres. "I couldn't count how many times I went to the Post Office and complained. I kept getting the runaround. All the mail gets delivered, it's a law of nature. They know. They got such an efficient system. And then all of a sudden I come home one night and find the power, the gas, is off.''

"Naturally,'' said Mendoza.

"Naturally,'' said Sanborn bitterly. "I take a morning off, I go see the companies, they say I haven't paid the bills and they've sent me notices I'm delinquent, that they're about to shut me off. So I go back to the Post Office and raise more hell. And get nowhere, and then I get a little worried about the house payments and I go to the bank.'' He sighed. "Everything gets done by computers these days, and I hadn't had the statements to send back so it hadn't got counted and I'm delinquent with the payments and they've slapped a fine on.''

"Frustrating,'' said Higgins.

Sanborn glanced at them briefly. "At least that gave me a little ammunition. I rubbed his nose in it, that assistant postmaster. God damn him. Three and a half months. He said he'd look into it, talk to my mailman. I know he never had, before. When I went back a couple of days later he had the goddamned gall to tell me it was all my fault. The mailman said he couldn't reach through the grill to the mailbox!—his arms were too short, he said! The postmaster admitted that of course the mailman should have reported it right away—do you know, that bastard had just been burying my mail somewhere, hadn't said a damn word to anybody! And that goddamned assistant postmaster says it's my fault—it's up to me to make the mailbox accessible.''

"Federal bureaucrats,'' said Higgins. "But the mailman should have—''

"They admitted that, but do you think anybody gave me one apology? They handed everything over then—all the mail due me for three and a half, damn near four months— bills, house payments, all the family's letters, the wire about Mother, a pile of junk mail—the goddamned mailman just sitting on it, of all the damned irresponsible— It took two days to get the power and gas back on, I'm still liable for the fine for the house payments—it was a mess. A goddamn mess. All that damn stupid mailman's fault—if he'd just mentioned it to somebody—! And then, by God, I find out he's not even going to get fired for it! That assistant postmaster wouldn't back down an inch when I told him, by God, they ought to pay the fine—no, it was all my fault because of where the mailbox was, and the mailman was what he called officially reprimanded and that was all. By God!

"You know, I'd never laid eyes on that mailman. But I'd been doing a slow burn ever since, and that day—it was the day after that—by God, if it was all I could do I was going to cuss him out from hell to glory! Really lay it on him! It'd cost me a day's pay but I figured it was worth it. I waited that morning, and just before noon I saw him coming up the street with that cart. I'd taken the grill off by then. He comes up on the porch, and I opened the door. He was a little shrimp of a sandy fellow, didn't look too bright, and I started to tell him what I thought about all the trouble he'd made for me, the money trouble and the rest, I cussed him, I said how would he feel if he didn't even know his mother had been dead for two weeks—and the stupid little bastard said, I don't have any family. And that did it—that did it— I just took hold of him—'' Sanborn gave a long deep sigh. "I never meant to kill the man. But there he was.''

"Manual strangulation,'' said Mendoza. "A fairly easy way to kill anybody, and you're a big powerful man.''

"Well, I dragged him into the house and wondered what the hell to do. He was a fool, but God, I hadn't any right to kill him. But there it was, I'd done it, and nobody had seen anything, nobody was around. Just his cart sitting out there. And I thought—if nobody could find out who he was, I might get away with it. I—well, I stripped him and late that night I drove him out to the freight yards and just left him. I cut up all his clothes and just put them out with the trash— everything on him. And I took the cart back to the Post Office because,'' said Sanborn unsmilingly, "I wanted everybody to get their mail. That's all. I'm sorry it happened—that's all I can say. It's been on my conscience, and I might as well pay for it and have it done with."

"You'll have to come in with us now," said Mendoza.

He nodded. "You'd better let me take that mower back to the clubhouse first."

PALLISER FINALLY FOUND some neighbors down the block from where the Damicos had lived who knew where they'd gone; they'd moved in with her brother because Damico senior had lost his job. It was over in the next street. Palliser went over there, but Tony wasn't home, they didn't know when he'd be home. Palliser cursed himself for a fool. Nobody in that family liked cops, and now Tony would be warned to stay clear, the fuzz was after him. Palliser would like to nail Tony for Sammy Keefer and Dave Packer.

Mendoza was over at Juvenile Court talking to a judge when he got back to the office, but he heard about Sanborn from Higgins and was amused. "It's not really funny, John, and you can see why he was so damn mad at that stupid little bastard, but the idea of murdering the mailman because he wouldn't deliver the mail is a kind of nice touch. Even the D.A. might be sympathetic. Anyway, I think he'll get charged with Murder Two and he's an honest man with a good record, he'll probably get a five-to-ten and serve three."

Palliser told him about Damico. "I'd like to get him, damn it, and now he's warned."

"Pity, but I don't know what we can do about it. I've got to type this damn report."

It was Grace's day off. Galeano and Glasser were out looking for that pal of Gurney's. Nobody seemed to know where Hackett was.

HACKETT HAD GONE OUT on a new call. The squad-car man didn't know anything about it, had just got a call to an unnamed trouble. It was a small ugly stucco crackerbox of a house over past the railroad yards, Penn Street. The body was on the kitchen floor, the body of a big husky red-haired man in old work clothes, a man about forty. There was a heavily contused area on his left temple which felt ominously soft: the skull had been cracked.

The woman sitting at the kitchen table was probably younger, but she had stringy dark hair straggling about a thin face with no makeup; she wore a faded blue cotton dress. She said dully to Hackett, "He must have slipped and fell. I was out to the market and found him when I came home. Yes, he's my husband. Bob Kaiser."

"Was he alone here when you left?"

"That's right. He must have tripped and fell and hit his head on something."

The man was a big heavy man, but even if he'd fallen with all his weight, it didn't look likely that the damage would have been that extensive—he was well away from the stove, the refrigerator. "Was he drunk, Mrs. Kaiser?" asked Hackett bluntly.

"No. He didn't drink or smoke. He must have fell. I'm glad my two girls weren't here, they're up the street with the Vanburen girls, they got a TV there."

Hackett decided to give it the full treatment, and called the lab. He stepped out on the back porch to look around the place, and there was a woman gawking over the fence from the next yard. He went out there deliberately, and she called. "You a cop? What's happened at the Kaisers'? I saw the police car come up—"

Hackett put on his best expression of stupid cop and said, "Mr. Kaiser had an accident, looks like. Hit his head on something—he's dead."

"No!" She was pleasurably excited. "Oh, poor Francie, she must be in an awful state—whatever can happen next, she's been so worried over one of the kids needing glasses, and getting laid off from her job—and now Bob getting killed, how could he get killed just like that? Big strong man—and she must've been right there and saw it—"

"I guess she was out somewhere, found him when she came back."

"Oh, no, she didn't go anywhere, when she came to borrow some milk awhile ago she said she was feeling too tired to go out to the market— Say, maybe I ought to come over, she might like another woman with her at a time like this—"

"Maybe later," said Hackett.

ZIMMERMAN called in a Code Seven at one-thirty, a little late. He parked the squad in the small lot behind the coffee shop, went in and sat at the counter. The man sitting next to him was a fat man in rather loud sports clothes; he had a diamond ring on his left little finger. He was talking to the man at his other side. Zimmerman ordered a sandwich and the waitress poured his coffee.

"The damndest thing I ever had happen since I been in business," said the fat man. "You never saw such a wad of cash, Tom! Fellow didn't look too bright either—maybe he'd just robbed a bank!" They both laughed. "Comes in off the street, looks around, points to this console TV, biggest one I got in the place, and says, I want that."

"How much was it?" the other man asked.

"With the tax it came to just over fourteen-hundred bucks. And naturally I expect, while I'm making out the ticket, he'll pull out a checkbook or charge card or whatever, but when I look up he's bringing out these wads of cash from every pocket he's got! My God, who carries that much cash with all the muggers around?"

"You sure it wasn't counterfeit?"

"Nah, nah, I've seen counterfeit stuff—this was all kosher. Mostly twenties and tens, and most of it still had the bank folders around it. It was all okay. But you better believe I didn't waste any time getting it to the bank! Left Millie alone in the store and chased right over. I'd had that console in four months, never expected to move it, tell you the truth."

Zimmerman had been one of the beat men first on that heist at the Security-Pacific bank last week. He debated over his coffee—there might be nothing to this at all, he didn't know what the front-office men had got on that heister, but just in case— The men were getting up to leave. He said, "Excuse me, sir, I couldn't help hearing what you were saying." The man stopped and looked at him. He was an honest citizen; Zimmerman saw the respect for the uniform in his eyes. "It does sound a little funny. Do you mind telling me your name?"

"Why, no, officer—I'm Bill Horvath. Do you think there was anything wrong with it?"

"I don't know. You have a store around here?"

"Yeah, Horvath TV and Electronics right up the block."

It might be nothing at all, but Zimmerman thought he'd pass it on to the front office at the end of shift.

SHE SAT AT GRACE'S DESK and Hackett, Higgins, Palliser stood around her. Tears rolled down her thin cheeks, slow and painful, but otherwise there was no emotion in her flat dull voice or her eyes.

"Somebody's got to take care of my two girls. If you arrest me, who's going to look after them? Had to do something—about him laying there on the floor—I thought if I said—" She was staring past them out the window. "The funny thing is, a lot of people thought he was a good husband—never an unkind word, always cheerful, didn't smoke or drink or chase around. But it just got to be too much—I don't know what came over me, I never planned to do it. He never had anything and he never understood that most people want nice things, something more than just enough and secondhand clothes—long as there was food for today he thought everything was fine— He didn't like to work for anybody, he'd take odd jobs when he bothered to look for them—I was the one had to work regular so we had enough for the rent and enough to eat—happy-go-lucky, people called him—he's forever sayin', oh, he never worries about money— Yeah, the only people don't have to worry about money are millionaires and fools—I'm the one has to worry about money—and I got no education, only jobs I could get are waiting on table in cheap joints. Here we are, we got nothing—nothing—all the clothes we got from thrift shops and the girls need clothes for school in the fall, and I just got laid off. The washer's broke and the laundromat costs too much—and I been so tired—he just didn't see how much there is to worry about—the school says Susan needs glasses and they'll cost nearly a hundred dollars—and Josie wants to be a teacher, that's college, and he says that's all crap, girls get married in five, six years and be off our hands. And I don't know what came over me—I was just starting to fix his lunch. I had the iron frying pan in my hand, he was sitting at the table, and I said how I was worried about finding another job and he said I worried too much and I'd find a job all right—and I just turned around and said why don't *you* get a job, you damn lazy son of a bitch, and I hit him as hard as I could—''

WHEN ANGEL went out to bring the children in, that dog was flat on his back between them with Sheila yanking on his tail and Mark stroking his mismatched ears.

"I think Laddie's the loverliest dog I was ever acquainted with," said Mark, his eyes shining. Mark liked long words.

"Laddie?"

"You said his name's Laddie."

"Oh, I did? But you liked the cute little white puppies we saw the other day, didn't you?"

"Yes. But they were awful little."

"Well, you'd both better come in now, Daddy'll be home soon."

The dog looked after them, sitting lopsided on one hip.

Wednesday was Art's day off, and he took the Monte Carlo in for an oil change, said he'd kill time at the library waiting for it. The children were spending a couple of hours every morning at a supervised playground a few blocks away. When she'd dropped them off, Angel came back and left her car in the drive. The dog was mooching around the side of the garage. She said, "Come on," in as severe a tone as she could. He followed her willingly down the street at a shambling trot, sniffing at every tree and bush, his long plumy tail busy. Every once in awhile he came back closer and gave her his silly simpering grin. He wore the insouciant air of the free spirit determined to accept what life meted out as cheerfully as possible. In the bright sun his black mottles shone, and his legs seemed to have lengthened overnight.

She found somebody at home at nearly every house. Some people said they'd seen the dog before, wandering around, and some said they'd never laid eyes on it, but everybody said it was a funny-looking dog.

The woman in the house at the end of this long block, down the hill, said, "It's a stray. You ought to call the pound. It's terrible how people are so irresponsible. With those legs, it could have come from miles away. Looks as if it's hungry."

She had kept the word firmly out of her mind. And those lean hound-type dogs always looked thin, but she took a second look at him as he nosed along the grass ahead of her, and his ribs were showing painfully.

He leaped the fence lightly, in his stride as it were. Angel came in and stood in the middle of the kitchen and said, "Damn, damn, damn." Then she opened the refrigerator, found the bowl of leftover stew, some odds and ends of vegetables, and the last of the hamburger. She put it all on a paper plate on the back porch. It vanished in about five seconds, and the dog rolled over and waved his paws at her.

There wasn't any natural water around for miles. She filled a bowl and set it in place of the paper plate. The dog came and leaned on her to be patted, and then suddenly sat down on one hip and began to scratch vigorously behind the mostly-upright ear. He was, she thought, probably covered with fleas.

THE OFFICE was humming along at a fairly brisk pace on Wednesday morning. There were more people out looking for Roy Fidler, Gurney's pal, than just LAPD Robbery-Homicide. He had skipped parole and disappeared. Of course they didn't know that he'd been the one on the caper with Gurney, but it seemed likely.

The search warrant for Gurney's Pasadena apartment had come in yesterday, and Grace and Galeano went over to have a look at it. It was a cheap old place with a few sticks of cheap furniture in it, and not much else but a meager collection of clothes. They went through all the drawers, all the pockets, and found odds and ends of unimportant things, but no loot.

Gurney had had an old clunker of a Dodge parked at the college, but that had been towed in and looked at yesterday; there was nothing in it but the registration and some pornographic paperbacks.

"They stashed it," said Grace, fingering his moustache. "Occasionally they show a glimmer of sense. They split it and it's banked under phony names."

"No bank books. Their minds seldom work that way," said Galeano.

"Well, sometimes they're cute. What are you looking at?"

"Just thinking of what the boss found—that funny case last March—stashed away in a place like that." Set into the ceiling at one side of the tiny kitchen was the square fitted trap to admit a workman to the crawl space above, to get at wires. This was an old house cut up into apartments, and things were a little makeshift. Galeano stood on a kitchen chair and pushed the trap. "Have you got a flashlight?"

"I saw one somewhere around—" Grace found it and handed it up.

Galeano flashed it around; there was nothing up there but dust. He descended with a grunt.

"Oh, he wouldn't have been such a fool, Nick," said Grace.

Galeano looked at him. "When you stop to think, ordinary people like you and me have an advantage. Growing up in ordinary times. We know money doesn't grow on trees in the back yard."

"Meaning what?"

"Well, what do we know about Gurney? Spoiled son of a doting mother, always had everything, never had to work very hard. Quite a comedown all right, when the money went, but all his life up to then he'd been able to take a casual attitude toward money. And I don't know," said Galeano, "never having tried it, but it's always seemed to me that's one reason the pros are so irresponsible when they do have it, throwing it around, gambling, buying things right and left. When it comes all at once in wads, so easy with a gun, it can't feel like real money."

Grace said again, "He wouldn't have been such a fool."

"Let's go and ask."

They drove back downtown, to the main jail. In five minutes a jailer brought Alan Gurney to them in an interrogation room. He was wearing the coarse tan jail uniform. "You again," he said. "What are you after now?"

"What did you do with the loot, Gurney?"

He laughed. "Wouldn't you like to know?"

"You know, this is a second charge for you and you won't get off so easy as you did before. It'll probably add up to a five-to-ten, and you'll do at least three."

"So what?" he said contemptuously. "I'll still be young enough."

"And you'll have a nest egg waiting when you come out?" Grace laughed. "Did you really have that much faith in Fidler? To let him keep it all? He's jumped parole and he's long gone, Gurney. With the loot."

"Who's—Fidler?"

"Now come on," said Galeano. "You knew we'd talk to your P.A. officer. And his. You got pretty thick while you were in the joint. He was the one with you on those heists, wasn't he? And he was keeping the loot for both of you, was that it?"

"I don't—believe you," said Gurney. "No, Roy wasn't on that job with me. You're just trying to get me to admit—I don't believe you."

"Would you believe your P.A. officer?" asked Grace. "He'll tell you the same thing. Fidler has skipped—and he did have the loot, didn't he?" It figured in one way, at that: Fidler was the more experienced pro criminal.

Gurney looked from one to the other of them, and they saw belief come into his eyes. The girlish mouth tightened in a little snarl, and he said, "That goddamn bastard—I trusted that goddamn—"

"Would you have any little idea which way he's gone?" asked Galeano.

"You're goddamn right I do, but you'll have to get a move on to pick him up!" said Gurney vindictively. "He's got a girl he's crazy about in Denver, and he was saving his share to go back and marry her when he's off P.A. Her name's Jean Sanderson and she's hostess at a Holiday Inn. That goddamned son of a bitch—"

They were already out of the door.

HIGGINS HAD WRITTEN the report on Sanborn, and got it ready to go down to the D.A.'s office. They had applied for the warrant when they brought him back, and it came through about four o'clock. Mendoza had been over in Juvenile Court with the judge and the public defenders again. He had said he might go to see the parents after that—they'd want to know what the probabilities were.

There was also the paperwork on Mrs. May Kaiser. Poor woman. When they had booked her into jail yesterday, Wanda had gone back to the house with Hackett and found the two girls, who were ten and twelve. That kind of news was bad to break too; Wanda would have done her best. The girls were at Juvenile Hall, but Mrs. Kaiser had told them that her mother lived in Portland, Mrs. Martha Swain. Hackett had called the police there, asked them to notify her. Any family would probably take the girls.

Just as Higgins finished with the report, a call came in from a Sergeant Wortman in Portland.

"We did your dirty work for you. I was sorry for the woman, naturally she was all shook up. There's another daughter here, married with two kids. She'll take the Kaiser girls, and they'll wire money if somebody can put them on the bus. I don't think they've got much money, but they seem like decent people. Can you arrange that?"

"Sure." Some efficient matron at Juvenile Hall could pack the girls' clothes, see them onto the bus, wire the arrival time. He took down names and addresses. He thanked Wortman, sat back and lit a cigarette, looking forward to his day off tomorrow. The heat was starting to build, but at least he didn't have to mow the lawn; Steve Dwyer had taken over that job. Higgins reflected a little sleepily on his good family.

GRACE AND GALEANO were down in Communications sitting on the wire to Denver. They just hoped they'd been in time to intercept Fidler. No telling how long he'd been gone; he could have taken off last Sunday after the heist on Saturday night. But the odds were slightly better that he'd decided to skip when he heard about Gurney's arrest. He could have called him: there was only one phone downstairs in the made-over old house, and the elderly woman who owned the house could be a prying landlady. In any case she'd been told on Monday or Tuesday about the search warrant to come, and it was possible that she would have passed that on to any supposed friend of Gurney's calling him.

If Fidler hadn't skipped until last night—they didn't know what planes were available, but say he had landed there some time today— And was there more than one Holiday

Inn in Denver? It was a good-sized town. If there was any delay in locating that Jean Sanderson— And there was an hour's time difference. Sometimes even an hour could change the luck.

They hadn't had any lunch, and sent one of the messengers up to the canteen for sandwiches. It had been about one o'clock when they had talked to Denver, two o'clock there. It was four-thirty here and five-thirty there when Denver, in the person of a Lieutenant Woods, called back.

"We picked him up okay. He had the loot in the glove compartment of a rented car. You really are spoilsports. We had to chase around a little after the Sanderson girl, only way to find him. Finally found her sister, and she knew where they were. And we'd have missed him by two hours except that Miss Sanderson's a nice respectable girl and wanted to be married by a minister. Wouldn't go to a justice of the peace. They'd have been married at City Hall by three and on their way to Hawaii by now—he had the plane tickets in his pocket—except that they had to wait for a Methodist minister to come home from playing golf."

Grace burst out laughing. "Thank you so much," said Galeano. "Will you ferry him back or do we send somebody over?"

"Be obliged if you would. We're a little busy."

"So are we, but we will. Let you know details."

MENDOZA HADN'T gone back to the office yet. He had had a depressing interview with the Gonzaleses and Gomezes, and of course that had set him thinking about Rosalie and Brenda. He ended up in Carey's office, and Carey asked what they were doing about it now.

Mendoza growled at him. "What the hell is there to do on it? We've gone all the indicated places."

"All right, I know."

"That's the kind that's always a bastard to work, you know as well as I do. How many of those men with the right records did we haul in to lean on, who couldn't give an alibi? Who could have been the right one on both of them, only no solid evidence to show it. That kind, a lot of them break at a touch, yes, I did it, but not all of them. And you also know that the chances are just as good that it's one we haven't got listed at all, that nobody's got listed.''

"Keep your hair on. I know that."

"¡*Válgame Dios!* Another thing, how often do we pick up one like that, in the act, or by a lucky fluke, and he comes apart and says, I been doing this for years, I killed one in Cleveland six years ago and another in New York—and we ask, and there the unsolved cases are, on the books for years. True crime!" said Mendoza. "When they finally picked up Peter Kürten in Germany, they never did decide how many women he'd accounted for—some estimates say over fifty."

"I know that too," said Carey.

Mendoza said, "Oh, hell," and got out a cigarette. "There's no point in getting stirred up about it. Fact of life. But I'd like to get that one."

"Anybody," said Carey, "who's got a little girl at home wants to get this one." After a moment he added, "I never got talking to Higgins until the other day. I had the idea he was a bachelor, but he talked a little about his family."

"Yes," said Mendoza.

"We're expecting a third one in August."

"There must be something catching going around this building," said Mendoza. "So are three of my boys. Thank you, the three we've already got are enough of a handful. Not to mention the livestock. ¡*Condenación!* I'm sitting here wasting your time." He stood up.

Carey was looking out the window. "It's funny you should mention the true-crime classics," he said abruptly. "Do you believe in fate? That some people are born lucky or unlucky? Things predestined to turn out right or wrong for them?"

"Having a logical mind, I can believe more easily in karma and past lives—at least some reason in the good or bad luck then. Why?"

"I always remembered that fellow—can't think of his name—in England. His wife and mother and daughter were all murdered by a lunatic while they were having a picnic together when he was at work. Whole family gone, no reason, no motive. Wrong place at wrong time. And ten years later a private plane crashed into his house and killed him."

"I don't know any answers," said Mendoza.

It was a quarter past five. He hesitated in the corridor; not much point in going back to the office. But out of force of habit he did. Higgins was yawning at his desk, and Grace and Galeano gave Mendoza the news about Fidler.

"John offered to go over and bring him back. Said he'd never been to Denver. He's getting a plane out of International at ten-forty."

"Good." Mendoza wandered down to his office, and three minutes later was back. "When did this arrive?"

"No idea." It was Zimmerman's note, which the desk downstairs had seen fit to relay this morning. "What is it?"

"Maybe something very suggestive. George, let's see if we can catch this fellow—hell, it's nearly five-thirty, but—"

"Which fellow?" Higgins got up.

"Bill Horvath. It's another little offbeat thing, but—"

At this hour everybody was on the freeway, and one of the convenient perquisites of the job is the right to park anywhere. Mendoza slid the Ferrari into the loading zone in front of Horvath's TV and Electronics just as a man emerged and bent to lock the door.

"Horvath?"

"Yeah?" The man turned. Mendoza showed him the badge. "Oh," said Horvath. "That cop yesterday— Say, are you detectives? Do *you* think there's something wrong about that money? Look, there couldn't be, my bank took it with no fuss—"

"We'd like to know what the man was like. The one who gave you all the cash for the console TV."

"Oh." Horvath considered. "Well, he was a big young guy—blond, short hair, no moustache or beard. He acted kind of simple."

"Had you ever seen him before, around here?"

"Never in my life."

"I take it," said Mendoza, "that you delivered the console? Do you remember where, have you any record?"

"Sure," said Horvath readily. "Come on in and I'll look it up for you, carbon of the ticket. It was Constance Street, I think—I know it wasn't far out of the area—"

THE RED-HAIRED freckled nurse checking the patient in the end room of this wing of the hospital was pleased to find that he was conscious. She glanced at the I.V. and bent over him: his eyes were open, and he stared up at her in a bewildered way. These two patients had been interesting in a sense; of course the old woman was terribly difficult, with her incomprehensible chatter. But the nurse was young and romantic and she couldn't help feeling sorry for them, thinking how it would be to come to a place where you couldn't talk with anyone, make friends. One of the doctors on this floor knew a Chinese from Taiwan interning at Hollywood Presbyterian, and had got him to come over last night, to try to talk with the woman, but he'd said it was a strange dialect to him, and couldn't help at all.

She bent over the young man—he'd been horribly beaten—and said rather loudly, "You—feel—better?"

He was supposed to know some English.

He just went on looking bewildered, as much of his face as she could see under the bandages. A broad flat face with one eye bandaged. She thought, as difficult as the old woman maybe, not very much English. She'd heard someone say they'd only been here a few months. She said clearly, "This—is—hospital. I am nurse. You understand?" He just moved his head feebly.

"Tump," he said weakly.

"What?"

"Tump."

Good Lord, she thought, we can't talk to this one either. But the police wanted to know when he was conscious. Better have somebody call them.

TEN

AT TEN O'CLOCK on Thursday morning Mendoza and Hackett went looking for that address on Constance Street. All these streets down here were old, and the houses on them, but this block seemed to be maintained neatly enough, with little rectangles of green lawn in front yards. The one they wanted was a small white house with green trim, and behind it, beside the single garage, was a rear rental unit, a tiny frame building matching the front house.

The woman who answered the door there was small and plump, pleasant-faced, ordinary, in late middle age. Mendoza said, "I think you had a console TV delivered recently, Mrs.—"

She looked surprised. "We didn't, no. Don did—that's the little house at the back. Who are you? I'm Mrs. Haney—and if there was anything wrong about it—was there?"

"Did you think there might be?"

"Are you from the place he got it? Oh, dear, I don't know—if he signed up for payments—I thought when he said it was coming, how much it must have cost, and when I saw it—haven't priced any lately, but it's awfully big—that boy just never does anything but watch TV every spare minute—who are you and what do you want?"

Mendoza told her. She put a hand to her mouth, and her eyes were shocked. "All that money! Where would Don get all that money? But I can't think he'd do anything wrong—he's a good boy. It's worked out real well, he's got on fine. But—all that money—even if he'd saved every penny from his job—I don't see how he could have all that—"

"Who is Don, Mrs. Haney, your son?" asked Hackett.

"Oh, no, he's not ours. Don Ogden's his name, he's twenty-four now, we had him since he was eighteen, and it's worked out fine, really. My husband didn't like the idea at first but as soon as he met Don he saw what a nice quiet boy he is.''

"Who is he, Mrs. Haney?"

She was looking frightened. "I don't understand how he could have got hold of all that money—Don wouldn't do anything wrong—he was brought up to be a good religious boy— It's that big religious orphanage out in Fullerton, the Christian Foundation for Children, you know, a private place, they raise the children right, and some millionaire left a lot of money to it, Helen says the children love it, they got good teachers and all."

"And was Don Ogden raised there?"

"Why, yes, he was left there when he was just a baby, parents killed in an accident and the grandmother about to die of cancer, she put him in the Foundation. And when he got to be eighteen, Helen was worrying about getting him started on his own, so he could take care of himself and get along. He's a little retarded, you see, but he gets along fine on his own, real independent. Helen—''

"Helen?" said Hackett.

"Miss Helen Rouse, she and I went to school together, she's one of the teachers at the Foundation. She thought of us because of the rental in the rear. They only keep the children till they're eighteen, and she thought if he could get some simple job and do for himself— She got him settled in, and Gene, my husband, took quite an interest in him. Our only son's married and lives in Phoenix. Gene went with him on this bus, showed him which one to take, and walked around with him till he knew the streets. He even took him in the van a few times, to see something of the city. Gene drives a delivery van for a big furniture store—Don liked that. Gene always says he's got more sense than people think. Helen found this job for him at a cafeteria uptown, he's a busboy there, makes steady money. And she wanted him to learn how to do for himself, so he could always be independent—he takes his own laundry to the laundromat and gets his own meals and all, he's got along just fine.

Takes the bus to work every morning, the cafeteria's on
Beverly Boulevard, and home again regular as clock-
work—he never wants to go out nights, just stays in to watch
TV, he had a little black-and-white portable Helen gave him.
I just don't understand—*police*—and saying about that
bank— Where did Don get all that money?''

"Well, Mrs. Haney, it looks a little suggestive," said
Hackett.

"Oh, no—Don could never think of doing a thing like
that!" But she was frightened. "He's held that regular job
all this while, we've all been pleased he's done so well, he's
not much retarded, you know, just a little simple—but a
good boy—brought up to go to church regular, he comes to
our church, the Baptist—I just don't understand this—"

"What cafeteria is it?" asked Mendoza.

"Clifton's—out on Beverly like I said—oh, I'd better call
Helen—"

"We just want to talk to him," said Hackett. She nodded dumbly.

They went out to Clifton's, an old place, a fixture in the
city for years, open twenty-four hours a day. They went in
and asked for Ogden. The thin gray-haired man at the
cashier's desk in front looked surprised, but pointed him
out; he was cleaning a table, methodically piling used plates
and cups on a tray. He was a big blond young man with a
serious expression, concentrated on his work. When Mendoza spoke his name he looked up and smiled. It was an
open, boyish face with round blue eyes. "We'd like to talk
to you, Don," said Mendoza.

"Sure, only I got my work to do."

"It's all right," said Hackett, "you can take a few minutes. We're policemen, Don, and we'd like to talk to you
about where you got all that money, to buy your new TV."

He didn't say anything, but suddenly his eyes looked
wary. "It was a lot of money to pay for a TV," said Hackett.

"I like to watch TV. It's a color one."

"Where did you get the money?" asked Mendoza.

"I—can't stop my work or Mr. Carew'll be mad at me. I can't talk to you."

"I think you'd better come back to the police station with us so we can really talk," said Mendoza.

"No! Mr. Carew'll fire me if I leave before five o'clock, I got my work to do—"

"Did you have any money left, Don, after you bought the TV?" asked Hackett.

"I won't tell you, it's none of your business."

"Because if you did, and we find it in your apartment, we can tell if it's money from the bank."

"No, you couldn't. I don't want to talk to you any more."

"You have to, Don—we're going to go on talking until you tell us all about it."

The cafeteria was nearly deserted at this hour, and the man at the cashier's desk was watching them. Don suddenly walked over there and said, "Make them go away, Mr. Carew. I don't want to talk to them, I don't want to—"

Mendoza showed the badge, and Carew said in a horrified tone, "My God, what did he do? Look, he's always been a steady worker, I've got to say that—I'll be damned. Listen, Don, you'd better go along with them. You'll be all right." He looked at Mendoza. "I feel a little responsible— listen, will you let me know what happens?"

They took him back to the office and went on trying to talk to him. He was mulishly silent at first, and all he kept saying was, the TV was worth all the money because it was a big picture and color. Then Mendoza had a bright idea and went out to get a newspaper, started talking to him about all the TV shows in the listing in the *Times*. Don brightened up at once and began chattering a blue streak, about which ones he liked best. He knew more about TV than Mendoza or Hackett, neither of whom was a fan. They led him on that track awhile and then Mendoza said, "Is that why you wanted the money, to buy the big TV?"

"The one I had was just a little old one, and no color like the ones in the stores."

Hackett said, "So you thought you'd get the money at a bank?"

He liked them better now, but he looked uneasy. "You know it was wrong to steal the money, Don?" said Mendoza.

After a minute he said tentatively, "It wasn't like steal, like from anybody real." And he looked at them sadly and said, "I suppose you make me give it back. And the TV too."

"Where did you get the gun?" asked Mendoza conversationally.

Don said, "Oh, that was easy. Mr. Haney, he's got a gun, he says it's for burglars, and I know where it is, in the drawer of the table. I have dinner with them Sundays and I just took the gun when Mr. Haney was looking at the newspaper and Mrs. Haney was in the kitchen. And I put it back next Sunday. Nobody knew I took it. I didn't think they would. I suppose you make me give the TV back now." He looked almost ready to cry. "Sure—I knew—I knew it was kind of wrong to do—but I wanted—I wanted—I knew just how to do it right! I knew because I saw it on TV, it was one of the long ones, I don't always like the long ones—" he meant movies—"but this was good. I saw it two times. The people talked funny like they do sometimes but it was good. It showed just how you get money from a bank. What to say to the lady and everything. I remembered it all good, about the dollybird and all." Mendoza and Hackett exchanged a glance. An old British movie. The answer was so simple when you knew.

"We're going to take you somewhere else now, Don," said Hackett. "But everything will be all right, don't worry."

"I suppose I got to give it back," he said unhappily. Hackett took him over to the jail, and that would be temporary. This wouldn't go to trial, there'd be a hearing before a judge and he'd be sent up to Camarillo, at least for a while. The poor devil seemed to be just capable of taking care of himself in daily life, but when he'd once pulled something like this, you'd never know what he'd take it into his head to do, and Mendoza didn't suppose he'd ever seen a gun before; it could have gone off in his hand.

He went back to Constance Street for the gun, and she had called her husband home. He explained, and they were shocked and sorry. "Never would've thought the kid would do a thing like that," said Haney heavily. "Like I said, more sense than you'd think. Imagine him noticing that gun—" He handed it over to Mendoza. It was a Colt .32 revolver, hardly used. Mendoza said, "We'll have to take this as evidence, Mr. Haney, but we'll see you get it back." Haney just nodded.

GRACE HAD GONE over to talk to Gurney. Gurney was quite willing to talk now, and was claiming that the whole idea of pulling the jobs was Fidler's—"It was a drag, you know, the damned boring job and hard work too, and the pay not so hot—Roy felt the same about that damn gas station— Sure, I was the one knew about the theater, but he planned it out really—"

Galeano had gone to the airport to meet Palliser bringing Fidler back; the plane was due in at noon. The warrant was out, but they'd have to try to get a statement from him too. In the last few nights there had been four new heists, and Henry Glasser and Wanda were coping with the witnesses coming in to make statements. Palliser and Galeano got to the jail by two-thirty and booked Fidler in, and started to talk to him. There would be a lot more paperwork to do.

Galeano had noticed in the night report that the hospital had called to say that that Chinese fellow had come to. He didn't know if anybody had followed up on it; they'd been busy. Grace didn't know either. "That was a queer one—but he may not know anything to tell us, at that."

HACKETT FINISHED TYPING the initial report on Don Ogden at three o'clock. He had seen the night report and he would have followed up on the call from the hospital then, but a call from a squad came in just then, sounding urgent, so he went out on that instead.

The address was on Coronado Street. The beat man was McConnell, and he said, "I was cruising down here fifteen minutes ago and this guy hails me, and all I can get out of him is that he's killed somebody. He doesn't seem to be high on anything, and I put him in the back of the squad, but you'd better—"

Hackett got into the back of the squad. "Can I have your name, sir?"

He was a man about sixty, tall and thin, with gray hair and glasses, and he sat there holding a big piece of paper in his hands very carefully, and tears were running down his face. "I've killed her. I've killed her. You've got to take me to jail," he said in a shaking voice. "I love her so much, my beautiful Stella, Stella my darling, and now I've killed her and I want to die too—she laughed at me, and so I killed her—"

"Try to pull yourself together, sir. Who did you kill and where?"

He pointed a shaking finger. "Up there. My wife—my darling wife—up there just now. They all said she was too young for me, but I was so lonely after Ruby died, I never thought I'd love anyone so much again, but Stella—and now I've killed her—"

"Can you tell me your name, sir?"

"I'm Robert Fontaine. I thought it would please her, she liked to go out dancing, I thought she'd come back to me if—but she laughed at me, so I killed her—"

"Where?" asked Hackett patiently.

"There—there—the Coronado Arms—apartment twelve, she's lying on the floor bleeding—"

Hackett took the piece of paper and looked at it. It was a fancily decorated and embossed Certificate of Proficiency in Ballroom Dancing from an Arthur Murray school. He left Fontaine with McConnell and went into the apartment building, climbed stairs and looked for apartment twelve. The door was slightly ajar and he went in, looking around for the body. A startled voice said, "Who in hell are you?" Hackett jumped. Standing in the doorway of the bedroom behind him was a lusciously stacked young lady in pink bra and panties, holding a towel to her head. She was in the early twenties, she had a good deal of reddish-blond hair, and a model's long-legged figure, but more generously supplied, and big brown eyes. There was a bruise darkening on one cheek, a developing black eye, and as she dropped the towel he saw that there was a gash on her temple, still bleeding slightly.

Hackett took out the badge. "Would you be Mrs. Robert Fontaine?"

"Yeah, but not much longer."

"Your husband seems to think he's killed you."

"He damn well might have—comes up here and begs me to come back to him—what did the old idiot think I married him for, his looks? Him with his own brokerage and a house in Beverly Hills! All I wanted was a decent settlement, he might have taken it like a gent, but when he shows me that damn fool paper I had to laugh, and he starts beating up on me—he might have killed me at that, I was out like a light for a while—gah, this eye's going to be a beaut, I can feel it— Believe me, now I take him for everything I can get!" She laughed. "The old fool, taking up dancing at his age!"

Hackett went back downstairs and managed to make Fontaine understand that she wasn't dead. But the man was obviously in no state to be let loose—maybe he'd had a stroke—so Hackett took him up to the hospital, to Emergency. He was still clutching his Certificate of Proficiency. They went through his pockets, found a billfold with I.D. in it, and Hackett called the house in Beverly Hills. The woman who answered said she was just the cleaning lady. She was sorry to hear Mr. Fontaine was took sick. He had a sister in Newport Beach, she could get the number. Hackett called the sister, who said he'd have been driving a brand-new Lincoln, which must be around somewhere. She did remember to thank him for calling.

By then it was after five, and time wasted on something that didn't even belong to Robbery-Homicide. He decided to go home early.

THE CHILDREN were tucked in bed and the house was silent. Hackett was stretched out in his big recliner reading tonight's *Herald*, and Angel had been wandering around uneasily doing nothing.

She came into the living room for the fifth time and stood in the middle of the room twisting her hands together and said miserably, "I can't do it. I just can't do it."

Hackett lowered the paper. "All right," he said cheerfully, "don't do it. What can't you do?"

Angel sat down on the couch. "I can't call the pound and tell them to come and pick up that dog. That dog! Somebody's turned him out—or left him—he's a stray—nobody wants him—and I can't do it. They only keep them about three days, and they use that horrible decompression chamber—and I—simply—can't—do it. Even when he was starving and thirsty, he *enjoys* life so much, and loves everybody—he's a great big idiotic lummox of a dog, but I can't do it to him." She was sniffling.

Hackett said, "Well, there's no law about it. Maybe we can ask around, find a good home for him."

"That dog?" said Angel. "Nobody would want him! Nobody!" She was crying a little.

Hackett said, "Hey." He went over and picked her up and sat down again, settling her across his lap. "There's no need to cry about it."

Angel sobbed once. "I w-w-wanted the cute little white one!"

Hackett kissed her. She sniffed and blew her nose and put her head on his shoulder. After quite a long silence she said, "Art. We'll have to build a higher fence all around. Quite a lot higher. About eight feet, I should think."

IT WASN'T until Friday morning that Hackett got over to the hospital. By then, he found, they had the young Chinese man propped up in bed. The nurse said, "He hardly knows any English, but you can try to talk to him, I suppose."

He was still all bandaged up, and his yellow skin looked sickly; a lock of lank black hair hung over the bandage on his eye. "Hello, Mr.—er—Chung," said Hackett. "I'm glad you're feeling better." Chung just looked uncomprehending. Resisting the impulse to start shouting at him, he said, pointing to his own chest, "Police. *Polizei*—oh, hell. Do—you—know—who—hurt—you?" He executed savage blows in the air, and raised his eyebrows as high as he could.

Dim comprehension showed in the black eyes. Chung ducked his head. "Tump," he said.

"What?"

Chung looked a little desperate, wanting to communicate: he frowned deeply. He was obviously trying to remember the bare smattering of English that he'd picked up. He sat up a little straighter in the hospital bed. "Bad," he said. "Father bad do—steal. Old place—" he gestured, and his hands moved up and down wildly—"water by—"

Hackett followed him vaguely. "Yes, yes, back where you came from, across the ocean—"

"Yess! No food. Steal okay. No here. Bad."

"Yes," said Hackett faithfully.

"Father—bad. Steal food."

"Do you mean that your father stole food from somebody, and that's why you were all beaten up?" They had had the autopsy report on the old man now; he'd had all sorts of internal injuries, broken bones, a fractured skull; the doctor said it looked as if he'd been knocked down and jumped on. Of course he'd been in poor physical shape to start with. Hackett looked at Chung incredulously. The black eyes were intelligent, but bewildered. "Steal food?—why—" and he beat the air again savagely.

"Yess!"

"Who?"

"Tump," said Chung. "Tump-see."

That was all Hackett could get out of him, and it didn't make much sense. He made several more tries at it, but got the same words, and gave up. He was down in the parking lot when suddenly something clicked in his mind and he thought, the man next door. Mr. Dempsey. But what the hell? Food?

He went back to the office and collected Higgins. "I don't know what the hell this could mean, but let's see if we can locate Dempsey. But what that woman said—"

They went back to the place on San Marino Street, and tried the doorbell of the house next to the poor little duplex. This time they got an answer. After they'd pushed the bell three times there was a dragging step inside and the door opened.

"Mr. Dempsey?" said Hackett. He held out the badge. "We'd like to talk to you if you don't mind."

He was a big old man, not fat but with a comfortable little paunch, and he was in bad shape. His face was blotchy, his eyes bloodshot and bleary, and he staggered a little and caught the door jamb for support. "Mr. Dempsey," said Hackett sharply, "do you know what happened to the people next door?"

Dempsey said thickly, "Not—people. Been expectin' you. I don't care. Nothin' don't matter now. She was—all I had. I been drunk for five days—six days—don't know. Never was drunk before in my life—'cept once when I was young—years ago. Years 'n' years ago. I couldn't stop crying—after I tried to kill 'em all—I hope I killed 'em all— and then I got a lotta Scotch and—I—been—drunk. So can't think—"

Higgins said incredulously, "But why, Mr. Dempsey? You said you were sorry for them—"

"Sorry! Sorry! I come home, couldn't find her—always right in the yard, come runnin' up—to me—get picked up— Trudy, my li'l Trudy, my own li'l girl—must've got out o' the yard, and I went—call and look all over—ask if anybody'd seen her— That goddamn heathen, they're not human, he hands me money—for what he stole—I—I—"

The hair rose slightly on Hackett's neck and he said sickly, "Oh, my God—you don't mean—"

Dempsey sagged on the door jamb and began to sob. "They they—they killed my li'l Trudy—*an' they ate her!*"

GALEANO, relaxing on his day off, went out into the back yard of the house in Studio City after breakfast, and stood looking around with tiny doubt growing in him. It was a fairly big yard, and he didn't know anything about yard work, taking care of things. Quite a lot of grass to keep cut. And Marta talking about putting in a garden, which he supposed meant digging.

She came up beside him and he said, "I was just thinking, it's going to be a lot of work, this garden of yours."

She put her arm though his and her dark eyes were smiling. "Oh, we will perhaps wait until next year after all, Nick. You see, I have a little feeling—oh, I am not sure yet, but I think—yes, I think we are about to enter the sweepstakes too, *liebchen*."

"What? Well, I'll be— You really think so?" Galeano started to laugh. "The boss must be right—there's something catching going around headquarters!"

WHEN HIGGINS GOT HOME that night and Brucie the Scotie came skidding across the kitchen to greet him, he picked up the rough hairy little body and hugged it. "You're a good boy. You take good care of my family, don't you, boy?"

"Wuff," said Brucie.

"Getting sentimental in your old age," smiled Mary.

"Well, I'm not going to tell you why until after dinner," said Higgins.

PALLISER CAME IN the back door and Trina greeted him lovingly. He smoothed her sleek head. "Good day, darling?" asked Roberta.

"Not," said Palliser, "particularly." He came to kiss her. "We had to book a fellow in for homicide that we all, well, felt sorry for."

"Oh. Why?"

"I'm not going to tell you. I don't think it would be good for you in your delicate condition."

"Men!" said Roberta.

LANDERS GOT HOME to the Hollywood apartment a little late, and Phil already had the salad made and beef patties ready to broil. "I don't think I'm very hungry," said Landers. "The salad will be fine."

"The heat's building up all right. Maybe you'll want something later. Tom—"

"It's just," said Landers, "that my father is a veterinary surgeon."

"Well, I know that. What's it got to do with anything?"

"Nothing," said Landers.

"Well, anyway, I've found something. It sounds like a bargain to me, at today's prices, and of course we'll have to go and look at it—it's lucky we're both off on Saturday—of course it'd mean a little drive, but you said yourself, the further out you go the lower the prices—it was in the *Herald*—"

"Where is it and what?" asked Landers suspiciously.

"Well—it's in Azusa," said Phil.

"My God!"

"No, listen, Tom, it really does sound possible—and the Foothill freeway runs right through town—just *listen* for a minute, you needn't rant and rave until I tell you about it. It's a three-bedroom stucco on a wide lot, and it's only seventy thousand because it needs a lot of fixing up. But we can do most of it ourselves—I'm a good painter, and—"

"Not in your present condition," said Landers. "If you think I'm going to have you standing on ladders—"

"Well, we can go and *look* at it. The freeway—"

"At the price of gasoline now—" In the immediacy of arguing with Phil he forgot Mr. Dempsey temporarily.

"WELL, THAT'S QUITE an interesting specimen you've got here, Mrs. Hackett," said Dr. Whittemore. Expertly he dodged both tongue and tail. The dog was wildly excited a these strange new experiences, the collar and leash, the car—and now here was another brand-new friend. "Quite a mixture. What's his name?"

"Laddie," said Angel in final capitulation. "What do you think he's a mixture *of*?"

The doctor stood back and looked. "Be interesting to know. I'd say there's a dash of collie somewhere, on account of that ear. Quite a lot of setter—Irish for choice—and considering the legs, there may have been a Russian wolfhound or an Afghan back there." Laddie simpered at him coyly, and he examined the bared teeth professionally. "I'd say he's about ten months old. He may have a little more growing to do."

"Oh, no," said Angel.

"I suppose he gets the works—rabies, distemper, parvo. Er—we can give you some good flea spray."

"Just tell me one thing. Is it possible to housebreak a dog this old?"

"Oh, yes," said the doctor. "It may take a little more persistence, that's all."

"Thank you," said Angel feebly.

ABOUT THREE O'CLOCK on Monday afternoon a call came in. Everybody else was out somewhere, so Mendoza took it. It was an old eight-story building out on San Pedro, and the squad-car man was Corbett. He wasn't too far from being a rookie, and he was looking sick. There was a man sitting on the curb there behind the squad, and he was looking even sicker, green in the face and sweating. He was wearing a tan jumpsuit with a red label on the pocket: *Porter's Service*.

"It's on the roof," said Corbett.

"On the roof, for God's sake?"

"That's right. There's been something wrong with the elevator, and the janitor had to call the company that installed it recently. That's the repairman there, his name's Ryan. He went up to look at the machinery, naturally, and found the body."

"No me diga. You don't say." Corbett led him into the building and now indicated a narrow wooden staircase.

"The elevator's shut off. He cut the power before he found the body, and he wasn't feeling up to doing anything after that. The elevator's been sticking between floors anyway."

"¡No faltaba más!" said Mendoza. "Adding insult to injury! I'm not as young as I was, *hijo.*" They stopped halfway for a breather, and he added, "My God, the lab will love lugging all their equipment up here."

"I don't suppose they'll have to," said Corbett. "It's been there quite awhile."

This building was higher than any other nearby. On the eighth floor a folding ladder led up to the roof, and Mendoza looked at it with distaste. "What is this place, a set of offices?"

"No, sir, it's all one business—manufacturer of women's clothes."

Mendoza climbed the ladder and emerged onto the roof, which was filthy with dust and dirt and bird droppings. Over to one side was the little building housing the elevator machinery. "It's just behind that," said Corbett. "It was kind of wound up in a big bolt of fabric of some kind. Ryan happened to prod it with one foot, and it sort of gave and he got curious and unrolled it. Which he's regretting."

Mendoza went over to look. The body was half uncovered from its wrapping of dark green wool; the fabric had insulated it somewhat, but the last few days had been warm, and it wasn't a pretty sight. It was a man, and he was wearing a beige short-sleeved shirt—his legs were still covered—and his left arm had been dragged across his chest with the fabric.

He was partly starting to mummify, partly to decay, but—Mendoza bent closer—you could still make out the tattoo on the forearm: the six-pointed star and beneath it, *born under a lucky.*

Mendoza began to laugh. "Well, I don't see anything funny about it, sir," said Corbett stiffly.

"Oh, there is about this one! You can sit on it for a while. I'll get the lab out, and how they are going to love me for those stairs!"

Back at Parker Center, he stopped off at Narco, and both Goldberg and Callaghan were there. "Like all good ideas, it was very simple," said Mendoza amusedly, accepting a cigarette from Callaghan. "Whether they had a fight, whether it was accidental or what, Crossland was stuck with Quinlan's body. Normally, it wouldn't have been once in ten years that anybody would have occasion to go up to the roof, and it's not overlooked. The elevator was new six months ago, it was unlikely it would need attention for years, and even if it did the body was behind the housing and concealed. The company just happened to send out a curious Irishman. The only other thing Crossland did that night was to drive Quinlan's car back home—"

"And phone his wife to come get him. Oh, won't we make his charge stick!" crowed Callaghan. "Put him out of business for good—"

"Until the Syndicate sends in a substitute," said Goldberg, blowing his nose.

"What I don't understand," said Mendoza, "is why in hell he didn't try to make up some excuse for not calling the repair service—"

"Oh, that's another joke, Luis," said Goldberg. "He didn't know anything about the trouble with the elevator. He and his wife are on a European tour."

JUST BEFORE the end of shift that afternoon, Lake came panting into Mendoza's office. "Squad-car man just called in, he says he's got your child rapist—"

Mendoza leaped up. "Where?"

"Corner of Severance and Adams."

Everybody had just left; he found Hackett waiting for the elevator and they went down together; out of the parking lot Mendoza switched on the siren in the Ferrari.

The squad was parked in a yellow zone on Adams, and its driver, Dubois, was leaning against its side looking angry and triumphant at once. There was an old tan Dodge sedan parked ahead of it, and a man in the back seat of the squad.

"Just call me lucky, Lieutenant—it was one big damn fluke I was there. This bastard ran the light, and I was just coming up to the intersection—I gave him the siren and pulled him over. By God, I thought I was just going to write a ticket! But when I leaned in the window—" he crooked a finger at them—"what was the first thing I spotted?"

They looked. On the front passenger's seat of the Dodge was a neat coil of thin rope and a roll of wide adhesive tape. "¡Ca!" said Mendoza softly.

"So I turned the flash on the back seat, and—" None of them made a move to open any doors: the judges so careful of criminals' rights. But there on the back seat of the Dodge, clearly visible in the flashlight beam, was an ordinary looseleaf notebook, and its cover had fallen open to show the first page.

"I know I was alone," said Dubois in deadly earnest, "and my sweet Jesus, I know that if it hadn't been open and I'd touched it without a warrant, the whole case could get thrown out by some shyster. But I take my Bible oath it was open, Lieutenant."

Nobody had told them that Rosalie Ybarra had had her school notebook with her. Carefully printed on the first page of it was *Rosalie Ybarra—Third grade—St. Ignacio's School.*

HE WAS A THIN, thin-faced blond young man in very dapper coordinated sports clothes, and his name was Gilbert Florian. He had I.D. on him, and at least some of the contents of his pockets was suggestive, notably a business card from a porno bookstore on Hollywood Boulevard. There was a case full of marijuana cigarettes, and a little address book. They hadn't asked him a single question yet; he sat across the office, his legs crossed casually, watching them with a little crooked smile.

Hackett stabbed a blunt forefinger at one page of the address book. "That stretch of Santa Monica Boulevard, Luis—"

"Oh, yes. The Blue Boy Club. Let's ask." Mendoza called Hollywood precinct and talked to a Sergeant Hummel.

"Sure we know it," said Hummel. "One of a lot of fag joints down there. Gets raided once in a while for the dope."

"Does the name of Gilbert Florian ring any bells with you?"

"He's the piano player there. He's got a little pedigree of possession, using—nothing serious," said Hummel.

"Nothing serious!" Mendoza laughed.

But the questions they threw at him, sharp and cold, didn't ruffle him. They had him, and the lab could undoubtedly pick up more solid evidence from the car. He listened to them spell it out, he listened as coldly as they talked, and finally he said, smoothing his blond wavy hair, "It's a pity I never noticed that thing had got left in the back seat. But you're not going to do much to me, you know. Any shrink will tell you I'm sick-sick-sick—you'll never put me in the gas chamber or even the joint." He smiled a little dreamily. "It was just, I'd done everything else kinky—you name it, I've done it—except *that*. Thought it might be a new sensation. I was going to try for a black one tonight, reason I was down there."

The night watch was on by then, listening in, and Mendoza said to Conway, savagely, "Oh, take him away, Rich—for God's sake take him out of my sight!"

They would find out in time whether a judge, a jury, would hand Florian any part of the punishment he deserved. But at least they knew about him, they had him on record; and if he was let out, the next time a little girl got hurt he'd be one of those to look for. They could only hope that he wouldn't be let out for a long while, but they would take no bets.

"WELL, THERE HE IS," said Angel. Laddie was tearing round and round the back yard, uttering a joyful bark now and then, with Mark and Sheila chasing after him.

"Good heavens, he is big, isn't he? But you know, Angel, he was sent to you," said Alison with conviction. "Just the way Cedric was sent to us, out of the blue. Maybe some day he'll save you all from a fire or something." Laddie came up and leaned on her, pleased to make another new friend. His long tail waved madly. He was filling out, and his peculiar coat shone.

"Well, Cedric hasn't been much use to you, has he?" said Angel.

"Of course he has," said Alison indignantly. "We all adore him, even if Luis pretends he's not a dog man."

"Anyway, you can see this one's hardly a prestige pet."

"You simply want a little imagination. When people ask what kind of mixture he is, you just put your nose in the air—" Alison lifted her tiptilted nose and squinted down it haughtily—"and say, oh, don't you recognize it, it's the very latest imported breed, very rare and not recognized by the AKC yet, he's an Upper Transylvanian Otter Hound and the ears are distinctive to the breed—"

Angel began to giggle helplessly. "Anyway, I've got a man coming to see about the fence on Wednesday."

THE FERRARI sailed through the gates, which closed politely behind it. The sunlight was still brilliant at a quarter to seven, what with summer and daylight-saving time. Johnny and Terry were playing on the hillside among the Five Graces, Cedric chasing after them; they waved at Mendoza as he passed. Mairí would be down to round them up for baths and bed presently.

He went in the front door and deposited his hat on the credenza in the hall, and looked into the living room. Alison was curled in her chair on one side of the enormous fireplace, reading *A Companion to Murder*. Bast, Sheba and Nefertite were in a complicated tangle on the ottoman by the chair, the baby was crawling happily around the floor, and

El Señor, paws well tucked in, was brooding on top of the seven-foot bookcase.

"Good Lord, is it that late?" She looked up in surprise.

"What a warm welcome, *mi vida*." He bent to kiss her.

"But I'm glad you're home, because I want to talk to you seriously about this Denmark-Sweden tour. It really sounds quite interesting, Luis. It starts August first, we fly to New York and—"

Mendoza wandered over to the big front window and stood looking out. "I don't like tours, *querida*. Being herded around by guides. We're going to the British Isles. I've got the plane tickets in my billfold. We leave from New York two weeks from tomorrow."

Alison just looked at him. "I'd like," said Mendoza thoughtfully, "to see Bateman's."

"Bateman's."

"Kipling's old home. And Pook's Hill. And we can go on to see Mairí's cousin in Scotland, and the place your father was born—"

"Dunnett Bay."

"Rent a car and go where we please."

Alison shut her eyes. "We'll both be killed, they drive on the wrong side of the road. You've been planning this out all along, haven't you? For weeks."

"No," said Mendoza seriously. "It just came to me suddenly—after some of the cases we've had in the last month—that I do need a vacation. In spades. *Es que ya me canso de las estupideces*—I'm tired of all the stupidities, *mi vida*.... I'm going out to get a drink before dinner, do you want one?"

El Señor understood English, and beat him out to the kitchen.

Order now the spine-tingling mysteries you missed in stores.

THE HABIT OF FEAR—Dorothy Salisbury Davis $3.50 ☐
New York columnist Julie Hayes struggles to regain her equilibrium
by traveling to Ireland in search of her father after a seemingly
random act of violence shatters her life. Her pursuit leads her into a
maze of violence, mystery—and murder.

THERE HANGS THE KNIFE—Marcia Muller $3.50 ☐
Joanna Stark's scheme to entrap one of the world's greatest art thieves
has gone murderously awry. Plunging deep into Britain's fabulous art
world and terrifying underworld, she must confront her nightmarish
past as she races to recover two valuable stolen paintings ... and stay
alive in the bargain.

KIRBY'S LAST CIRCUS—Ross H. Spencer $3.50 ☐
Small-time private eye Birch Kirby has been noticed by the CIA.
They like his style. Nobody can be that inept, they believe, and they
need somebody with imagination to save the world from ultimate
catastrophe. As he goes undercover as the bull-pen catcher of the No
Sox baseball team, Kirby keeps an eye on the KGB, whose secret
messages cannot be decoded.

Total Amount	$ _____
Plus 75¢ Postage	_____ .75
Payment Enclosed	$ _____

To order please send your name, address and zip or postal code with a check or money order
payable to Worldwide Library Mysteries to:

In the U.S.	In Canada
Worldwide Library Mysteries	Worldwide Library Mysteries
901 Fuhrmann Blvd.	P.O. Box 609
Box 1325	Fort Erie, Ontario
Buffalo, NY 14269-1325	L2A 5X3

Please specify book title with your order.

MYS-14

 **WORLDWIDE LIBRARY**®